The Lilliput Game

A Novel

by

B. R. Wilson

SPIRITBOOKS

SpiritBooks, an imprint of Portal Center Press
Newport, Oregon

www.portalcenterpress.com

ISBN: 978-1-936902-24-8

Printed in the USA

Virtual reality is inevitably going to become mainstream - it's only a question of how good it needs to be before the mainstream is willing to use it.

~ Palmer Luckey

Chapter 1

"Just tell me one good reason why I can't have my tongue pierced."

"Infection. Look, give me a break, here. I have to keep my mind on the traffic."

"Come on, mom, pierced ears haven't given you an infection."

"That's different. Pierced ears don't interfere with my diction."

"You always say I talk too fast. Maybe a pierced tongue would slow me down."

"Ever think of having it removed entirely? Emily, watch that grocery bag, it's leaning. . ."

A grinding crash and a splatter of glass later, Emily Ross fought the airbag away from her face and saw that her mother's airbag had failed to open. She jumped to her feet, heart pounding, then realized she was having another flashback.

The accident had happened six months before. Her mother was dead, and she was in her father's office, waiting for her ride home after cheerleading practice. Now, the only place Becky existed was in a VR videogame, created by her husband Josh, who would probably never get over losing his wife.

At least so Emily thought, and blamed herself even more than she had already. If only she hadn't had so many fights with her mother. If only she had kept her mouth shut that day. If only she had been able to like Becky enough not to go nose-to-nose with her over every little issue, like cutting the hems of her dresses to six inches above her knees. Emily flipped her social studies book noisily shut. Maybe, she thought, the problem was that she had loved her mother so much that she couldn't really like her, not the way she liked her dad. When you love someone the way Emily loved Becky, you expect a lot of her, wanting more than you could get. And when you don't get what you expect, you tend to resent the person who let you down. At least that was how Josh had explained it to her, when she complained to him about Becky.

Emily always called her dad Josh, just the way Becky had, which made her feel grown up—and ever since her mother's death Emily had been feeling that she had to grow up fast. Her thirteenth birthday was a week away, which gave her hope that soon she would be considered a real person. When you're only twelve, Emily muttered to herself as she paced the office, people acted like you were still a kid, even if you were a freshman in high school. That wasn't fair, since she was smart enough to have skipped a year and such a genius at the computer that her older brother occasionally loathed her. Everyone in the family said she had inherited Josh's gift for computer science, but she would happily have settled for her mother's waist-length blond braid and the tennis serve that even her big brother, Dan, couldn't return.

Her dad's job was making up computer programs and video games that had a virtual reality feature, like the one he had put Becky into, so he could still see her after she died. No one could blame him for being crazy about his wife. Becky had been tall and slender. She had played tennis like Serena Williams, won medals in archery, and earned a doctor's degree in eighteenth-century literature. Emily gloomily measured her looks and talents against her mother's, a comparison that never failed to depress her. Emily's shoulder-length hair was so dirty blond that it was almost mouse-brown. She was short and skinny. Her shoulders tended to hunch over from so much time at the computer. One of history's mysteries was that she had several wannabe boyfriends, who claimed that she looked something like Katniss, the Hunger Games warrior, only without the great hair and the flames shooting out of her head. Emily would rather have looked like Becky, but her DNA had not been so kind.

No matter how hard she tried, Emily knew she would never be as smart, gorgeous, and confident as Becky Ross had been. Becky used to say that Emily's problem was just shyness and that she would get over it. But here Emily was, nearly thirteen, and she still wanted people to keep their distance. Except, that is, for their neighbor Jake Cohen, a hunk any girl would want up close and personal. He was her brother's best friend, which gave her a chance to stare at him without having to talk. Sometimes he would ask her a question about computers, but then she would turn red and forget everything she knew. Maybe when she was thirteen, Emily thought, some magical shift would take place that would allow her to utter at least one clever word when in the hypnotic presence of Jake Cohen.

Avoiding her social studies book, which might commit her to nailing a homework assignment, Emily went over to her father's desk and studied his massive computer apparatus. He had told her never to touch his work station, but he hadn't said anything about just looking at the new videogame that was on the screen. The graphics of Lilliput were mostly hers, anyway. Besides, Josh was twenty minutes late, and what was she supposed to do with herself while she waited? Meditate? His office was not, after all, the Shaolin Temple. It was a messy little dump with papers and soda cans all over the place. More than one beer bottle, too.

Emily hit a few keys and watched the screen as her mother came to life, along with a bunch of strangers wearing uncool clothes and talking like they came from a book too old-fashioned even for the school library. The weird thing was that they were all tiny. You could tell from the size of the furniture in the room. Any one of them could run right under the couch, easier than a mouse.

That's where they were running in the game, because a cat was chasing them, sticking its paws under the couch, trying to pull them out. Altogether, there were four little people. Emily's mother, Becky, was one of them and was dressed in a tight Robin Hood-type green bodysuit and high boots. She was carrying a tiny little bow, a quiver of arrows, and a knife stuck in her belt, none of which looked like it could do much damage, except possibly to a gnat.

With her was a plump woman in a long dress, a bearded tough-looking man with hairy hands, and a gentleman in clothes like the ones on the covers of her mother's eighteenth-century books. Emily recognized her graphics—a barmaid, a blacksmith and a gentleman, just the way she had drawn them. Josh had given her some illustrated books from her mother's library to show her how the tiny people were supposed to look. The men wore tight knee-length pants like bikers, and the woman wore a big-skirted dress, with the top cut so low, you could just about see everything she owned. If Emily had ever tried to go out wearing a top that low, her mother would have body-blocked her at the door, not that Emily had much hot anatomy to show the world. Josh might, she reflected, have given her credit for all those computer graphics. He owed her one and would hear about it, when the moment came for a favor.

Just then, Joshua Ross came into his office, turning his head toward the hall to talk to someone. Emily had barely time enough to log off before he saw her. She was glad she hadn't tried to use his virtual reality glove, though it would have brought the whole computer game to 3-D life.

"Haven't you put in the holographic feature yet?" Emily stood a distance from the computer, not wanting her father to know she had messed with it.

"Let's keep that little item a secret from the guys in the hall, okay?" Josh put his hand over her mouth and whispered in her ear. "Colonel Sharpe has some bogus plans for Lilliput that I'd rather not see happen."

Josh Ross was a tall, lanky man, forty-something in age. Behind his aviator glasses, he had big, kind blue eyes like Emily's, only without her long lashes. He was considered good-looking, but not in a movie-star way, having just a dad sort of face, with a long thin nose and an easy smile. He wasn't smiling now, though, probably because the man he'd been arguing with had gotten the last word. Josh hated it when someone else got the last word, just the way Emily did. Her mother had always finished every fight with a flip remark to which any reply would sound wimpy. Now it was Josh and Emily who competed for the verbal smackdown that would send the defeated opponent sobbing from the room.

"Em, how about setting up at this desk with your home-work?" Josh pushed some papers off a small table in the cor-ner. "I've got a bit more to do here before we can leave. Have a slice." He put a cold, limp piece of hours-old pizza in her hand, and went back to work.

She wanted to move the chair to the side, so she could see the monitor, but he insisted on her facing the wall. Once he had gotten back to work at his computer, Emily managed to turn her chair slightly so that she could peek at him in a mirror that was hanging above the desk and even catch a glimpse of the screen. Josh put one hand in his virtual reality glove and started up the program. The other hand held a slice of pizza at a perilous tilt over the keyboard.

The four little figures on the screen were crashing through the window of an eighteenth-century British pub. They seemed to jump right out of the screen, and Emily automati-cally pushed her chair back. Even through the mirror, it felt like they were coming right at her. A crowd of people their size, dressed the same way, like Munchkins in white wigs, greeted them with cheers and raised tankards of beer. Josh's secret invention, the holographic feature of the VR program, had kicked in and brought the whole scene to life, right in the middle of the office.

Suddenly Josh swore and slapped at the keyboard, having spilled some pizza sauce on it. The computer whirred and clicked, responding to Josh's hitting a random combination of keys. Just as the computer whirred its ominous, expiring fare-well, the tiny Becky figure stood in the middle of the desk in a glowing holographic haze and held up a bottle of beer. Josh's gloved hand opened to take it. With another click-whir, the scene disappeared, leaving on the monitor screen a Pacific Electronics logo with the words "HIGH-FIVE! YOU MADE IT BACK TO LILLIPUT!"

Josh slipped his hand out of the virtual reality control glove and removed his headset with its thick, outer space goggles. He put them down on the cluttered worktable along with a tiny bottle of Guinness Stout. Emily clapped her hand over her mouth and suddenly pretended to be doing homework. The bottle, she realized, was the same one the Lilliputians had put in the hand of the virtual reality glove. Josh sat looking at the bottle, kind of stupidly, it must be said, as if he wondered where it had come from. He glanced back to the computer, then at the bottle again.

"Holy moly," he said under his breath, "You're not real. I turned you off." When he was a kid, Josh had always admired Captain Marvel. He still had a yellowing pile of comics in the garage and talked like the red-caped super-hero whenever he got excited. From time to time, Josh would try to cajole his children into reading the comics, but little Jamie was the only one who cared about them. Jamie became so sure he could fly that he had broken his arm the previous summer by jumping off the garage roof, expecting to be supported by his mother's red opera cape.

Like his father, Jamie lived in the umpteenth dimension most of the time. After that awful day of the car crash, her lit-tle brother had been telling everyone he was raised in the Sha-olin Temple and was a living weapon. It was true that Jamie had taken kung fu lessons for two years, but he was hardly in the ninja class. People thought he was weird, talking about the

Temple all the time, and the school nurse had recently been sending home notes that she thought so too. It was embarrassing, and Emily hated being embarrassed worse than anything.

She watched through the mirror as Josh stared at the bottle as though it was going to blow up any minute. Carefully, he gripped the neck, then touched the bottle to the monitor, as if he expected the bottle to slide back where it came from. Nothing happened but the cold clink of glass on glass. Emily kept her head down, as if for the first time in her life, homework seriously engrossed her, and Josh sat with the little beer bottle in one hand. With the other, he saved the combination of strokes that had brought the bottle out of the Lilliputian tavern and into his hand.

Just as he got the right combination and leaned back with a loud "OKAY!" two men came into the room. One put a hand on his shoulder. Emily recognized Mel Glatt, head of Pacific Electronics, and her father's boss. Glatt had greasy hair and a nose that wiggled like a rabbit's when the man was agitated, which was most of the time. He reeked of anxiety and Brut cologne. Behind him was someone she hadn't seen before, but supposed was Colonel Peter Sharpe, "certified hero of the Aryan race," Josh called him. Sometimes Josh imitated Colonel Sharpe at dinner, describing the Colonel as a cross between a Manhattan advertising executive and the Terminator. Sharpe wore a perfectly pressed full dress uniform, medals and all, along with spats, which Emily had seen only in old war movies.

The Colonel, she had heard during Josh's conversations with her mother, was exactly the person who shouldn't know what had just happened, that Josh's virtual reality device could pop out real stuff. Josh had told Emily that Glatt wanted a military contract from Colonel Sharpe, and the Colonel wanted some technological breakthrough from Glatt that would bump his rank up to general. Both had their eyes on that little bottle as if it had the makings of a fusion bomb.

Glatt grabbed the open bottle out of Josh's hand and held it up so he and the Colonel could have a closer look. Then he slammed it down on the desk, where it fizzed all over Josh's papers.

"No booze at the workstation, Josh. You know that. We're under Colonel Sharpe, now. Army R & D." Glatt loved to act like Josh was his slave, even though Josh was the brains of their operation.

"Like I could get smashed on half an ounce of beer," Josh muttered under his breath, blotting the spilled drink with his sweatshirt sleeve. "And I never signed up for the military. Discipline is not my thing."

"Obviously." Colonel Sharpe picked up the bottle and thoughtfully held it up next to the monitor, like he was guessing where it came from. His eyebrows moved up and down indicating, Emily guessed, that he didn't quite believe what he was thinking. "So, where'd you get a bottle that looks just like the one in your video game?"

"Search me. I'm just a technician." Josh stared morosely at his keyboard, and then closed his eyes. Emily was sure he was repeating the crucial combination to himself, not daring to write it down in front of the Colonel, but not wanting to forget it, either. The save might not have worked, and then he'd have to remember.

"Dr. Ross," said the Colonel in a voice hard and sweet as a gummi bear, "I'm not asking for your help, I'm demanding it. You owe your research to your country. And your country will be generous in return for your work. Trust me." He stood at attention and his voice sounded like he was using a karaoke microphone. Emily halfway thought he was going to salute.

Mel Glatt looked like he was palpitating at the thought of Pentagon bucks. If they would pay $800 for a toilet seat, what wouldn't they pay for a virtual computer that could pop out anything you programmed into it? Glatt stared hard at Josh, daring him to diss Colonel Sharpe and blow a big government contract.

Josh got the picture. "I'd take you through the program, but at the moment, it's less than user-friendly. Some new data has to be punched in." He rubbed his stubbly chin. "Give me a couple of days."

Clutching Josh's shoulder, Glatt leaned on him. "Exactly how many days are we talking?"

Colonel Sharpe pulled Glatt off Josh. He was being the good cop, Emily figured, softening up her father. "Take your time, Dr. Ross. Quality research is a slow dance. I'll check back when you're ready. And enjoy your beer."

He handed the bottle to Josh, with one of those phony, man-to-man grins you see on TV when a crook hands some poor dude a bagful of counterfeit bills. While he was leading Glatt out of the office, Colonel Sharpe glanced at his watch, not for the first time. A controller, Emily thought. Pathologically time-conscious, like Jamie's gym teacher, who couldn't wait for class to end so he could follow the cute little school nurse into the faculty lounge. Emily would warn her father that the Colonel was not as friendly as he seemed, but Josh probably wouldn't listen to her. It was Emily's fantasy that when she turned thirteen, her father would take her seriously and listen to her the way he used to listen to her mother. Only a week left for the transformation to take place, she thought, and no sign of it yet.

As Glatt left, he shot a nasty glance at Josh, like he wasn't fooled about his employee's intentions. Josh smiled back at him, and waved a friendly good-bye. It's something Emily had learned from him. When somebody at school gave her a hard time, she acted like it was fine by her, and smiled. It irritated them and satisfied her. Also, it made her seem a lot cooler than she felt. Her mother used to say that people create their own reality, and she hoped to create one that would fool the world into thinking she was as tough as Becky.

When the two men had left. Josh slumped back in his swivel chair, taking a deep breath. He seemed not to remember that Emily was in the room.

"Yo, Colonel Putz," he said, slipping the tiny beer bottle in his pocket. "What would you want me to pull out of this little box? Not just a bottle of beer, I'll bet my mortgage."

Josh set quickly to work, writing the combination of strokes on his hand, removing disks and components, wrapping up the virtual reality equipment and packing it into boxes. Remembering Emily, he turned around.

"You can help me carry these boxes to the car," he said. "They aren't safe here anymore, and neither are we."

Josh and Emily loaded his computer boxes into his van, careful to prop sleeping bags and other accumulated junk around them to keep the precious contents from falling out or getting knocked around. Once they had settled into the front seat, Josh switched on his micro-bug, so they could hear any conversation in Mel Glatt's office.

"I've been snooping," Josh told his daughter, in an ashamed sort of way. He wasn't the crooked type, and Emily could see he wished he didn't have to eavesdrop. "We need to know what's going on."

Glatt's voice was sweetly reasonable. "I know, Colonel, Josh Ross seems like a flake, but let me tell you why. His wife died in a car crash six months ago, and he's been hell to live with ever since."

"You got that right," Emily whispered under her breath, not wanting her father to hear.

"First rate physicist, though, even when he's off the wall." Glatt sounded like a salesman making a pitch for his product. "Don't forget that."

"So says his background check," said Sharpe. "Along with the information that he could care less about cooperating with the military. He has a neighbor we've been questioning. Plus, one of my men has orders to get the school nurse's help. We'll have to carrot-and-stick Ross along. Whatever works."

Josh turned off his radio. "You can't buy me, Colonel Putz. Don't even think about it."

Wondering what kind of stick the colonel had in mind and who the neighborhood snitch was, Emily said nothing. She kept her hand firmly on the box containing the virtual program and her tiny, unpredictable mother.

Chapter 2

The Ross living room looked the way you would expect with no maid and no mom to ride shotgun on the pants. Books, videos, and food containers were all over the table and the floor. Seven-year-old Jamie stood in front of the TV watching a *Kung Fu—The Legend Continues* video, practicing his killer moves while scarfing down popcorn. He was none too careful about where the popcorn landed. Scruff, the Ross family's huge, hairy mutt, followed Jamie around the room, grabbing any popcorn that landed on the floor. Whenever he got a hard kernel, he spat it onto the rug and batted it around with one over-sized paw.

While Josh stashed his computer boxes in the study, Emily opened her own computer on the dining room table, booting up the Illustrator, her art program. She had promised her father to draw some more pictures for his game, and wanted to get the job done before dinner. Since everybody was eating now, she figured the meal wasn't about to happen anytime soon and decided to raid the cupboard for some cookies.

Dan, a thin, serious-looking boy who was shooting up to be as tall and lanky as his father, was curled up on the couch with a book on his lap. He kept his eyes on the pages while he cracked nuts and dropped the shells on the rug, where Scruff idly knocked them around when he was tired of swatting popcorn. Dan held up *Gulliver's Travels,* so Jamie could see the picture of a giant man tied down with what looked like string.

"Hey Jamie, look at this. Gulliver just woke up stranded on an island with people the size of his thumb. But they took him down. He can't even get up to pee." Dan closed the book and looked out the window. "Mom used to say anyone with kids would know just how Gulliver felt."

Jamie sat down beside him. "It was her favorite book. She used to read me the easy parts." He flipped open the book, then changed moods without a beat. "Wow, cool!" he cried, pointing. "Look at that teeny sword sticking in Gulliver's belly button." He carried the book toward the dining table. "Maybe I can make a sword on Emily's Illustrator."

Emily tore out of the kitchen, popping a cookie in her mouth and stuffing another in her pocket. "Don't even think about it, Jamie!" she warned. "You can't use my computer unless I'm helping you. In how many languages do I have to tell you no before you get it?" She grabbed his hand hard and pulled him away.

"You're breaking my hand," Jamie howled. "You're breaking every finger I have."

Releasing him, Emily turned to inspect her computer. "Never, never, touch this computer unless you want to die."

"You can't tell me what to do," Jamie yelled at her, throwing a fistful of popcorn at her. "You're not my mother."

Immediate silence muted the room. Jamie's face crumpled as he tried not to cry, and Scruff whimpered, licking Jamie's hand. Emily and Dan looked uneasily at each other, knowing a line had been crossed, but not knowing how to retreat. Jamie had a habit of milking the family tragedy for all it was worth. It made living with him very uncomfortable in the emotional department.

"Em, you said you didn't like Mom bossing you around," Dan said finally, when the silence had become as painful as a stuck car horn. "So lay off Jamie, okay?"

Leaning over to pick up the popcorn and walnut shells, so no one could see her face, Emily said, "Are you saying I didn't care about Mom?"

Her way of defending herself had always been to attack. Everyone had told her that the accident wasn't her fault, but whatever they said, she blamed herself. The fact was that a watermelon had fallen out of the grocery bag Emily was holding on her lap. She and Becky had been arguing about Emily's insistence on getting her tongue pierced. At that moment the watermelon had bounced onto her mother's foot, making the accident happen. Emily still woke up from nightmares, hearing the crash and seeing her mother slumped over the wheel. Yes, it had been her fault, and no one could comfort her. She wouldn't let them know she needed it.

A rabbi had visited the funeral home with Jake Cohen, Dan's best friend. The rabbi had talked to Emily about how her mother still lived in the memory of family and friends. It was the Jewish idea of immortality, Josh explained to Emily later. If you forgot the dead person, she really was dead. But if remembering hurt so much, Emily thought, wouldn't it be better to let the dead person disappear from your mind? Then she felt guilty all over again, as if she were killing her mother twice.

"You were the only one that didn't cry at the funeral." Dan had obviously been keeping this deadly missile underground until just the right moment.

"I never cry." She wanted to say, 'not like some people I know,' but realized that would be too low a blow. She hadn't seen Dan cry for a lot of years, but he sure had cried a bucketful at that funeral. Emily had done her own crying while locked in her room, but would never admit it.

Relenting a bit, she put her arm around Jamie and steered him over to the computer, wiping his popcorn-slimed hand with her sleeve. "Ok, Jamie. Look, I'll show you how I do mice."

With Jamie staring absorbed at the screen, she began sketching mice and coloring them. Jamie was eager to take a turn, forgetting his grief for a moment.

"Wow, cool, blue mice." He danced up and down, trying to wedge his hand into the action.

"Let's put'em in the kung fu temple, eating cheese. How about that?" Emily's hands worked fast and expertly, stopping only to bat Jamie's fingers away.

"Mice don't eat cheese. Mom said so, and she had a PhD." Dan took on the superior tone that always infuriated Emily.

"That makes her an expert in mouse diets?" Emily got the last word, as usual.

Dan threw a handful of walnuts at her, and Emily turned her back to the computer, protecting the screen. Getting into the spirit of the fight, Jamie struck a kung fu pose and waddled over to Dan, keeping his center of gravity low and his hands at an angle. Emily wished one of Jamie's jump-kicks on Dan. She didn't like being reminded of her mother's infallibility.

The doorbell rang, and Emily answered it. It was their neighbor, a divorced woman with a big, gooey red mouth. She thrust her ticket of entrance at Emily, a casserole for dinner. She usually waited till Josh had driven up so she could smirk at him and so the kids couldn't say no to the food. Emily and Dan had it figured out that Andriette Hale had designs on their father and tried to fend her off. Emily opened the door only enough to let the woman's arm in.

"Thanks, Mrs. Hale, but we've already got dinner planned…"

Before Emily could close the door, Josh came in from the study, brushing the dust from the boxes off his hands. Over his shoulder, Emily could see that he'd already set up the virtual reality computer on his worktable, and she wondered if the cartridge with the game she had seen was still in the 3-D-drive. Josh looked tired and his thick, curly hair stood up on end, as if he'd been scratching his head.

"Thanks, Andriette, we'd love a casserole. Sorry I can't ask you in, but we're having a family moment." Josh took the food, smiled sweetly at the pesky neighbor, whose foot was about to come down on the threshold, and closed the door.

Forgetting about his attack on Dan, Jamie ran to his father and hugged him around the hips. "She's brought us okra cas-serole again, Dad. With kidneys. I can smell 'em." He peered triumphantly at his brother under Josh's arm. "Dan told her you always forget to bring home dinner."

Josh laughed and ruffled the indignant Dan's hair until it looked like his own. "I do. That's a fact. Can't seem to get the hang of being a mom."

The four of them stood awkwardly in a circle, looking at each other, waiting for a lost, invisible Becky to make things all right again, as only she could do. Her mother had always been the center of the show, having all the best lines, getting all the attention. Compared to her, Emily felt clumsy and stupid, not able to make small talk or joke in a way that used to make Josh laugh until he had to sit down and pull Becky onto his lap. Josh used to sit Emily on his lap, but he had not done that for the last couple of years, saying she was too grown-up for cuddling now. As if her mother wasn't even more grown up, but Josh didn't mind cuddling her. He said it was different for married people, the point of which wasn't clear to Emily. After all, she was related to her father by blood, while Becky was not. It didn't seem fair. Fairness was a big thing with Emily, but she saw precious little of it in the world. What dreamer had ever made up the idea of fairness anyway, she wondered, absently playing with Scruff's wiry hair.

Jamie broke the tension, by making one of his usual complaints. "I hate okra, Dad. It tastes like slime mold."

"And how would you know what slime mold tastes like?" Josh laughed and picked Jamie up.

The other two followed him as he carried Jamie into the study and turned on the virtual reality computer. Emily held her breath, wondering if the scene with Becky would appear again. But all that came up was a series of symbols Emily had never seen before. Jamie was quickly bored and got down. For some reason, Scruff growled and cowered behind Dan, keeping his shining black eyes on the screen, as if waiting for something small and tasty to jump out. Emily braced herself, expecting a beer bottle any minute.

"I'm running a diagnostic, Dan," Josh said. "Keep an eye on it while I heat up this killer casserole."

While the others were occupied in the study, Jamie had taken the opportunity to sneak into the hall and put on Emily's roller blades, a totally forbidden act. He began to zoom around the living room, spreading out his arms in a parody of Emily's graceful gestures. Emily pursued him down the hall toward his bedroom.

"Say the temple prayer for sudden death, Jamie," she cried. "You have absolutely had it. My skates are sacred."

Jamie locked himself in his room before Emily could catch him, figuring he didn't want slime mold casserole anyway. While Emily pounded on the door, shouting lethal curses, he skated around the room backwards, finally collapsing in a heap when he fell over his box of Harry Potter figures. Not bothering to remove the skates, he began setting up the little people and talking to them about initiation into the Shaolin temple. Jamie explained to the Hagrid doll that it was an unlikely candidate for learning kick-jumps, but could definitely find work as a temple guard. With the Harry figure, he discussed the intricacies of adapting kung fu moves to broomstick flight. He didn't even hear Emily quit pounding the door.

Josh had followed Emily down the hall. "Let him alone, honey. You know we've got to give him some extra space. He's the one who lost the most when your mother was killed."

Emily felt as she always did when Josh spoke of her mother's death, that she was to blame for everything. Becky would be alive if it weren't for her clumsy, dumb daughter's dropping that watermelon. Jamie would have a mom. Josh would have a wife. All would be right with the world, an eternal springtime. If Emily weren't such a klutz, life would be beautiful. She felt a lump rise in her throat as she remembered how it felt to have a mom to cry on, complain to, and skate with. Swallowing hard, she tried to put her mind someplace else, but it was hard to find a place her mother had not shared.

Jake Cohen's rabbi would say that was a good thing. Emily was not so sure.

Maybe the minister who spoke at Becky's funeral was right, and Becky was waiting for them in heaven with Jesus. That idea was a little easier for Emily to handle because it put Becky far away, into a future that wouldn't happen until Emily died herself. Since that event seemed to Emily in the same unimaginable category as the sun going nova, she could feel comfortable with it. If you were thirteen, death was something that happened to other people or, if it happened to you, it was so far in the future that you didn't have to think about it. Yes, the minister was probably right, or at least she hoped he was.

Then there was Dan's idea, picked up from looking at Jamie's Shaolin temple videos. People kept coming back to life again, in other bodies, trying not to make the same mistakes they had made before. Emily tried to imagine her mother coming back like an avenging fury, making her daughter's life miserable. After all, who was to blame for Becky being dead? Maybe Becky would come back as Emily's daughter someday and cause Emily to crash her hover-car, or whatever she might be driving when she was thirty-something. Not wanting to imagine Becky coming back in any form at all, Emily shook her head, trying to clear it of her mother's image in Josh's computer. As she followed him down the hall, she hoped the Lilliput game would crash, and Becky's image with it. Then she felt guilty all over again.

When they got back to the study, Dan was fooling around with the computer. Josh roared at him, and Dan jumped away. Scruff whimpered and squirmed outdoors through the dog flap built into Josh's study wall. It was almost too small for Scruff now that he was grown, but the dog was determined to escape the bad vibes.

"I was just wondering if you finished the Lilliput game." Dan smiled at his father humbly, with lots of teeth showing, like a cartoon villain. "You know, Dad? Like you promised?"

Jamie had crept back into the room and was getting too close to the VR set-up. Emily noticed that the skate wheels were getting tangled in the tassels of the oriental carpet and saw her chance to grab him before he could get away.

"Gotcha."

She sat on his stomach and wrenched the skates off his feet, none too gently. Jamie screamed as if he had suffered amputation.

"Enough already," Josh said, exasperated. "Out of my room, guys, and stay out, or the Lilliput game is history. Dan, set the table. Emily, pour the milk. Jamie, just sit and meditate until the temple gong rings for dinner."

Jamie was reaching out to touch the little people on Josh's computer screen, and Emily grabbed his hand. She sat him down in his chair at the table, and then followed her father into the kitchen. It was about the only time she was ever alone with him, except for the few minutes when he drove her home from cheerleading practice. For a moment, she pretended she was her mother, presiding over the crisp white kitchen with its green marble floor. True, on Becky's watch the kitchen cabinets never had jam stuck to the doors and the floor gleamed. No sticky peanut butter patches or dried up milk puddles stuck to your shoes. In your stocking feet, you could skate like Sarah Hughes on Becky's kitchen floor. Emily made a mental note to clean and wax the floor so perfectly that her father could see his face in it.

Opening the oven door, she looked at Josh over her shoulder. "Did you use my little people in the game, Dad? I drew 'em just the way they looked in Mom's books."

Josh burned himself while pulling out the casserole and swore under his breath. "Yes, Emily," he said with exaggerated patience. "I used your little people. You want a medal?"

Emily followed him to the dining room table, carrying four plates. She decided to see how far she could push her luck. "Just my name in the credits, right? You promised." She put the plates down on the placemats Dan had laid at odd, careless angles on the scratched mahogany dining room table. Becky had always covered it with a clean, cheerful tablecloth. But now no one wanted to bother with extra washing.

"Hey, it was my idea to do the Lilliput game," Dan protested. "Mom gave me the book. Anybody can draw."

"Oh yeah? Let's see you do it, Picasso." Emily served Dan a large helping of okra casserole and put only a single spoonful on her own plate.

"I am of the temple." Jamie said, rocking back and forth in his chair. "I eat no slime mold."

"Eat the casserole tonight," Josh urged, "and tomorrow I'll bring home a bucket of Kentucky fried. Deal?"

"Deal!" Jamie and his father gave each other a high-five and then dug grimly into the casserole.

"I thought temple priests were vegetarians." Emily moved the food around on her plate so it would look like she had eaten some of it.

"Kentucky fried is okay," Jamie said, after some thought. "Trust me. I have experience in these matters."

Emily brooded on the prospect of trusting Jamie about anything. Certainly, she couldn't trust him with the secret of the tiny beer bottle that Josh's computer had popped that afternoon. Of course, she would have to tell Dan, if she was going to carry out her plan for a midnight raid on the VR computer. You were dead if you didn't have a back-up for military operations, and an assault on the VR computer would be one.

Josh holed up in his bedroom early that night, and Emily figured he was probably writing in the journal he used to keep with Becky. Emily had often sneaked looks at the little notebook, so now she could imagine what he was saying. He would probably look at Becky's previous entries in the joint journal, things like "Love you, Josh, but you might come home from work before the stew fossilizes." Then he would write that Emily had an attitude, or that Dan was living too much in books, or that Jamie needed a shrink before he went completely around the bend and shaved his head.

The light in Josh's room was on for a long time, and Emily sat at her open door, waiting. She had a book handy and a pencil, so if Josh came out, she could pretend to be on her way to ask him a homework question. Her heart beating hard, Emily kept her eyes on Josh's door until the crack under it went dark. Then she slipped down the soft, carpeted hall floor into Dan's room and shook him awake.

"Dad's down," she whispered. "Let's go."

Dan rubbed his eyes. "You know, he'll kill us if we screw up anything on his computer. Grounded for life is what we'd be."

"Well, let's not screw up, okay?" Emily pushed her brother toward the door. "Go, go! Before Jamie hears us."

They moved carefully down the steps, trying to avoid the one that creaked. Almost at the bottom, Dan yawned and stumbled, landing with a thud at the foot of the staircase.

Emily froze. "Oh, nice work, Dan. Now we'll have them both on our necks."

They waited a few moments, but heard nothing from upstairs. Feeling their way into the living room, they stopped at a tall bookshelf. Dan pushed a chair in front of it and Emily climbed up, while he held it steady. She pulled a carved wooden box from the top shelf of the bookcase, opened it, and took out a key. After replacing the box, she jumped down. Dan pushed the chair back against the wall. They had performed this maneuver enough times that neither had to say a word.

Just as they unlocked the door to Josh's study, Jamie whispered from the darkness behind them "You thought I didn't know. But I got psychic powers."

Dan sighed. "Right. Temple training does that for a guy. Go back to bed, Jamie. You can't be in on this one."

Jamie followed them into the study, smiling. One front tooth had just fallen out the past week, and he knew his jack-o-lantern grin made people nervous. "I'll tell," he hissed.

"Count on it." Emily stopped and looked at Dan. "If he's not included, we're toast."

Dan closed the door softly. "Okay, but I'm oldest. I go first."

"I'm a girl. Me first." Emily tried to push past him to the computer.

"Might makes right. Mom said so." Dan blocked her way let. "Remember? 'I'm the mommy, that's why.'"

"I didn't like it then, and I don't like it now," Emily grumbled. She stuffed a few cushions against the door to block the light, and then flicked the switch.

The lamp in Josh's study was fluorescent, throwing a harsh, bluish glow over the tan leather sofa, oriental carpet and white utility table with a small microwave for heating coffee. Becky had hated that light, saying that it made her look as blue as a corpse and that Josh only used it to keep her out of his study. He had refused to let her or anyone touch his stuff. Piles of books and papers cast sharp, angular shadows around the corners of the room.

Emily looked around uneasily when she heard a rustling sound, then sighed, relieved, when Scruff wiggled his bulk through the plastic dog flap and ran around the room wagging and whimpering softly with the pleasure of seeing them again. You would think it had been weeks since their last encounter, Emily said to herself, wondering why dogs lived so much in the present while humans lived so much in the past. If she could stop living in the past, remembering the accident, Emily thought, she could be as happy as Scruff.

She was still back there in the bad old days with Becky, duking it out over what to wear. Memories that stuck like glue and never stopped haunting her. So many times she had wanted to tell her mother that she loved her, no matter how they fought. But the words had caught in her throat. Like a lot of things, talking about love embarrassed her. Maybe if she ever ran into Becky in heaven, love would be an okay topic of conversation. Maybe the only topic of conversation. In that case, she and Becky would finally be able to talk to each other. But heaven seemed a long way off, since Emily planned to live as close to forever as she possibly could.

Dan was already at the computer. He slipped on the VR headphones and glove. Emily handed him the card on which she had copied the combination of strokes Josh had written on his hand, the strokes that had brought Lilliput to life. Dan worked slowly and methodically, checking each stroke before he made it. Suddenly the screen came to life.

"I think we're in!" Dan said. "Me first."

"Second," Emily whispered, trying to be sportsmanlike. Actually, what she wanted to do was to tear the gear off him and shove him out of the chair.

"Last." Jamie's voice was small and resigned. He never got to be first and did not expect to be now. He stood by Scruff, twisting one floppy dog ear nervously between his fingers.

"It's my turn," Emily said impatiently. "I have the blue mice cartridge. You got nothing, Dan, just the Lilliput credits." She noticed that her name was now right there along with Josh's, and felt a rush of pride.

"Wait, wait," Dan said. "We need to bring down the menu. Now, put in the cartridge." He shoved his hand into the V-R glove.

Emily slipped in the software and stood first on one foot, then the other. It was worse than having to go to the girl's room when there was a long line. "The colored mouse file is the one we want. There. Click, Dan."

"Yeah! Look at that!" His voice was so loud Emily put a hand over his mouth. "Wow, you can even feel the fur. Okay, okay. Your turn, Em."

Scruff was growling and lashing his tail. Little blue mice in 3-D brought out the wolf in him. With one hand, Dan held him back, and with the other he handed Emily the VR glove.

Emily put on the headset, then the glove. As she opened the plastic hand, she almost shrieked, stifling her voice with the other hand. A blue mouse jumped out of the glove and stood up on its hind legs. The three of them looked at the mouse and the mouse stared back.

"This is outrageous," Emily whispered in an awed tone, first looking into the empty glove and then at the mouse.

"I don't believe it." Dan started to reach out toward the mouse. Having second thoughts, he pulled his hand back and put it behind him. Electronic rodents might, after all, have unknown powers, not to speak of lethal diseases.

Jamie dove after the mouse as it ran under the couch. "It got away. This is one weird mouse." He kept sticking his hand under the couch, and it kept coming back empty.

"No way that thing could have come out of the V-R," Dan whispered, backing away from the couch. "Unreal!"

"Wanna bet? Didn't I tell you?" Emily hardly realized she was jumping up and down.

"Get that mouse, Jamie," Dan pointed to the small, furry blue face peering at them from under the couch.

"I can't," Jamie panted, lying down on the carpet and groping under the couch with both hands. "It's a magic mouse. You can tell from its color. No way we'll ever catch it."

Scruff tried with both paws, making harsh gasping noises like he was choking to death. He was one-part terrier and loved to chase small things that ran faster than he could. Emily always wondered what he would do if he caught one, but he never had.

"Go on, Scruff," she urged. "Get that mouse. A leftover kidney is all yours, if you do."

Suddenly the mouse leaped out from under the other end of the couch, then sped over to the dog door-flap. Scruff loped after it, panting and thumping. When the mouse leaped against the flap and rolled outside through the opening, Scruff followed, barking up a storm.

"Everybody upstairs," Dan ordered. "Dad's going to be wondering what Scruff's after."

He grabbed Jamie by one arm and pulled him out of the study, while Emily turned off the computer and locked the study door behind her. It took only a moment to restore the key to its box. Emily and Dan were so busy trying to get this job done that they didn't notice Jamie staring at them, looking from the chair to the box on the high shelf.

"Hide," Dan insisted, pushing them both under the staircase. "Dad's coming."

"Who's there?" Josh called, playing his flashlight beam down the stairs. "Scruff? Knock it off, dog. We're trying to sleep here."

When Josh had gone back to bed, Dan announced that the coast was clear, and the three of them dashed upstairs.

"I gotta go," Jamie said, heading for the bathroom.

"Well, go then," Emily replied, "But if Dad catches you out of bed, don't tell about the mouse, y'hear?"

Chapter 3

Emily and Dan disappeared into their rooms and their lights went off. Jamie waited a minute, looked at all the closed doors, and then tiptoed downstairs. He wasn't sure at first how to get at the carved box, but piled Dan's *Gulliver's Travels* on top of *The Life of Samuel Johnson* so he could climb high enough. It took him only a few moments to unlock his father's study, prop cushions against the crack under the door, and fumble the light switch on. He paused over the computer keys, and then remembered the card with the combination of keystrokes. Emily had left it right beside the computer, so he was in luck.

"Just one more blue mouse," he said softly. "I want to hold it for a minute, like Emily did."

He glanced around the room, waiting for the computer to boot up. It was fun pretending he was Dad, and he hitched up his pajama pants as he had seen his father do. Then he walked over to the little microwave on the bookcase and, after a moment's hesitation, opened it. Inside was half a cup of Josh's morning coffee. Now he could really pretend to be Dad. With a quick grab, he seized the cup and tossed down a swig, thinking it must taste terrific, given how much of it Josh drank. It didn't taste terrific. It tasted horrible, like the way dishwater looks after the dishes are done. He wanted to spit it out, but knew better than to make a mess. Swallowing again and again to get rid of the bitter taste, Jamie replaced the cup, closed the microwave softly, and sat down at the computer again. He suddenly felt very young, not like Dad at all, and wondered if he would do something really bad to the Lilliput program by turning it on without help. Maybe even lose the image of Mom forever. He wiped his cold, damp hands on his pajama top and didn't take his eyes off the screen.

When the Lilliput scene of small people in the tavern suddenly flashed on, Jamie sat back, not sure what to do. Slowly he put on the goggles, watching the tiny figure of Becky hand out bottles of beer.

"Mommy!" he cried. "Mommy, you're in there."

Emily swooped up behind him. "Shut up, Jamie. You wanna get us all killed?"

"I thought you were asleep," Jamie whimpered.

"Think I'd go to sleep and leave you capering about?" Emily shut down the computer fast, and picked Jamie up.

"You promised you wouldn't give us away," Dan said. He was standing in the doorway, the key in his hand. "Now upstairs, both of you, before we're destroyed."

"How come Mommy is in the computer?" Jamie cried softly. "Do people go into the computer when they die?"

Dan and Emily looked at each other over his head.

"Dad just scanned her picture into the video game, that's all," Dan said, as they hid the key in the box.

"She's really there. I saw her. I touched her." Jamie's voice was getting louder and Dan shook him before pulling him up the stairs.

"It's not really her, dork," he said. "It's only a program Dad made up."

"The mouse was just part of Emily's program and it came out," Jamie insisted. "Emily, you gotta make Mom come out too."

Emily put her arm around Jamie and steered him into his room. "We want her back as much as you do, Jamie, but Mom's gone. That's how it is. Come on, punkin." She tucked him into bed. "Pretend you had a dream."

It took Emily an hour to get to sleep, since she had to keep an eye peeled on Jamie's door across the hall. No way was he going to get past her again. She listened to the cuckoo clock in the hall ticking and cuckooing until her eyes drifted closed, and she dreamed that she was six inches high, skating around the living room with a beer bottle in one hand and a blue mouse in the other. Then, suddenly, she was dancing on skates with Jake Cohen. He and Dan were two years ahead of her in school, which made them totally superior in their view and her as pathetic as a house-elf. At least until it came time for computer science homework. Then, even Jake had to give her some respect. Emily smiled in her sleep as she dreamed of Jake spinning her around at the skating rink until she was dizzy.

Josh stopped at his office the next morning before dropping the kids off at school. Mel Glatt met him at the door and followed him so closely down the hall that he stepped on Josh's heels.

"Get something straight, Josh," he whined softly, like he was scared Colonel Blitzkrieg was just around the corner. "You gotta realize it's the Department of Defense that wants your research. The guys that pay eight hundred dollars for a toilet seat, remember?"

Josh did not bother to turn around, just pushed his office door open and started taking papers out of the files. "I'm working on it, Mel," he said vaguely.

Taking a look around the room, Mel Glatt tugged at his blond, thinning hair. "Working on it? Man, it isn't even here! Where. . ."

Josh shoved the papers into his briefcase and snapped it shut. "I took the equipment home. Something as important as this, I don't want to limit myself to office hours. I'll bring the computer back as soon as I've transferred the files to my home office." His voice was patient and unmoved, the way it sounded when he was insisting that his kids brush their teeth.

Glatt pounded on Josh's desk with both fists, losing it completely. "You get that VR computer back here and working right now. If I don't see finished cybernaut software in forty-eight hours or less, I'll have you arrested for stealing government property."

Shrugging his shoulders, Josh brushed past him into the hall. He was not as calm as he looked. The cybernaut software was what he had been working on when he switched over to the Lilliput game for a break and by inspired accident accessed what he figured had to be the Higgs-Boson Field. In this most elemental level of reality, Josh knew nothing has mass until high energy and weightless photons, tiny bits of light, run into each other, stick together, and make something solid.

In the Higgs Field, the figures of the Lilliput game were just as real as Josh and his remaining family. People said the Higgs-Boson field was like God because it was pure energy, pure spirit. Josh's religion was the belief that God was the unified field, the underlying cause of everything. For Josh, that meant that somehow, somewhere, he would meet his Becky again. In the Field that was the Source of everything, Becky was not dead. She was in Lilliput, and he could go there with her whenever he wanted to, no matter what Glatt said about Lilliput belonging to the army.

Josh knew his software was classified top secret and that Colonel Sharpe had big plans to apply the new program to spy activities. The idea was that Josh would come up with something Sharpe called nanoprobes, having seen too many science fiction movies. Josh had explained that he couldn't make nano-anythings. He had no wish for the kind of karma that would happen if he created microscopic entities that would be injected into the brains of spy suspects to find out what they knew. Messing with anybody's head was not something Josh could be bought to do.

As he ran down the steps to the car, Mel Glatt still behind him, yelling like the place was on fire, Josh shuddered, imagining what the Aryan Terminator, aka Colonel Sharpe, would do with tiny objects, let alone people, from a VR computer. They could be forced to blow up an enemy's nuclear facilities after being stashed inside a lunchbox. Or they could pop out of an enemy computer and blow lethal gas all over a military complex. Not being an army man, Josh could not begin to imagine uses his discovery could be put to. All he knew was that Lilliput belonged to him, not to the government, and that he had to protect his creation from being turned into a weapon.

Josh had his reasons for being afraid of the military. His older brother was still wheezing and tooling around in a motorized wheel chair after breathing enemy chemicals in Iraq. Josh practically worshipped his brother, and swore that he would never, ever help the US military get hold of sneaky weapons, ones that were not fair. Actually, he didn't want to help with weapons at all. He didn't want to wind up with a bad conscience like his friend, Plummer, who had worked for Colonel Sharpe building military robots. Josh had not known Mel Glatt was signing him up to work for the government until the deed was already done. Now he just seemed to be sinking deeper and deeper into a hole with money and mayhem at the bottom. If he didn't take a stand soon, he would turn into the kind of guy he hated, with no principles and a headache that never went away.

Dick Briglia, the elementary school gym teacher, kicked open the door of the nurse's office. He was pulling Jamie Ross by one arm. Briglia was an army reserve officer who had never served in combat, but he liked to pretend he had. He was also the ex-boyfriend of Carmen Rochas, the school nurse, a pretty Latina who thought he was scum. She had been his girlfriend for about two weeks, until she found out that he picked his nose, ate what he picked, and cheated at cards. He was one bad dude, everybody said, even though they liked the heel lights on his gym shoes and the cool army hat he wore all the time.

Briglia had caught Jamie napping in gym class, just a few minutes before. Kicking Jamie awake, he had called out, "Rise and shine, soldier."

The gym teacher liked to pretend he was running an army camp, not just a gym class of seven-year-old boys. His hope was to run his own army reserve platoon one day, but so far, he had been blacklisted, owing to a long history of irritating his superior officers.

Jamie rubbed his eyes and sat up on the mat. "I just fell asleep for a minute, Mr. Briglia, honest. I feel sick."

"Yeah? We'll see how sick you are." Briglia dragged Jamie up by the collar of his gym shirt."

"You guys do twenty push-ups," Briglia called over his shoulder to the class. "I'm taking Jamie to the nurse before he totally wimps out."

"I'm okay, Mr. Briglia. I can play. Just try me." His voice trailed away as he was pulled out the gym door and down the hall.

Briglia pushed Jamie in the nurse's door and stuck his head in to say, "We got unfinished business, Carmen. I'll see you later. Don't make plans."

Carmen Rochas stood up as Jamie came in, her mouth open to answer Briglia, but the gym teacher was gone before she could say anything. She was very small and thin, a mix of Hispanic and Indian, with a long black braid, big brown eyes, and a round little mouth that looked like she was always surprised. Everybody thought she ought to be in the movies, she was so gorgeous, but she just wanted to take care of sick kids.

Jamie stood in front of her, not saying anything, his head hanging. He just looked at her tiny white shoes and her ankles, covered with white stockings. Carmen Rochas wasn't that much bigger than he was, barely five feet tall, and she was smiling. Jamie was relieved, glad to be with someone he could handle.

"Hi," said Carmen, putting an arm around his shoulder. "What's happening?"

"Mr. Briglia's mad because I went to sleep in gym class."

"You feel sick?" Carmen laid her cool hand over his forehead.

"Not exactly." Jamie chose his words carefully, mindful that he had told Mr. Briglia something was wrong with him. "I'm tired, that's all."

Carmen felt the glands under his jaw, then tipped his face up to meet hers.

"You look okay," she said, studying his eyes. "Been going to bed late?"

Jamie let his voice quiver. His grief-stricken child act worked with just about everybody, so he figured it would work with Carmen Rochas. Besides, he really was grief-stricken, so the act wasn't a lie. "Sometimes I can't sleep. Since Mom. . ."

Sitting him down beside her on a bench, Carmen rocked him against her. "Yeah, I can believe it. But you're not sick? Not enough to miss gym class?"

Jamie shook his head. He didn't mind going back to gym class since it would be over in five minutes. "I'm fine," he said cheerfully. "Terrific."

"Back to class, then." Carmen gave him a hug. "But you come see me again if you can't sleep, okay?"

Jamie looked back at her as he walked out the door. His heart was beating hard, and he figured he was probably in love.

When Jamie had left, Carmen consulted her computer file, picked up the phone and punched in Josh Ross's office number. She knew Jamie's mother had died not long ago and was wondering when he would register some grief. It wasn't healthy for him to go on like nothing had happened.

"I'd like to speak to Joshua Ross," she said, in her coldest, most professional voice. "He's not there? Well tell him to call his son's school nurse when he gets in. It's about Jamie falling asleep in gym class." She gave them her number and hung the phone up hard. If there was anything she hated, it was solo fathers who treated their kids like unpaid bills. The letters she had sent home to Josh Ross in the past had been answered by vague, hastily-scrawled notes or not at all.

This Dr. Ross might be a nuclear physicist, Carmen thought, but to her he was just one lazy, uncaring dad. She would let him know her opinion of him. He was probably like Briglia, her ex-boyfriend, Carmen said to herself, filing away Jamie's health records. The gym teacher had never been her favorite date, and she went out with him the first time only because he pressured her; told her he was "in crisis," since his divorce. Carmen had a soft heart and didn't want to believe anybody was a lost cause. Briglia changed her mind. The second date, he tried to push his way into her apartment and pounded on the door when she closed and locked it. The next time he tried to get her to go out to dinner, Carmen had said no. Briglia flipped out and pushed her against a brick wall so hard she had a goose egg on the back of her head for a week. After that, Carmen got a court order to keep Briglia away from her. She could understand why his ex-wife had dumped him and fled.

Besides being violent, Briglia couldn't hold a conversation that was not about himself and his disappointments. Of course, he occasionally talked about her too, how pretty her long black hair was and how smooth her olive skin felt to the touch. It didn't take long for her to get tired of being told what a beautiful woman she was, a line that Briglia always trotted out when he couldn't think of anything else to say. Finally, she let him know that he had only two topics of conversation, herself and him, and that she was sick of both. After that, he talked only about himself.

Carmen looked up when her door opened and stood to protest when she saw the intruder was Dick Briglia. "The court order said to stay away from me, Briglia." She picked up a paperweight that weighed as much as a bowling ball.

"Easy, sweetheart," Briglia said, leaning against the wall, his hands in his pockets. "Just checking on the kid. Jamie's okay? No drugs?" His voice sounded almost hopeful that she might have found out the poor kid was sniffing coke, just so he could lean on Jamie some more.

"He's sleepy, that's all," Carmen said coldly. "You boring him like you bore me?" She picked up her briefcase and tossed her coat over her shoulder.

Briglia followed her out the door and down the hall. "How about a burger tonight? I got time off from Guard duty this weekend. We could…"

Carmen didn't look up at him. "You sent Jamie to me as an excuse to get in my face again. Forget it."

She turned abruptly into the women's room and Briglia barged in after her, refusing to be brushed off. The six women inside screamed when they saw him, and he backed out, crashing into the school principal as he went.

"I've been meaning to talk to you, Briglia, about the classes you've been cutting short," the principal said, shaking his finger at the gym teacher. As the swinging door swooshed closed, Carmen smiled, glad someone other than herself was on Briglia's case.

That night Jamie seemed to Emily to be even more antsy than usual. His leg jiggled against the table like a metronome, and his fingers tapped the edge of the plate. Of course, he might be trying to avoid eating his tofu, which sat in ghastly pale, drooping piles around his plate. Emily decided to chance a rebellion, given that at least one person was going to be on her side.

She pushed her dish away and folded her arms. "If botulism had a taste, it would be like tofu."

Dan looked up from his dinner, which he was chowing down like it was spaghetti and meatballs. "It thinks it's going to be poisoned," he mocked, pointing his fork at Emily.

Ignoring the attempt of Dan and Emily to escalate their perpetual war, Josh turned to Jamie. "Nurse Rochas called me at work today. She says you fell asleep in gym class."

Jamie tried to change the subject. He called the maneuver word-judo, and he was very good at it. "Isn't she a 10, Dad? Dan says she is."

"Shut your hole, Jamie," Dan muttered, red-faced, pretending to hunt for stray bits of tofu on his plate. "I never said that."

"I only heard her message on my machine," Josh said. "What's going on, Jamie? How come you're sleeping in school?"

Emily froze, nearly dropping her fork on her plate. She and Dan exchanged glances, and Dan crossed his eyes dramatically, the way he always did when they were about to get into trouble.

They need not have worried. Jamie was in his best form, smiling like an angel. The kid ought to be an actor, Emily said to herself. His angel routine could win an Academy Award for best con artist of the year. First, he would screw up his pouty little mouth as if he was about to cry, then straighten it out, in a heart-breaking attempt to look manly.

"It's just that. . .sometimes I can't sleep at night. I keep remembering how Mom used to read me a story at bedtime."

Emily relaxed. What a load of hoo-ha. This kid never asked for a bedtime story in his life. He went to sleep before his head hit the pillow.

Jamie's act always melted Josh, and was melting him now. "I know, son," his father said. "Haven't been sleeping so good myself. How about calling out for some pizza?" Josh's answer to every emotional crisis was always junk food. A chorus of cheers around the table seconded his motion.

"Can I order it?" cried Jamie. "I want to order it!'

"Don't let him." Dan got up fast, knocking his chair over in his hurry to be first at the phone. "He'll get that pineapple kind again."

"No Honolulu pizza, Jamie," Josh said firmly. "I'll be listening on the other line."

36

Chapter 4

That night Jamie lay awake after the others had gone to sleep. He was belching garlic because Dan had insisted on double Italian when the pizza was ordered. Now his stomach was sending up waves of odorous discontent, almost as bad as the night before, when he had drunk Josh's day-old coffee. Jamie stirred restlessly, then sat up, trying to keep the garlic stuff from rising any further up his throat. If he couldn't sleep, maybe it was a signal to go down to the computer and visit mom again. Maybe she was even calling him, like she did in the dreams of her that he often had.

Jamie had watched a movie about a kid who could see dead people. Maybe that was happening to him. Sometimes he experimented with trying to summon up ghosts, invoking the powers of the Shaolin priesthood. Emily had said he must have ESP, because he always knew what she and Dan were planning. Jamie had been the same way with his mother. The two of them had been so close they sometimes believed they could read each other's minds. He had to ask himself why she was calling him and not the other kids, but that must be because he had psychic powers and was the youngest. There had to be some perk to being the youngest, and maybe this was it.

He checked the hall to see that nobody's light was on, then held tight to the banister, afraid he might noisily tumble down the stairs in the dark. This time he would not wake up the others. He got into the study easily, having had his dry run the night before. Before turning on the computer, he slipped back to the door and looked upstairs, checking to see if a light had gone on. The hall was still dark, so he pushed cushions against the crack under the door and went to work.

Jamie had memorized the sequence of keystrokes needed to get in, and didn't care that the card with the instructions was gone. He slipped his hand into the glove after putting on the

VR headset and waited. The same scene came up that had been there the day before. His tiny mother was still in the old-fashioned pub having a beer with her friends. Jamie put out his gloved hand. The plump, pretty lady bartender was leaning over the counter telling Becky something and both glanced up at the ceiling.

Just then, Jamie closed his eyes and grabbed, sticking the glove practically into the screen. He felt something move. Several somethings. It was like holding a handful of lizards before putting them in his terrarium. He opened his eyes and stared at the glove. Four tiny people, among them his mom, were spilling out of it and looking very mad.

Turning the computer off with his spare hand, Jamie set the four down on the desk, so fast that three of them tumbled over. Becky, managing to keep her footing, stared up at Jamie, while he stared back. Meanwhile, the others scrambled to their feet and looked at their surroundings with varying degrees of dismay.

"Oh, bloody hell," said the tallest one, a fellow who looked like a woodchopper in a fairytale book. "Not that glove again. Another of them giant blokes, is it?"

The gentleman with a wig brushed off his black suit and looked with interest at the computer. "This one is smaller. A child, I presume. Let us hope he does not take us for toys."

"E's not so ugly as the big ones yesterday," said the plump bartender lady, who adjusted her lace shawl modestly over her low neckline. "Who is 'e, Becky? It seems you know 'im."

Becky kept her eyes on Jamie. "Are you real?" she said in a soft voice. "Am I?" She held her head with both hands. "It hurts to remember so much at once."

Trying to keep his voice just as quiet, Jamie leaned toward her. "Mom? You're real! I made you come back."

He picked her up gently and held her close to his face. She kissed the tip of his nose.

"Honey, I'm not supposed to be here. I'm not even supposed to be there. I'm supposed to be dead."

"So are we," said Samuel. "Just send us back and we'll sort out the theology later."

Jamie's heart beat so fast he thought it would burst. "I want you here, Mom," he blurted out. "I'll never send you back. Never!"

With one quick gesture, he grabbed the four of them up in both hands and held them close to his chest. Then the thought struck him, how would he get out the door if he couldn't turn the knob? He looked around and his eyes fell on a small empty box in which Josh had packed the keyboard. It would have to do. Carefully, he set the four little people down and closed the cover over them, making sure a crack was left for air. Jamie hadn't raised lizards and mice for nothing. Keeping one hand on the box cover, he picked up a nearby flash drive, slid it into the computer, and saved the Lilliput Game onto it. Then he removed the copy, stuffing it into his bathrobe pocket. Lilliput was his now, Jamie said to himself, and so was his mother. He crept out of the room, kicking the door closed, and tiptoed up the stairs.

After zipping the back-up Lilliput cartridge into his worn teddy bear pillow, Jamie sat on the edge of the bed, swinging his feet and trying to think. He toyed with the idea of keeping this secret to himself, but realized a lot was at stake. The lives of the little people, for one thing, and keeping Josh from finding out, for another. He peeked into the hall, and seeing no one, carried the box carefully out of his room. Emily's door was ajar, and he went in, bumping the door closed with his rear. Scruff had been sleeping at the foot of the bed. The dog got up, stretched, and trotted over to sniff at Jamie.

Jamie clutched the box close when Scruff growled and lashed his tail. "No, Scruff. They're mine. You can't have them."

Emily sat up and rubbed her eyes. "Jamie. . .what's the matter? Shut up, Scruff, you'll wake Dad."

"Looky," Jamie hissed, his whisper almost as loud as a scream. "I did it! Mom's here!" He tumbled the little figures out on her pillow.

"Are you crazy?" Emily turned on her light. "Who's here?"

When she saw a tiny Becky trying to balance on the curve of the pillow, she froze "Holy sh. . ."

"Emily, sweetheart," Becky said, her tiny hands on her tiny hips as she looked up at her daughter. "Make just the tiniest effort not to talk like a tart."

"You sound like Mom, but you can't be." Emily's voice was tight and she had to swallow before she could go on talking. She wanted to believe her mother had been resurrected but knew it couldn't be true. Whoever this little person was, she wasn't Becky. "You're dead. I mean, she's dead."

As she surveyed the rat's nest that was her daughter's room, Becky shook her head. The desk was heaped with unwashed clothing. So was the floor. Schoolbooks and papers were piled on top of a bookcase in which most of the books were turned backwards, sideways, and upside down. Wet towels hung over the back of a pine straight chair, taking off its finish as surely as turpentine. In the corners dust balls the size of mice rolled gently in the breeze from the open window.

Scruff trotted across the room carrying in his mouth items of underwear that he certainly hadn't found in the per. Emily looked at her mother, trying to fight down the blush that was blotching her face with guilt. It was true she had not cleaned her room since the slumber party a month ago, and only then because Jake Cohen's sister was invited to the party.

"Dead, is it? Well, she's back," Becky said, "and none too soon, apparently. Em, this room hasn't been cleaned since the rocks cooled." She pointed to the torn picture of a scroungy-looking guitarist, with every aperture in his head pierced and studded.

"Who's this pathetic twit? And where's that Picasso print I gave you?"

It was true that Emily had replaced the picture of a girl in a flowing white dress with the grungy guitarist, so the friends who came to her slumber party would think she was cool. She spoke slowly, kneeling down to put her face near Becky's.

"You really are my mom. I've missed our fights." She gave Becky a cautious kiss on the cheek, which caused the tiny woman to drop backwards onto the pillow in an undignified heap.

Looking a little sad, Becky picked herself up and adjusted the quiver of arrows on her back. "I hope you've missed more than that, Emily. I have. Remember what I've told you about negativity making your world ugly."

Emily bit her lip. She wanted to tell this tiny hologram that for the past six months she had struggled against guilt and tears every day, wishing she could undo what she had done in that terrible moment. But no words came out. Her mother's philosophy had always been to look for the best in whatever happened. If it's happening, she used to say, it's for your good. Believe that and everything will turn out well. If you set your mind on good things, they will come to you. Your mind will create them. Emily wondered how her mother felt now that a falling watermelon had ended her life. She imagined what Becky would say if her daughter came out with such an idea. Becky would probably remind Emily that now she had an eternal life in her beloved eighteenth century, just where she'd always wanted to live.

"I've missed you, mom," Jamie insisted, his voice so loud that his sister put her hand over his mouth. "I've missed you so bad the school nurse thinks I'm having a nervous breakdown. She told Dad so." He subsided when Emily shook him. "Well, she prob'ly told him that," Jamie finished lamely.

The door opened and both kids turned around fast. It was only Dan, rubbing his eyes and muttering. His hair was sticking straight up, and his top was unbuttoned so you could see little chest hairs starting to sprout. Dan acted very proud of them and never buttoned up unless he was made to.

"Chill it, you guys," he said in a cross voice. "It's the middle of the night."

Emily jumped off the bed, so quickly that Becky fell over again, half-vanishing in the soft pillow. "Look what Jamie went and did!"

Lifting his mother carefully and holding her in both hands, Jamie stood in front of Dan. "I got mom out of the computer, Dan! Me! It's just. . ." he paused and looked down. "It's jus' that she's kind of small."

"Mom? I don't believe this… It's really you." Dan blinked, and his eyes were wet at the corners. He bent down, clumsily trying to pat her on the head. Becky leaned indignantly away.

"Hey, big guy, don't you patronize me." Then she grinned and opened her arms as if she was going to try a hug. When all she could encircle was Dan's thumb, Becky gave up, shrugging. "We're totally out of scale, here," she said. "I feel like Alice in Wonderland after eating the wrong cookie."

"More like one of Gulliver's Lilliputians, mom," Emily said. "You came out of Dad's Lilliput video game."

"Dad!" Dan slapped his hand to his head. "Now we've got to tell him."

"If we get her and the others back in the VR program," Emily argued, "we won't have to tell him anything."

For a moment, the three of them turned and stared at the other Lilliputians, who were standing silent, politely waiting to be introduced.

Becky waved her hand at the burly, wigged gentleman in knee britches. "This is Doctor Samuel Johnson, kids. Mind your manners. He'll notice if you don't and will make a cutting remark."

Not knowing exactly how to greet an eighteenth-century gentleman, the famous scholar who invented the dictionary, Emily bobbed an awkward curtsey, while the boys nodded.

Samuel doffed his hat and bowed. "'Twill do, Becky, though I've seen my chimney sweep turn a more elegant ankle than any of these three."

"This is the twenty-first century, Samuel," Becky said. "We may have indoor plumbing, but our manners leave much to be desired. Children, meet Molly, pub owner and barmaid."

The plump little woman curtseyed. "And this other one is 'Enry, the blacksmith." Henry's bow was a good deal less polished than Samuel's, and if the scholar hadn't caught him, the blacksmith would have pitched forward and landed face first on the rumpled sheets.

"I guess you want to go back into your pub, right now. Yes?" Emily looked at them hopefully, wanting to get rid of the evidence as fast as possible.

"Just a minute," Jamie said. "You can't put her back. If you do, I'll tell Dad you taught me how to get into the Lilliput game. I will! I'll tell!"

"Mom, help." Dan turned back to Becky. "Explain to him there's no way you can stay here."

Becky folded her arms stubbornly in a way they had all learned to read as 'forget about it.' She spoke in her loudest voice, which came out like a mosquito's, despite her efforts to shout. "Let me talk to your father. Then I'll go back."

"You had better do as she says, boy," Samuel said, looking at Becky with fond admiration. "It's no use arguing with her. If her pistol misfires, she's the sort who'll knock you down with the butt end of it."

He backed up, pulling Becky with him as Scruff pushed his way in between the kids, trying to sniff and paw the strangers, especially Becky, for whom he felt a dim recognition. She didn't smell like anything he remembered, though. The dog managed to slobber on the head of Henry, before the blacksmith furiously pulled off his cap and wiped it on his pants leg, as Emily grabbed Scruff's collar.

"I say, giants," cried Henry, "call off your beast before 'e drowns me."

Scruff was licking his chops as Emily pulled him back. "Not to eat, Scruff," she scolded. "Cut it out."

The dog whimpered, then sank down on the floor, putting one paw over his eyes in his gesture of shame. Dan had taught it to him when he was still a pup and occasionally paid attention to directions. Sadly, Scruff had had many opportunities to practice this trick over the years.

Jamie got in front of the dog and bowed politely to the little people in his best kung fu style. "I am Jamie," he announced, using his fake Chinese accent. "I will help you."

"Knock it off, Jamie," Dan said, in a bored, superior tone. "These guys never heard of kung fu. They're from the seventeen hundreds. All they got to watch was dancing bears and dog fights."

Hearing the word 'dog,' Scruff lifted his head hopefully, wondering if he was forgiven. When no one noticed him, he let his snout drop on both paws and was instantly asleep.

Samuel returned Jamie's bow and smiled at him. "Samuel Johnson, Sir, at your service. I say, you seem rather smaller and more civil than these other giants. Since you are the one who took us out of our world, perhaps you are just the one to put us back."

Fanning herself with her handkerchief, Molly interrupted hysterically. "'Enry, if you don't make the giants send us home, you've 'ad your last kidney pie!"

"We aren't giants," Dan explained, stung at the implication there was something wrong with his wonderful new height. "You're Lilliputians. And you'd better give us some respect, if you want to get home."

"Never you fear, darlin'," Henry soothed Molly, one arm clumsily around her shoulders, "I'll see to it. Me Molly's kidney pie is worth any risk, even the terrible teeth of that there beast."

The beast under discussion was snoring, with mouth open and tongue lolling between his pointed canines. One look at him and Molly shuddered, burying her face in her hands.

Becky stamped her foot and shook a fist under her daughter's nose. "Okay, kids. Let's not turn this into a mini-series. Either you wake your father or I will. Which is it going to be?"

Emily took a deep breath. It was hard for her to stand up to her mother, even a mother only six inches tall. Becky somehow always wound up being right or at least getting the last word. But she'd been gone long enough to be out of touch with reality, Emily figured, and would have to be clued in.

"Not going to happen," she said. "Dad would ground us for life. Or take our computers away, which is just as bad. You'll have to deal with us."

Becky was clearly desperate, her usual straightforward tactics having gotten her nowhere. Size, it seemed, was everything. 'Might makes right,' as she used to say. Her voice softened and went into guilt trip mode. "Look, sweetie, you owe me. I got killed because you dropped that watermelon on my foot, remember?"

"Don't remind me," Emily said in a muffled voice. "It's not like I meant to drop it."

Becky looked down and scuffed one pointy green shoe on the other. "I know you didn't mean to, baby. And I wouldn't have said that if I weren't desperate to talk to Josh. You have to help me. I know you will."

Emily sat down on the floor, held her hands over her ears, and rocked back and forth, trying to pretend the scene was a dream. She had to believe that or face the possibility that Josh would maybe put her in reform school for habeas corpus, a felony that TV crime shows had taught her was something like kidnapping. After all, this was his game and she had stolen it, busted into his VR computer without permission, and probably deserved Jamie's favorite idea of a punishment, death by a thousand cuts.

"I want to help you, mom," she whispered, "but not if it means telling dad you're here. It's just a friggin' mess."

"Becky," Samuel said in a shocked voice, "you're not seriously acknowledging these young guttersnipes as your children?" He shook his head in sympathy, and his rimless glasses slid down his nose.

"They are, God help me."

It was the first time she had ever seen her mother look embarrassed. Emily stared at the floor guiltily, wishing she had learned Scruff's shame gesture and the trick of falling asleep before being blamed for anything. Like always, Becky was making her feel as if she was imperfect as a serve smacked into the net. Hardly bigger than a thumb, Becky could still make her daughter feel small. Emily slumped like a fallen soufflé.

Molly squinted, staring at the giant children, then turned to Becky. "Beggin' your pardon, luv, but you don't seem quite large enough in the hips to have whelped these bairns."

Holding her head distractedly, Becky muttered, "I used to be bigger. I haven't been working out."

Henry gulped and stared at her. "You used to be a gulliver? 'Orrible!" For someone who was the biggest of the four Lilliputians, he seemed overly dismissive of size.

"Not at all, Henry," Samuel remarked with a philosophic calm, examining their situation with scientific objectivity. "Proportion is relative. In the eye of the beholder. . ."

Dan interrupted, pulling Emily by the arm to get her attention. "We got no time for talk, here. How'd these guys get out of the computer?"

"From the game," Emily said, with exaggerated, scornful emphasis. "I made them, remember?"

Henry was fairly hopping up and down with fury. "Like 'ell you did. I got no Gulliver wench for me maker!"

"We're immortal, we are," Molly asserted proudly, smoothing her apron. "Made by Jonathan Swift in the year of Our Lord, 1726. Ye might 'ave a bit of respect."

Emily stared at the plump little woman, considering how often she herself had felt like she was being dissed. Probably

Molly felt the same way. They must seem truly awful to the tiny barmaid, as if they had no manners at all. Hadn't her mother told her that in the eighteenth century, manners were a major deal? Becky must be thinking that her kids were even worse-behaved than they had been when she was around, a misconception Emily would do her best to correct. She curtsied awkwardly to Molly.

"Sorry, ma'am. We know where you came from and just how you feel about going home. It was a total accident, us bringing you here." She turned to Dan. "We gotta put 'em back. Right now."

Henry took a swig from the flask at his belt and looked around him with interest. "I say, luv, let's 'ave a look around while we're here. There's plenty of time to go back 'ome."

"And 'ow about you keeping your brains clear for once, 'Enry?" Molly tried unsuccessfully to grab the flask out of his hand. "Next thing, you'll be laid out on the floor and we'll 'ave to carry you."

Samuel rocked back on his heels, hands in his pockets and contemplated Henry. "The trouble with drink is that it makes a man mistake words for deeds. What we need is action."

"Right," Dan said, "exactly what I think. If we don't get you guys back soon, you might start evaporating. How long does computerized molecular structure hold together, anyway? I guess only Dad would know."

"So let's go ask him," Becky said furiously. "If you'd just listen to me."

Emily decided to ignore her, having had plenty of practice. "I don't know how long, Dan. Let's just get them back fast, and we don't have to worry about whether they're falling apart as we speak."

Screwing up his face preliminary to a crying fit, Jamie quavered, "You can't put mom back in the computer. She's mine. I got her out, not you." He reached out to grab Becky, but Emily slapped his hand away. Jamie jumped backward and stepped on Scruff's paw, waking up the dog.

Scruff yelped and snapped his jaws rather too close to Henry for the little blacksmith's comfort. As Henry threatened the dog boldly with a slingshot grabbed from his pants pocket, Jamie hauled Scruff back. Henry snapped his rubber weapon, and Scruff whined, putting his tail between his legs.

"I say, giants," Henry's said, sounding suspicious, "you will try to put us back where we came from?"

Dan scratched his head until his hair stood straight up. "We'd like to, but the truth is, we don't know how."

"Then figure it out. God knows your brains must be big enough." Molly twisted her shaking hands together, and then put them under her apron, presumably not wanting anyone to know how scared she was.

"Not so big it won't take a while," Emily said, wondering if she might think of a non-incriminating way to ask her father how long virtual reality figures would last when separated from their program. No sign of disintegration yet, so maybe they had a while to make a plan. Turning to Dan, she said, "We'll keep 'em in my dollhouse and lock the closet door. Dad never comes in my room."

"Do it." Dan hurried out of the room. "I'll head for Dad's study and check his notebooks for how long computerized molecules last."

Becky waved her fists like a prizefighter. "I'm your mother, Emily. You can't lock me in the closet."

Using both hands, Emily picked Becky up, rather enjoying herself. "Wanna bet?"

Jamie trailed after his sister carrying the other three little people close to his chest. When Emily had opened the closet door, she kicked aside some dirty clothes to expose the dollhouse. Though filthy, it was large and comfortable. Emily had not played with the dollhouse for years, but she refused to get rid of it. Because Josh had made the dollhouse for her, it had sentimental value, even though its floors slanted slightly and the windows and doors were stuck closed. Emily lifted off the top and deposited her mother in the upstairs bedroom. Jamie set down his charges in the next-door sitting room on a green plastic couch. Once the heavy wooden rooftop was in place again, Emily was reasonably sure her mother couldn't escape, but she pushed the top down hard, just to make sure.

After getting Jamie settled in bed, Emily went back to her room and tried not to hear the scufflings and high-pitched conversations from the closet. She spent some time punching her pillow, turning it over, and holding it against her ears before finally falling asleep. Emily dreamed that she was a blue mouse being shot at by her mother with a shower of arrows. They pricked her skin, and she was sure her mother had drawn blood. Somehow, in her dream, she wound up under the table in the dollhouse, smallified as her mother had been, and fending off arrows with her bare hands. She woke hearing her own voice groaning out protests against mothers in general and Becky in particular. It was not a night she wanted to remember.

Chapter 5

In the dollhouse, the four Lilliputians filed down the tiny winding staircase to the living room. Running her fingers over the plastic piano, Becky grimaced at the dust. Henry went to each window and door, testing it, but couldn't break through. Finally, they all sat down on the carpeted floor and stared glumly at each other. The crack under the closet door let in just enough of Emily's night-light that each of the little people could see the worry lines on the faces of the others.

Becky had whiled away a few hours giving Henry lessons with the bow and arrow, as she used to when they frequented the pub together. Since Henry was strong and a natural athlete, he had become almost as good an archer as she was. But the lack of air in the dollhouse had made both of them feel faint, and they had to quit. The only fresh air came through the chimney. Becky noticed the opening, and stuck her head into the fireplace, looking up.

"I think I could climb out," she said, "but it'll be a tight fit. Have to leave the bow and arrows behind."

"Maybe you could find this 'usband of yours," Henry said. "'E could make your children send us back."

"Leave 'er be," said Molly fiercely. "You think it's enough just to tell a woman wot to do and she does it. Which is why I'm in no 'urry to marry you and let you run me pub."

Henry rubbed his rough, bearded chin on Molly's cheek, trying to be sexy, but succeeding only in being slapped away. "Now Moll, it's an easy matter, this is. The gullivers got us in, and they'll get us out. Right, Becky?"

"I'll tell Josh to send you three back," Becky said, laying her bow and arrow on the coffee table. "But I'm staying."

Samuel smacked his hand to his broad forehead. "Heat dry up my brains! The woman's lost what small wits she had.

You heard what the children said. We could disintegrate at any moment. Something about molecular structure, whatever that is."

Bracing herself against the walls of the fireplace, Becky began to climb. "I have to stay," she said. "They're my family. My kids, my husband."

Molly pulled her down again. "And what do you expect to do for your 'usband, luv? Kiss 'is ankles?"

"I'm twice the woman I used to be." Becky shook the other woman's hands off and climbed up the chimney to the top. "As Sam says," she called down to them, "dying concentrates the faculties wonderfully."

A light popped on in the bedroom and streamed under the closet door. As Emily opened the door, Becky slid down the gutter from the roof, ready to run. When the door moved, she scuttled out of the closet between Emily's feet. As her daughter tried to grab her, Becky ran under the bed straight into a cluster of rolling dust bunnies. They covered her face in a dark web and wrapped her hands like mummy bandages. Sneezing and choking, Becky slapped them aside and ran out of Emily's room into the hall. Strands of dust hung from her braid and trailed behind her like a veil.

Emily was glad she hadn't bothered to clean under her bed, since a face-full of dust bunnies might just slow Becky down. But her mother zigzagged down the hall like a football player, eluding Emily right to the open door of the master bedroom. Emily's gasped and lunged, her arms flailing as she tried to head her mother off at the door. With a squeal of victory, Becky rolled between her daughter's feet, then slipped into Josh's room. Emily stood still, her hands falling to her sides. It was all over, then. Becky would find Josh and tell him what they'd done. Emily trembled and waited.

Suddenly a blue mouse ran out through Josh's bedroom door with Becky right ahead of him, just as scared as he was. Emily pounced, falling to her knees on the bare hall floor, so that Becky ran straight into her waiting hands. Behind her,

Scruff came skittering down the hall toward them, his nails scratching against the wood floor. His bright black eyes were focused on the mouse, who was inches from obliteration. Scruff was making harsh, predatory noises in his throat, obviously thrilled that he was about to make his first kill. The mouse barely made it down the stairs and through the dog door outside, while Scruff panted and pounded after him. Emily had just grabbed her tiny mother and stuffed her into her pajama pocket when Josh appeared at his bedroom door, shaving as he walked.

"Emily, you'd better set a trap. We've got a mouse. Odd color."

Emily tried to sound nonchalant. "Yeah, I saw it, too. Must have been one of Jamie's. I caught him painting a mouse the other day."

Becky was fighting to get her head out of Emily's pocket. She waved her hands between her daughter's fingers and called in her mosquito-like voice, trying to get Josh's attention. But the sound of Josh's electric razor drowned her out. Emily rushed back into her bedroom and slammed the door shut.

"Couldn't you just trust me this once?" Emily held her tiny mother up so they could look each other in the eye. "You always have to be in charge. You always had to be the best athlete, the best everything."

Saying the words, Emily remembered all the times she couldn't return her mother's tennis serve, couldn't duplicate her mother's straight-A average in school, and couldn't get her father's attention when Becky and he were talking. It came over her suddenly that if she lived to be a hundred, she couldn't learn to do all the things her mother had done effortlessly and with grace. She was a hopeless klutz in the kitchen, would never fill a bra, and her hair wouldn't ever grow past her scrawny neck. Her heart hardened into a knot, and she glared at her mother.

"Well, who'd you want for a role model anyway?" Becky stood her ground, her lips firm. "Betty Crocker?"

"Just someone I wouldn't have to look up to all the time," Emily said, her voice unsteady.

"That's not exactly our problem now, is it?" Becky wound her hair into a fresh braid and tossed it over her shoulder. She looked as much in charge as if she was six feet tall.

Emily took a step back. "Our problem's the same as it's always been," she muttered. "You wanted me to be just like you, and I couldn't be."

Becky reached out to her daughter, but couldn't stretch far enough to touch her. "Sweetheart, you were fine. Just had too smart a mouth. More like me than you think."

"I wish." Emily put her mother down in the dollhouse, wishing she really could be like this wild, self-confident woman. With Becky's long hair, full figure, and quick tongue, Emily could swagger through the school day, the envy of all the girls and encircled admiringly by all the boys. Especially Jake, who Emily liked to imagine abandoning football and following her around, like Scruff looking for a handout.

Scruff pushed past her and stuck his furry snout into the dollhouse. He saw all the little people, and did what he always did when people couldn't stop him. He began joyously licking them from top to toe. Slapping at the long pink tongue Becky shrieked, "No! Bad dog," and ran behind a plastic chest of drawers.

"Down, Scruff," Emily said, turning around to see her little brother coming in the open door. "Jamie, you aren't supposed to come in here without knocking. Now you've let in the dog, and he's slobbering all over mom." She dropped a tissue into the dollhouse and Becky, looking grateful, began to wipe herself off with it.

"I brought 'em some food," Jamie said brightly. "They gotta have breakfast, right? Here Henry, Samuel, try the chocolate ripple before it melts. It's mom's favorite ice cream." He crowded into the closet, followed by Dan, who was carrying a demitasse cup full of orange soda.

"Don't you try to bribe me, you bullies," Becky said, setting down the tissue and looking hungrily at the shot glass of ice cream Jamie had set down on the dollhouse floor.

Henry was already shoveling it into his mouth, using both hands. "'Ave some, Molly. It's even better than your porridge. 'Ow about some more of that ripple, young master? I could give up my gin bottle for that stuff, I could."

Jamie was awkwardly stroking his mother's head with one fingertip. Then he picked her up, wanting to move her closer to the ice cream.

"Be careful," Emily warned. "She almost got away a few minutes ago. Tried to run into dad's room. Tell him not to pick her up, Dan."

"Bro, it's not respectful to pick your mother up. Bad idea." Dan began pouring orange soda into the tiny teacups of Emily's dollhouse set. He had a v-shaped frown between his heavy dark eyebrows. "Em, don't you think. . .I mean, if she's really mom, maybe we should, like, listen to her? Do what she says?"

"Look, we don't mean her any harm," Emily said impatiently. "Our intentions are good, right?" She started brushing her fine, flyaway hair very hard, wanting what she said to be true.

Samuel came up behind Becky and put his arm protectively around her shoulders. "Intentions be damned. You may shoot a man through the head and say you intended to miss him. But the judge will still have you hanged. If you mean well by us, young giants, you'll consult your father, just as your mother told you to do."

"That's right," said Henry, licking the ice cream off his fingers. "Maybe you don't mean to send us back at all? Maybe we're just your bloody toys." He pushed the shot glass away and folded his arms challengingly across his brawny chest.

Suddenly the door opened and they heard Josh's voice. "You better get dressed, guys. School's just a burnt pop-tart away."

Emily jumped toward the dollhouse and clapped her hand over her mother to shut her up. Retaliating, Becky bit her daughter's finger, making Emily swear and pull her hand away. But Josh had continued down the hall, not noticing Becky's shrieks. The three children sat down on the floor, weak with relief, and looked at each other.

"Okay, genius," Dan said to Emily. "What now?"

"We get ready for school. Jake's going to be here any minute and we aren't even dressed." Emily got up and jammed the dollhouse roof back on.

"Everybody out. I got this thing handled." She closed the door behind them.

As she pulled on her jeans and tie-dyed crop top, Emily wondered just how her mother was feeling, hearing those words she herself had said so often. Maybe Becky was right, that the two of them were more alike than not. Emily smiled at the thought, wondering if there might not be some magic moment in the future when she would turn into a fearless, gorgeous grown-up with a man of her own. The smile faded when she realized that Becky would not be there to see it happen. Because of one careless moment, they had missed sharing the rest of their lives, and nothing she could do would change that. But at least there was now, Emily said to herself, sliding the brush through her hair with a final stroke. She would take good care of her small, stubborn mother and get her home safely, however much Becky tried to stop her.

Jake was banging on the back door calling for Dan before their pop-tarts had popped out of the toaster. As if Scruff had never seen Jake before, he barked like a Rottweiler in heat and threw himself against the door. Choking on her milk, Emily put down her glass, forgetting to wipe her upper lip. She had hoped to be ready when Jake came. If she was ready, maybe he and Dan would let her walk to school with them, but her books were still scattered over the dining room table.

"Cool it, Scruff," Jake said, patting the dog behind the ears and letting the screen door bang behind him. "You guys look like something out of a Hogwarts dungeon. What's up?"

He lounged against the door, hands in his pockets, a shock of red-blond hair hanging over his high forehead. Emily thought he looked good enough to eat, a lot better than pop-tarts. Maybe because of his height and broad shoulders, Jake seemed older than Dan, even if they were in the same class. More like a man than a boy, even though Jake was only fifteen. His jaw had some blond prickly hairs on it, so Emily could tell he was working on the five o'clock shadow that all the guys aspired to sprout. Jake was one of the few who stood a chance.

He glanced at Emily's white mustache and smiled. "Got milk?"

Turning red, Emily grabbed a piece of paper towel and cleaned herself up. Why could she never look right? Probably he was even noticing that her belly button ring had come apart and was threatening to pop off if she took a deep breath. Since Jake was smiling at her, she guessed he was only looking at her mustache.

"Here, you didn't get all of it," Jake said, taking the paper towel away from her and dabbing at her upper lip. "That's better. You should smile more, munchkin. You got a great mouth."

Emily leaned weakly against the table, sighing. She couldn't think of a single clever comeback, and wished, not for the first time, that she could suddenly be grown up and have her mother's gift for smart remarks. She smiled shakily at Jake, and fumbled with her belly button ring. Sure enough, before she could click it closed, it dropped to the floor and rolled toward Jake. Emily watched it with horror as it fell over at his feet. She could feel her face turn red and shut her eyes, trying to blot out the whole scene.

Jake picked up the ring casually and handed it back to her, acting like nothing had happened.

"I think this is yours," was all he said.

"I think you're right." Emily replied. As she took back the ring, she decided Jake had to be the coolest guy on earth. Giving him a slight smile with her great mouth, Emily went to the dining room to gather her books and reaffix the ring to her midsection in private.

When she came back, Dan tossed his book bag over one shoulder. "Hey, Jake, you're the class expert in physics. Got any idea how long the molecular integrity of a virtual reality figure might hold up outside the box? Hypothetically, of course."

Jake looked thoughtful. "Can't rightly say. I'd guess maybe a few days, a week. It depends on a lot of variables."

"So we've got a reprieve at least till tonight," Emily breathed softly. "They'll live that long."

"Who?" Jake turned to her again, his dark blue eyes piercing hers. "Whatever you got going here, I'm in. Trust me."

"Maybe after school," Emily said, putting her books in her bag. "I'll think about it."

What she was really thinking about was how much she would like having Jake share their secret. That would bring him closer to her and her brother, mainly of course to her. It was the moment she had been waiting for, the moment when she had something he wanted. Now maybe he would start being her friend as well as Dan's. Emily hummed a punk song and swung her non-existent hips as she joined the two boys on the front porch. Jake stepped aside so she could walk between them and took her book bag.

"Let me carry it," he said. "Brawn should serve brains. Or something like that."

"Dan's the brain." Emily looked up dreamily into Jake's face and nearly tripped over a crack in the sidewalk. "Not me, except with the computer."

"What else counts?" Jake smiled down at her. "Now, tell me what's going on. I can keep a secret."

Chapter 6

Carrying a slip of paper from his teacher, Jamie walked slowly down the empty school hall. Everybody else had gone to class, but he was all by himself, his shirt torn and his face dirty. He was trying to think how he was going to tell the school nurse why he had gotten in a fight on the playground. At least he could tell her he had won.

He rehearsed the fight in his mind, picking out the best parts, so he could impress Carmen Rochas. Taunting him with the cry of "Your mom isn't alive any more. She's not coming back," Ronald, the class bully, had pushed Jamie down. All Jamie had said was that he had proof his mom wasn't dead. He didn't say a word about the Lilliputians, having promised Emily that he never would. Ronald pushed him down anyway, and Jamie returned the favor, nailing Ronald in his fat gut with a fast kung fu kick. Ronald had gone off sobbing and roaring his complaints to the teacher on playground duty.

That was why Jamie was now walking down the hall with a note that seemed to burn his fingers. The playground teacher had not understood that a martial arts kick was fair in battle and the note made Jamie look bad. He hated to think of Nurse Rochas frowning at him with her big, liquid brown eyes. Carmen was just about his favorite person in the world except for his tiny mother.

She was standing by the window starting to adjust the blinds so the sun wouldn't slam-bang its way into the office, as it was doing now. Motes were flying in the air, and Jamie fixed his eyes on them, not wanting to look at Carmen. He squinted as if he was studying the mote pattern under a microscope, working hard at it. Sometimes he wondered if everything that seemed solid and real was just like dust motes whirling in the light. Jake and Dan said everything that felt real was only electrical charges stuck together. So maybe it was true that nothing existed except positive and negative particles flying around like tiny, invisible dust motes. That might mean his tiny, pixilated mother was no less real than he was, which Jamie deeply wanted to believe. Hadn't his mom always said that 'real' was whatever you thought it was? Didn't that mean that if you wanted something badly enough, you could make it happen just by thinking hard?

Coming over to him, Carmen put her arm around his shoulders. "Jamie, what's wrong?" Her long black hair hung down near his face and smelled like lilacs.

He hung his head, ashamed to say what had happened, not wanting to get into the whole story of his mom's accident and the other kids' cracks about how he was an orphan. He just wanted to go home, take his mom out of the dollhouse, and hold her.

"I guess you don't want to tell me that you've been in a fight," Carmen said. "You don't have to tell me. I can see that for myself. What were you fighting about?"

"Ronald said my mom wasn't coming back." Jamie's voice quavered. "And then he pushed me down. So I kicked him."

"Kicking isn't the right way to fight, Jamie." Carmen shook her head and her jetty hair rippled like water. "You know better."

Jamie straightened up. "The way I kick is okay. It's kung fu. I'm a living weapon. The kids all know that and don't bother me. 'Least not till today."

Carmen sat him down beside her on a hard bench. "And what's this about your mom not being dead? We better talk about it."

"My sister says I can't tell." Jamie realized that he'd half-let it all out already. Now it would be hard to pick out what he shouldn't tell from what he could.

"Dead people don't come back, Jamie." Carmen was looking into his face so intently that Jamie wanted to close his eyes to avoid hers.

It was impossible. He could no more tell Carmen a lie than he could get the Lilliputians back into the computer.

"They do," he said, the words falling out faster than he could make sense of them. "They do come back, if you got my dad's virtual reality computer and the right code. Dan says it's a secret and the military will come and take mom and the others away if I tell. You won't tell, will you?"

"Wait a minute," Carmen said, pulling him around to face her. "You're telling me that your mom is alive? That she came out of your dad's computer?"

Carmen was looking at him as though he had suddenly turned into an orangutan. If he didn't explain, Jamie thought, she would have him in the principal's office for lying, not to mention fighting.

"You gotta believe me." He folded his hands in front of him as if he was praying. "I really did bring her back. Only," he faltered, "only it's just. . . she's smaller than she used to be."

Bringing her heavy black brows together in a frown, Carmen reached over to grab her pen and notebook. "How small? Smaller than me? Explain." She was ready to write down whatever he said, her pen poised above the paper.

Jamie looked around him wildly, hoping for inspiration. Finally, he put his palms six inches apart. "This small. She's brought some friends with her. Now they're going to be my friends too." He smiled the tremulous smile that usually got sympathy from grown-ups.

Instead of looking sympathetic, Carmen looked distinctly worried. "You could try making friends with some of the other kids. Maybe then Ronald wouldn't push you around."

"I like mom's friends better. They aren't mean like kids are." He had a quick idea and it was out of his mouth before he could think about it. "I tell you what. Tomorrow I'll bring the little people here, like in show 'n tell.. Then you gotta believe me."

Carmen raised an eyebrow and paused, waiting for him to take the words back. When he didn't, she sighed. "Okay, Jamie, you do that. Now, I want you to sit outside my office door while I make a phone call."

When Jamie had gone, Carmen let her breath out with a long whoosh. She stuck her notes in Jamie's file, pulled out a telephone number, and then dialed Dr. Josh Ross's cell phone.

Josh had no intention of being in his office at the corporation for long. He slipped in, checking the hall behind him and closed the door. Running his fingers over the spines of some tech books on virtual reality, Josh muttered to himself. There had to be a way of deactivating the holographic VR feature of his program so that no one could remove live parts of it. He had nightmares about Colonel Sharpe snatching the people from Lilliput and putting them in a heat register to spy on the Iranian embassy. Just the thought of his Becky being used as a weapon made the sweat break out on his forehead. He should have thought twice about putting her in the game, but he missed her so. Keeping her on his screen in 3D seemed at the time a harmless indulgence of his fantasies.

A way had to be found to stabilize the Lilliput program, and he would need every virtual reality book in his office to find it. Clutching his books under one arm, Josh opened the door, but stepped back fast when Mel Glatt stood in the doorway confronting him.

"Remember what I said about stealing government property?" Glatt's words gurgled in his throat, as if he was snarling instead of talking. "That's what this whole office is, Josh. What you and I are."

Josh brushed his boss aside and started out the door. "Speak for yourself, Glatt, not me. Whatever we were when we worked together before, now you and me got nothing in common except a fly."

Barring the other man's way by hanging onto the door jamb with both hands, Glatt shoved his face into Josh's. "Maybe you don't care about the job or yourself, but Colonel Sharpe reminds me you might care about your kids."

The cell phone played its musical hello and Josh grabbed it out of his pocket. He walked to the window, wanting to get as far away from Glatt as possible. The man squirted out meanness like a skunk squirted stink. What did he mean about Sharpe threatening the kids? Was Glatt lying? Sharpe didn't seem that bad. But if the stakes were high enough child-stealing might be the tactic of choice. Josh spoke into it curtly.

"Josh Ross, here."

A high, melodious female voice sang through the earpiece. "It's Carmen Rochas, the school nurse. You need to come to school right away. Jamie's got a problem I can't solve."

"Ok, Ms. Rochas, I hear you. But I got problems of my own right now. I'll have to see you later."

The voice became a little more shrill and less melodious. He could tell that Nurse Rochas would not listen to any excuses. She'd probably heard them all, over her years in that office.

"You got a problem here, is what you got. Jamie's flipping out. He needs your help and he needs it now. Nothing's more important than this child, you hear me?"

Josh held the phone out a foot from his ear. "How could I not? Just hold it, Nurse Ratchit or whatever you call yourself. I'm on my way."

He pictured a tyrannical, white-garbed nurse with a large, red-glossed mouth and muscles like Arnold Schwarzenegger's. She was probably another man-hunting harpy. He was tired of fighting off all the wanna-be Mrs. Rosses, like his next-door neighbor, Andriette, who was always trying to turn her gift casseroles into an invitation to get better acquainted with the bereaved father of those poor, helpless darlings, as she called his three children. Josh turned off the phone and headed for the door. Mel ran after him, frantically hanging on-to the back of Josh's sweater.

"Wait a minute. You can't just walk out of here. Colonel Sharpe expects…"

Josh turned around, slapping Glatt's fingers away from his handmade Bolivian sweater, a last gift from Becky. "When my wife died, you told me I had a week's family emergency leave coming to me. I never took it, right? So I'm taking my leave now. Get over it."

Frothing spit at the corners of his mouth, Glatt yelled, "I'll shred our partnership papers. You'll be out of here on your blue denim ass without a job."

Josh kept walking, glad he'd made copies of those papers. "You dump me for taking entitled family leave, and I'll see you in court." He smiled without turning around. "Go ahead, Mel, fire me. Dissolve the partnership. Make my day."

His voice cracking as he shouted, Mel Glatt slammed his fist against the wall. "Don't push it, Josh. Remember, the Colonel has taken hostages. And you got some to take."

Josh felt his face turn pale and cold as he heard the words. It was true, his three kids were vulnerable to any scheme Glatt and the Colonel might cook up. He thought about Dan's kind, serious eyes behind his glasses, Emily's slow, gorgeous smile, Jamie's wistful, vulnerable little face. He would have to guard them well. Becky would expect that and would have done it herself, if she was still alive. For the first time since his wife's death, Josh felt despair. He wasn't up to being both father and mother. Without his wife, he was not just a lonely single, but half a person.

If he could have, Josh would put himself into the VR pro-gram with Becky, plus their kids, and never come out. He was beginning to think the real world was a lot more dangerous than any video game. And besides, the game he played with Becky in it was becoming more real to him than what went on in the office. He looked forward to hanging out with her on the Lilliput game even more than he looked forward to leaving work. Hadn't there been a president who thought his administration was a reality show, who had so blurred the line between real and unreal that he couldn't tell the difference?

"What is real anyway?" he asked himself. Maybe the world everyone calls real is just a holographic dream, and he was no more substantial than his lost wife. For all he knew, some Great Designer beyond the multiverse had created the program that was his life, just the way Emily had designed the figures in the game of Lilliput. The more Josh thought about being just somebody's dream, the more fragile he felt. How was he going to help Jamie if he too was freaking out? How was he going to stand up to Glatt and Colonel Putz, if he wasn't even sure he was real?

Becky had always been the one who grounded the family in everyday life. Now that she was gone, Josh shivered as he found himself wondering if he were just a momentary collection of pixels in somebody else's video game. Well, if he was, then Glatt and Colonel Putz were too. That he could happily live with.

Slumping over the steering wheel, Josh reached out to activate his bug system. He had it rigged not only to cover Glatt's office, but the other laboratories in the complex. Glatt might be a partner, but Josh had learned that the man why he was so desperate for money and so could not be trusted. Glatt had a mortgage and a BMW to pay off, but more, he'd lately been dropping his money into Las Vegas slot machines like pennies into a wishing well. Once Glatt had borrowed gambling money from Josh, which was how Josh learned about his partner's habit. Sharpe's government contract was Glatt's last chance to pick up some quick bucks, and nothing would stand in his way–maybe not even scruples about child-stealing.

He could hear the door to Colonel Sharpe's lab open and close. Josh knew all about that lab, which made his own look like a third world classroom. Sharpe's golf clubs would be leaning against the lab table and his hi-tech metal tennis racket hanging over the desk. Probably some of his clumsy miniature robots would be bumping into each other on the polished floor. He'd seen the colonel's technology and didn't think much of it. Artificial intelligence was an oxymoron; you couldn't get an artificial human to think. The only way he had been able to program his VR Becky was to load her program with so much text that his wife's hologram had even more speech and action possibilities than the original game had, and that was a lot. The colonel's little robots couldn't begin to compete with her.

Josh leaned close to the receiver in his car, turning up the sound.

"Hewitt," Sharpe said to his assistant, a cold, metallic-skinned man that Josh had often thought was a robot in training, "take down the new mini-robot. Let's see what the little guy can do."

Hewitt's voice rang hollowly. "Like the flakes say, small is beautiful." There was a clunk and the mini-robot was ready for action.

Sharpe sounded pleased with himself and his product. "Slugger's my favorite so far. Should be able to cut his way through enemy missile circuitry without missing a microchip. Ten inches tall. If he does what I've programmed him to do, the Joint Chiefs are going to snap him up. Along with us and this whole lab."

"Like you say," Hewitt was fawning all over his colonel, "it's about time the President went after all those missiles pointed at us."

"Never mind the President." Sharpe's voice rang like a gong. "He's just a front man. My friends at the top run things. They want to crash the enemy's missile circuitry and leave us with the only viable weapons. North Korean missiles, Arab missiles, Iranian missiles—all gone. We just need a reliable mini-robot to infiltrate enemy weapons. Maybe Slugger is go-ing to be it."

"His outer shell is pure titanium," Hewitt said proudly. "57 magnum bullet capacity. Plus, rotating titanium knives replace his climbing-grasping claws in case of attack. This dude's got it all."

"Everything but brains." Sharpe sounded more doubtful than his assistant. "Let's try the little bugger out. If he's as good as you say, the U.S. could wind up the only country with working nuclear weapons. Maybe the only country, period."

Out in the car, Josh turned on the visual component of his bugging device and pulled over to the curb. "This I gotta see," he muttered.

As he watched, Sharpe sat down in his VR seat, a massive device that looked like a combination of a Beverly Hills dentist's chair and the defunct Shah's Peacock Throne. The Colonel put on the glove and headset. A wall-sized screen blinked on, showing the scene from the robot's point of view. The robot waddled stiffly into an obstacle course, then whirred and clacked, bouncing stupidly back and forth between the walls of the course. Finally, after a final bounce that smashed his insect-like face, Slugger spun around and fell flat on his back, legs in the air.

"Okay, Hewitt, explain why this dog won't hunt." Sharpe's voice sounded like he was about to assign a whole drill team to latrine duty.

Hewitt scooped up Slugger, who was still clicking, whirring, and waving his claws in the air like a crazed lobster. "Software glitch. Same as before. We'll take him down to the raw circuits and start over till we…"

Sharpe cut him off, not interested in excuses. "You do that. Meanwhile, I know where I can find a software cybernaut that can think." He picked up his cell phone and dialed. "Glatt, get in here."

Josh sat back in the driver's seat, wiping the sweat off his face. He knew Sharpe had the Lilliput figures in mind and would not be surprised if Glatt went along with the plan.

The lab door opened.

"You took your frigging time, Glatt," Sharpe hissed at him. I want Josh Ross's cybernaut software, and I want it now."

Nervous-nellying around the lab, Glatt alternately tittered and gulped. "Colonel, you gotta believe me. I tried. But Josh's gone off the wall again. Took all his stuff and disappeared. Says he's gone on family leave." Glatt fumbled nervously with Slugger and jumped back when the robot kicked him in a last mindless spasm.

Sharpe looked thoughtful and distant. "Hmmm…We'll have to do something…You stay out of it, Glatt. This isn't going to be a tidy-bowl."

Glatt backed out of the room, obviously glad not to have had a worse chewing out. When he was gone, Sharpe flicked through the address book on his computer terminal. Josh had to manipulate the viewer to zoom in, so he could see the colonel's screen. Sharpe paused over one name.

"Carmen Rochas, nurse at Lincoln School. Ex-boyfriend, Dick Briglia, gym teacher, lieutenant, Army Reserve, Violent. Threatened her. Court order for him to stay away from Rochas…"

He reached for the phone without taking his eyes from the computer terminal and punched in seven numbers. "Get me Lieutenant Briglia. He's busy at football practice? I don't care if he's refereeing the Superbowl. Get him."

After switching off his bug, Josh keyed his cell phone before pulling out into traffic. Colonel Sharpe's plans were clear enough not to need any more of his attention. He was going to catch hell for keeping Nurse Carmen Rochas waiting. Right now, what he needed to do was to make his peace with this formidable person. Her ex-boyfriend was about to be used to get hold of the Lilliput game, and she might be able to stop him.

Chapter 7

Josh dashed up the school staircase, two steps at a time. His heart was pounding. What if Jamie really had wigged out? The kid had good reason for making whatever improvements on reality he could manage. His brother and sister ignored or made fun of him, his mother was dead, and his father was living in some VR cloud-cuckoo-land trying to get her back, if only as a hologram. Becky would never forgive him if he let Jamie be put on Ritalin or shot up with Thorazine, or whatever it was they did to spaced-out kids these days. Oh God, he prayed, let me have Jamie back. I'll make it all up to him. Let him be okay, and I'll get him Kentucky Fried whenever he wants and pizza on the side. I swear it.

While he was swearing to swell every fat cell in his youngest child's body, Josh almost tripped over Jamie's legs, which were stretched out from the bench in front of the nurse's office. Josh dropped down on his knees beside his son and put his arms around the child.

"Jamie, are you okay? Talk to me."

Jamie looked down at his scabby little knees. "I'm in trouble, Dad. Nurse Carmen thinks I've gone around the bend, but honest, I haven't. It's just that I can't tell you." He put a finger to his lips. "Sworn to secrecy by the Shaolin brotherhood. You know how it is. You break your word to them and you die the death."

"I know," Josh sighed. "Execution by a thousand cuts. Jamie, we'll talk about the secret later. Right now, I'm about to be executed by your school nurse. Wait out here."

He knocked on the door and let himself in. As he closed the door behind him, he stared at Carmen Rochas' long braid hanging down her back over her white sweater. She was looking out the window, not at him. The braid whipped into the air as she turned around, just the way he remembered Becky's braid flying over her sturdy shoulders. Carmen's big brown eyes slanted over her high cheekbones and her round little mouth had turned into a stern line.

"Well, Dr. Ross," she said, keeping her tense voice low. "I see you've managed to tear yourself away from your research long enough to check on your kid. Didn't you get what I was saying in those letters I sent home? I have a mind to call Social Services and tell them we have a case of long-term parental neglect."

Josh shuffled his large feet and stared down at them to avoid Carmen's eyes and to avoid telling her that Dan was right, she was a perfect 10, just as Becky had been. Then he mentally smacked his own face for irrelevant thoughts and came back to earth.

"You're right on, Ms. Rochas, and I'll try to do better. But some big problems have just come up at the office and . . ."

Carmen walked over to him, toe to toe and tipped her head back to look up into his face. "You got problems? Are your kids dealing drugs? Getting knifed at recess? Hombre, you oughta spend some time where I come from and your problems wouldn't look so bad. I hate it when you rocket scientists come here telling me how you're suffering from overwork. Take a look at the rest of us that are holding down two jobs, then tell me what your problem is."

"That's not fair, Ms. Rochas." Josh was stung enough to fly right back at her. "I got the Terminator in spats trying to steal my cyber-software and maybe my kids and a VR game that's pooping beer bottles. . ." He stopped dead, wanting to confide in her, but remembering that she was somehow connected to Don Briglia, his colonel's hit man. Better not to trust her, warm and sweet-faced though she was.

Stepping back and looking him up and down, Carmen said unsympathetically, "So you're scared the military's out to steal your video game and blow up the world with it? I don't think so, Dr. Ross."

She knew more about him than he wanted her to, and he suspected Jamie had been too free with his mouth, as usual. "Look, I can't explain, but I have a responsibility to clean up what I started."

"Dr. Ross," Carmen said, her voice a bit softer and her frown receding, leaving her café-au-lait face as smooth as a child's. "Why not just let the world take care of itself? Your first job is to take care of Jamie. If you don't, I have to call up Child Services and tell them he might need a foster home."

She put her finger on his lips to stop him from jumping back into the fight. "I might take him home myself."

Her touch sent an electric shock through him that he attributed to the static generated by the carpet. It had been a while since he'd been this close to a woman who rated a 10 on anybody's scale. Not since Becky had chewed him out for forgetting to come home for dinner three nights in a row had Josh felt such remorse. He had lived too much in his lab, he realized, stuck in a made-up reality. It was time to come home to his family. Becky would have said, "high time," and she would have been right. He opened the office door and swept Jamie up in his arms.

"Okay, son, we're going to go home and make a real dinner. No more junk." He remembered some of Becky's favorite recipes. "I have in mind chicken salad with raisins and pineapple. Sound okay?"

As he turned to say good-bye to Carmen, he thought she looked impressed, which was exactly what he'd been counting on. She was one person he wanted to have on his side, and it looked like he had done a good day's work on that score. Maybe next time, he could convince Carmen Rochas to come home and share a dinner with the family. Emily would resent her as she had resented Becky, but Dan's enthusiasm would make up for Emily's lack of it. Yes, Josh thought as he whisked Jamie home, he needed to invite Carmen to dinner.

He slapped down his fantasy before it could get started. Time to focus on Jamie. Romance would have to wait.

Still, he turned around to look at the school a last time before driving off, and caught a glimpse of Carmen in the window looking down at him. When he saw a military car drive up the curving driveway to the front door, Josh froze. Colonel Sharpe got out, leaving the driver and the car blocking the main entrance. After a few minutes, Josh saw the blinds of Carmen's window being closed. What could Sharpe be saying to Carmen? Getting information on Josh's kids? He would really have to call Carmen Rochas, now. And not just about having a romantic dinner.

Lieutenant Briglia, carrying a large bouquet of zinnias and chrysanthemums so bright they looked like they'd been dunked in acrylic paint, knocked on Andriette Hale's front door. He hoped she'd be an easier assignment than Carmen Rochas had been, though she couldn't be any prettier than his ex-girlfriend. The middle-aged female who opened the door was definitely not prettier than Carmen, but she wasn't too bad. He liked the way her white-blond hair stuck out all around her head like a halo and the way her big red mouth shone.

She must be using that new-fangled lipstick, he thought, the kind with sparkles in it. He hoped it was also the kind that didn't come off on a guy's face, since he might have to kiss her before their interview was over. Sharpe said that her husband had dumped her, that she was desperate for a man and that she had been trying to hit on Dr. Joshua Ross. The desperation should make his job easier.

Dick Briglia introduced himself and had no trouble getting in the door. Andriette Hale appreciated tall men like him and said so, as she put the garish flowers into an even more garish vase.

"Now, honey, you just sit down with me and have a little sherry," Andriette purred, pulling Briglia over to the couch.

She had been born in Georgia and after thirty years away from home, still used her southern accent when talking to available men.

She poured a glassful for each of them, then sat down close beside Briglia. "I just bet you got a sweetie at home, handsome guy that you are," she said in her husky voice. "I bet you might even have a wife."

"Sadly, no," Briglia said, feeling hot under his collar. He stuck a finger in between the collar and his neck, trying to get a little air. It was the first time a woman had ever told him he was handsome, given his lantern jaw and teeth like the shark in *Jaws*. "I'm looking."

"So am I," Andriette whispered. "I got a lot to offer."

"Right now all I'm looking for is information," Briglia said. Seeing that Andriette pouted and drew back a little, he went on, "I hope you'll offer some of that. But later, we'll talk about you and me."

Andriette brightened. "Okay, soldier," she said, "What do you want to know?"

Briglia sipped his sherry thoughtfully. "Your next-door neighbor, Dr. Ross, has stolen some military secrets. My colonel and me, we want to keep an eye on him. Could we ask you to help?"

Tossing down her sherry, Andriette frowned. He guessed that she had pretty much given up on Josh Ross and was ready to track another prey. "Sure. I'm in with the family. They'll talk to me."

"It would help if I could come here often and use your house as a base," Briglia said, setting down his glass. "It would help a lot. How about it?"

"Anytime," Andriette smiled. "It's my patriotic duty, right?"

"Yeah." Briglia got up to leave. "Just like hanging out the flag."

"Are you going to start spying on them now?" Andriette stayed close to Briglia as he went to the door.

"Yeah. Want to come along? The kids know you, so if we're seen, you can tell them you're looking for your cat or something. How about it?"

"I'm with you, sweetie," said Andriette, stepping on his heels in her hurry to follow him out the door. "You couldn't keep me away."

They crouched down and sneaked across the lawn between the two houses. Briglia explained to her in a whisper that if he could get hold of some information about what Josh Ross was up to, it might mean a promotion for him and maybe something for her, too. He meant only that he would take her out for dinner at Sizzler's, but figured she'd read more than that into his words. Andriette Hale could think anything she wanted, Briglia said to himself, so long as she cooperated with the Colonel's plan.

Chapter 8

Inside Emily's closet, rebellion was brewing. Four small people had had it with the dollhouse. Henry had created a lasso made from the cord of Emily's bathrobe, and had tossed it with a mighty heave, looping it neatly over the closet doorknob.

"Well, me friends, what do you say to that bit of expertise?" Henry chuckled. "In me youth, I spent some time in the London streets gaining entry to gentlemen's 'ouses for no good purpose. Lucky for us that I did."

"I figgered ye had a criminal past," Molly said, her brows coming together in a frown. "Though I must admit, it comes in 'andy given our current predicament."

Becky pulled on the rope to be sure it held, then climbed up it until she could peer through the keyhole. "No one's in there," she said. "I think we're good to go."

She used her bow to twist the handle on the closet door, turning red with the effort. Finally, the door popped open, and she slid down the lasso to the floor. The others followed her into Emily's room, which had been cleaned and put in perfect order. No underwear or skates to be seen. Becky looked around, wondering what had gotten into her daughter. Emily had always resisted cleaning her room or letting her mother do it, maybe for fear that something would be found that would incriminate her. Not that Becky had been the sort of mother who would read her daughter's diary or check out the lyrics of her rock albums. They had always respected each other's privacy, a fact Becky had taken great pride in and Emily had chalked up to her mother's being too busy to care. Whatever the reason, Emily's room now looked like the "after" half of a home renovation TV show.

Molly cocked her head to one side and admired the room. "There now, she's not such a bad wench, is she, Becky, luv? Yesterday this room looked like soldiers had barracked in it overnight, and just look at it now."

"Let's stop gawkin' and look for this machine that thinks, say wot?" Henry pulled at his mustache and frowned. "The sooner we find it, the sooner we're 'ome."

"It's not enough just to find the computer, Henry." Becky paced around the circles woven into the carpet. "Somebody has to know how to use it. God, I wish I'd studied something besides archery and eighteenth-century poets."

Samuel, too, was pacing. Suddenly he stopped and shook his head, making the short, wispy tail of his wig scratch on his stiff collar. "Curious," he mused. "I seem to remember mathematics I couldn't possibly have learned at Oxford. Electronic circuitry, too. Elegant patterns, I must say."

"I wonder if Josh programmed you to know what he knows." Becky ran over to Samuel and stared hard into his face as if she was trying to see through his skull bone into his brain. "We have to find out. Let's go. We'll hide in Josh's study. Quick, before the kids come home."

When they had climbed down the stairs, using Emily's bathrobe cord to link them together like mountain climbers on tough terrain, the four Lilliputians found themselves up against a door that Becky figured was probably locked.

"You can't know that, luv," Molly said, slipping the rope off her waist. "'Ow about another of those rope tricks, 'Enry? Maybe we can open this 'ere door like we did the other one."

"Not going to happen," Becky said, starting down the hall for the living room. "Emily's door had a lever, but this handle is round." She stopped and thought for a moment, then spied the dog door flap into the study. "Come on, Henry. Help me pull some of Jamie's building blocks into the hall. I very much doubt that he's put them away. He never did."

The others followed her into the living room. Bright colored blocks of all shapes and sizes lay around in piles, looking like an ancient city tossed by an earthquake. They each dragged a few pieces to the study door, and then piled them in a staircase until the top step reached almost to the bottom edge of the dog flap.

"I'll swing down first on our rope," Becky said, putting one leg over the ledge. "Henry, you hold the other end. When we're all down, we'll catch you."

Except for Molly's getting her wide skirt stuck in the dog door, the four broke into Josh's study without incident. Once inside, the Lilliputians surveyed the problem. They would have to climb up on Josh's computer desk. Maybe via the lamp cord, Becky suggested. Since the others didn't know what a lamp cord was and recoiled from touching it, she offered to climb up carrying Emily's bathrobe belt, which Henry had retrieved after his jump into the study. Then she could fasten the belt to the innards of the pencil sharpener and wind it up with the handle as the others hung on. Luckily, Josh had screwed the device firmly to his work table. The plastic cover had to be pried loose with the point of a pen, and Becky was sweating by the time it fell off.

"Why does everything have to be so hard?" she muttered as she worked. "Being small is the pits."

"Now you know 'ow your children feel, luv," Molly said with a laugh. "If you cast your mind back to childhood, you may remember how it feels to be struggling all the while."

"To be reduced to childhood after one has already endured it is a bloody insult," Samuel said, hanging onto Emily's belt for dear life as Becky turned the handle of the pencil sharpener. The pencil sharpener's spiral insides groaned as the cloth wound around them.

After all four were safely on the desk, Molly and Henry wandered around while the other two studied the computer. On the sill of the open window was a mousetrap, which Molly leaned over to inspect. "Ah, cheese," she sighed. "The smell of it. The power of it over me nose. I think I'll just have a bite."

"Molly, no!" Becky cried. "Stop her, Henry. That trap could kill her if she springs it. Both of you come on back to the computer, so I can keep an eye on you."

"I can't make anything of this thinking machine," said Samuel, walking on some papers that Josh had left beside the computer and bending over to read them. "It seems I have a lot to learn. Not easy when every word is twice my size."

Henry peered over his shoulder. "'Ow do you know what you 'ave to learn first?"

Unsheathing his sword and using it as a pointer, Samuel answered without looking up from his work. "Sir, does it matter what you learn first, any more than it matters which leg you put in your britches first? You may stand disputing which leg to put in, but in the meantime, your bum is bare. Now sir, let me think in peace."

They were all so busy watching Samuel puzzle out Josh's instructions that they didn't notice what was happening at the open window. Holding up some branches as camouflage, Andriette and Briglia arranged themselves carefully, so that only their eyes would be visible from the room. They stood still, hardly breathing, and gaped at the little people. Briglia was chewing his gum noisily, and Andriette had to jab an elbow in his ribs to shut him up. He gasped so hard at the pain that he swallowed his gum, turning a pale blue trying not to cough as it stuck in his throat. Fearing he would make a noise, Andriette pulled him under the window for a moment until the gum had gone down. Then the two cautiously lifted their heads to the level of the window sill again.

Henry got bored with Samuel's attempts to study the papers and walked restlessly around the desk. He spied an open bottle of wine, the tiny kind you get on airplanes, and managed to pour some in his mouth.

Seeing Molly's disapproval, Henry said, "Improves me mind, it does." He wiped his mouth and belched appreciatively.

Molly pulled him away from the bottle so fast that it teetered and almost fell over. "No, 'Enry, it only makes you insensible of your defects." She slapped him on the shoulder in a friendly sort of way, as if she didn't want him to know how much she liked him.

"Now, Molly," Samuel said, looking up briefly from his reading, "some men are improved by drink as some fruits are improved by rotting. Let the poor fellow be." He tapped his sword point in the middle of the page. "By Jove, I think I've got the combination we need to get into the machine. Becky, have a look…"

Scruff, barking as if he'd lost his mind, suddenly jumped through the door flap into the study, his rear legs scrambling the blocks with a fearful racket. He skidded up to the computer desk and nosed Samuel, whose sword flew into the air, landing on the windowsill. Edging as close as he could to the window, the dog barked, lunged, and panted like he was having a seizure.

Becky swung around and saw two sets of eyes devouring them all. "We have to get out of here," she cried. "Somebody's seen us. Come Scruff, come, boy."

The dog, who had been nosing a dishful of little chocolate footballs on Josh's desk, rushed over to her, his ears twitching, his tail wagging so hard it looked like it would fly off his rump. Becky hopped on his back, then climbed under him, hanging from his belly fur.

"Get on, everyone," she ordered. "No, not on top, get underneath, so Scruff can take us through the flap without knocking anybody off. Go, Scruff, out the door!"

"Me skirts are all awry," Molly moaned, trying to do as Becky did. "I look a sight, I do."

"A pretty sight," Henry reassured her, "petticoats and all. Let's go, beast. Through that flap-door, like the lady said."

As Scruff leaped through the dog door, Briglia reached in under the half-open window, wanting to raise it so he could climb into the room. His hand felt around, then touched the cheese. With a loud sprong, the trap shut.

"My fingers," he bellowed, "it's got my fingers." Briglia danced around the yard, roaring as if he'd been shot.

"Shut up, the neighbors will hear you," Andriette hissed.

Briglia pulled the trap off his fingers, stomping and moaning. After a few minutes, he calmed down enough to think. "We've got to climb in the window and get those little guys. Do it!" He rubbed his fingers and moaned some more.

"It's too late," Andriette replied calmly. She felt along the windowsill for the sword, then closed her hand around it. "They're gone, but we've got the evidence. Here." She handed Briglia the sword and smirked at him as if to remind the man that she was worth all the attention he had been paying her. The Ross family had gotten its last kidney casserole from Andriette Hale.

Briglia ran to his car and dialed a number on his cell phone. "Colonel Sharpe, fast," he said. He paused a moment, then hung up, saying softly, "Maybe I'll just bring them in myself and get me a promotion. Carmen's gotta go for them captain's stripes."

Andriette was right behind him. "Carmen?" She stormed. "Carmen?"

"Take it easy," Briglia said. "She's just some babe I used to know. Deal with it."

Not answering, Andriette looked back at the lighted window of the house next door. As Briglia walked to his Porsche, she said under her breath, "This time I'm going to sneak in by myself. Deal with that, Briglia."

"Okay. You told me I'm in," Jake said to Dan and Emily as they walked up to the door of the Ross house the next afternoon. "So what's it all about?"

"You're not going to believe this," Dan said cautiously, opening the door. "It's so high tech, we hardly believe it ourselves."

"Try me." Jake turned and smiled at Emily. "I got a real flexible belief system."

"You have to swear you'll never tell," Emily said. "Swear on whatever you believe in."

"How about the *Guinness Book of Records*? I believe in that." Jake looked around the living room for a bookcase. "Good enough?"

Dan slapped his palm against Jake's. "Good enough. We need your help."

Emily broke in nervously. "Some Lilliputians are in my closet. We're trying to send them home through the virtual reality program. Trust me. It's true."

"Oh—kay," Jake said very slowly, indulging her. He obviously didn't believe a word, and stood half-turned away, surreptitiously scratching one of the zits almost hidden by his almost beard. "So you got little tiny people in your closet, Emily. Let's see 'em."

She led the two boys up the stairs. "Be quiet, now. We mustn't scare them."

"Oh no," Jake said sarcastically, "Tiny people are sensitive. We gotta walk on eggs, right Dan?"

Emily hated the way Jake winked at Dan, as if they were both humoring her. "They're here, honest. Just look." She flung open the closet door and lifted off the dollhouse roof. "Well, okay, they're not here. Dan, what happened? Did Jamie take them?"

"They've got to be here someplace." Dan looked under the bed and sneezed. "Jeez, Emily, you got dust bunnies like I never saw." Scruff nipped at his heels, panting and barking.

"Well, who cleans under a bed?" Emily flared at him. "You only need to clean where people can see."

"Right," Jake said, patting her on the shoulder. "Under the bed is where I kick all my stuff."

Emily threw him a grateful glance. "The little people must be loose in the house," she said, her voice strained and hoarse.

"Downstairs! Quick. Dad'll be home any minute. Scruff, find Mom. Where is she?"

Scruff looked up at her, his head cocked to one side, and wagged his tail slowly, not sure what Emily wanted, but willing to follow orders if they made any sense to him. Could she be asking him to find her mother? Becky had been gone a long time, and Scruff could barely remember her scent. He cocked his head to the other side and waited, hoping Emily would make herself clear.

"Never mind," Emily said. "We'll find her ourselves."

"Mom would be in the kitchen," Dan said. "It's where she always was when we came home from school. Careful, just push the door open an inch, enough for us to see in."

"Yep, they're in there," Jake cried. "Holy sweat, they really are. Let's go. Everybody grab one."

They ran into the kitchen, followed by the dog. Each stopped short, looking at the mess Becky and her Lilliputian friends were making on the counter. Scruff was already lapping the black granite. Ashamed, he lay down quickly, his head next to the tiny people, his tongue popping in and out of his mouth, trying to taste the results of whatever they were making. Becky was turning on the juicer and Henry had climbed onto the handle. He was trying to peer in, and was vibrating with the machine.

Dan grabbed Henry just as the little blacksmith was starting to lose his balance. "Watch out, unless you want to be juice," he cried, cradling Henry in both hands.

Molly was investigating the toaster, which popped out a piece of iron-hard bread and knocked her flat. She lay there stunned, her feet in the air. "It's some kind of bread cannon," she moaned. "I'll 'ave a bruise big as an egg, I will."

Spying Samuel, who was examining the interior of the open microwave, Emily dove for him and slammed the door shut. "Don't go in there, Sam, ever. It's a hot box. Bad idea." She picked him up, one finger around his substantial belly.

With exaggerated patience, Becky said, "Look, Emily, I've got everything under control here."

"Sure you have," Emily frowned at her mother. "Don't you realize they haven't got a clue about appliances? Are you trying to kill them?"

"They're my friends, not yours," Becky answered, standing on her tiptoes to make herself bigger.

Emily looked down at her mother and put her hands on her hips. "Might makes right. Seems like I remember hearing that once upon a time when you were bigger than me."

Becky ran her hands over her hair, which had become somewhat straggly what with no way to wash or comb it. She did not look or feel like the glamor girl of old. "Maybe I said that once. Maybe it was PMS or a grad paper due, or a bad hair day, like now. Maybe I'm not as perfect as you thought. Come on, Emily. I did my best for you. Give me a break."

Leaning on the counter, Emily reached out to Becky. She had to admit that her mother looked tired and undone, not at all like her old self. It occurred to her that she had her whole young life ahead of her, full of whatever surprises and good stuff young lives could usually expect, while Becky was either dead or a disintegrating computer hologram, neither of which was a safe thing to be. Of course mom isn't perfect, she told herself, staring down at the little person who was ankle-deep in spilled juice. Nobody is. It's time I grew up enough not to expect so much. And not to blame people for being less than I expect. Poor mom, she was going to lose either way. It's like I set up a real trap for her. No matter what she did, good or bad, I saw it as the wrong thing for me.

Emily straightened up and tried not to care. If you cared, you were down the drain. Everybody would know you had a weakness, and they wouldn't let you forget it. Besides, Jake was there, and she wouldn't show weakness in front of him, anymore than she would have let people see her cry at the funeral. She turned away from her mother and said nothing.

Molly stepped in front of Becky trying to defuse the tension. She pointed to the picture on the raisin bran box and smiled winsomely up at Emily. Her eyes were kind and motherly, and Emily would have hugged her, if Molly been big enough. As it was, the little barmaid would have been sausage meat if Emily had done what she felt like doing.

"'Ow about one of those flakes, Emily, luv? Some hospitality is in order. We 'ave to civilize these young giants of yours, Becky."

"Be my guest." Becky sat down on the bowl of a spoon, the only dry place on the counter. "I've had no luck at it."

Gesturing at the raisins in the picture on the cereal box, Molly said earnestly to Emily, "Oh, and you can leave those cockroaches in the box, dearie. I've seen too many o' them in my time, I 'ave."

Hearing a noise, Scruff looked at the window, then began to paw the floor and snarl, lashing his tail. No one noticed, and he paced back and forth, huffing and gasping, dismayed at his failure as a watchdog. Briglia was taking pictures through the window, clicking one after another, his mouth wide open in concentration. Not for the first time, Scruff was wishing he could talk. Other than hurling the humans to the ground and stomping on them, the dog had no way of getting their attention, caught up as they were with cockroaches, if he was hearing rightly. Not that he saw any cockroaches, and he had dutifully looked, as soon as he heard the word. His humans were totally clueless about reality, the dog decided, flopping down on his belly, spreading out his back legs, and going to sleep. If they didn't care that someone was peering in the window, neither would he.

Emily set out one flake per person on a piece of plastic wrap and poured a drop of milk over it. To Molly she gave a bit of coffee out of a medicine dropper. The little woman sipped it with wonder and delight.

"It's far nicer than tea, luv," she cried, gesturing for more. "Gives me 'ead a bit of a buzz. Let's 'ave some more."

Emily was just beginning to serve up coffee to them all, when the front door slammed. Scruff leaped up out of his sleep, his eyes rolling, and bumped into Jake's leg. The dog realized that the one person who could take responsibility for the intruders was now at home. Loping into the hall, he greeted Josh while standing on his hind legs, pawing and muttering imprecations at irresponsible children and peepers into windows. Josh was too busy fighting down his insistent dog to notice what else was going on.

Dan, Emily, and Jake chased the Lilliputians through the kitchen, slapping at them desperately. Zigzagging every which way, Becky and her friends managed to reach the dining room. Jake dove after Samuel, who stepped neatly out of his way like a judo-master, then rubbed his hands together with a smile, glad to have beaten the giant at his own game. Emily managed to grab Henry with one hand and Molly with the other, trying not to hold on hard enough to hurt but hard enough to keep them between her fingers.

"Mom," Dan whispered, "just give us a chance to get you and your friends back into the computer. Just one more night is all we need."

"No way," Becky shrieked, in her high-pitched, mosquito voice. "I'm going straight to the top." She grabbed Samuel's hand and pulled him toward the hall archway.

With a last, frantic lunge, Jake threw himself on the floor and grabbed the small area rug between the dining room and the hall. Becky and Samuel cried out as they fell, clutching each other. Emily took the edges of the carpet in one hand, bagging her mother and Samuel. Taking time only to drop Henry and Molly in with the other two, Emily dashed upstairs to her room. Over Becky's shrieked protests, she set all four of them on a high bookshelf. Then she ran back to face Josh's wrath over the mess in the kitchen.

"What the devil happened in here?" Josh said, dropping the grocery bags on the kitchen floor.

Jamie followed him in, eyes wide. Scruff circled them, growling and tucking his tail under him, hoping they would recognize his signals that peeping toms were lurking about. Josh shook his head, ignoring the dog and began half-heartedly putting the kitchen to rights. Scruff curled up on the floor and gnawed a paw in frustration.

"Let me do that, Dad," Emily said, rushing into the room. "It's my job."

"No, Emily," Josh said sadly, squeezing out a foul-smelling rag that he had used to wipe the counter with. "You're only a kid. It's not your job."

"We were just chasing Scruff," Dan faltered.

"I'm gonna bail," muttered Jake. "Catch you later."

He was through the door before Emily could say goodby. So much for her hopes that Jake could stay and do homework with her and Dan. Home was an embarrassment, Emily said to herself. She could never expect that a boy she liked could come in without seeing something all wrong, like stinky slush on the counters and Lilliputians trying to get into the micro-wave. Her throat tightened, and she stood in front of her father, feeling as if she was about six inches tall, just like Becky.

"It sort of got out of hand," Emily murmured, feeling her voice droop like one of Jamie's wind-up toys when no one had wound it for a while.

Josh gathered the three of them in his arms. "The whole family's in meltdown, is what's happening, guys. Carmen's right. We gotta fix it, and we will."

Bouncing up and down as if he sensed a junk meal coming, Jamie cried, "How 'bout we fix it at MacDonald's?"

"Sounds good to me." Josh went toward the door and stopped short as he opened it. Carmen Rochas was on the front steps, holding out a big bowl overflowing with paella, little mussel shells and pea pods sticking up out of the glistening yellow rice. She wasn't wearing her nurse's uniform, just a pair of skintight jeans and a red turtleneck sweater. Her hair wasn't in a braid, but poured down her back in a black, shining river. She looked even better than the paella did, and that was saying a lot.

"Hey, Ms. Rochas. Nice to see you," Josh said as if he'd been expecting this combination of culinary and female gorgeousness. "I can't believe you'd want to set foot in this nest of serpents. But please…come in if you dare."

"Carmen," she said. "To all of you. Dr. Ross, I owe you an apology."

"It's Josh," he said, taking the food with one hand and her arm with the other. "I think we might have a clean dish or two."

"Careful," Carmen said, steadying the large bowl. "I carried it all the way across town on the bus."

Josh surveyed the dining room. "Is this a table that I see before me, or a hog wallow? Get busy, guys. Carmen, how about a glass of wine?"

She nodded and started to follow him into the kitchen, while the three children started excavating the dining room table, removing layer after layer of accumulated junk.

"On second thought, you'd better stay here," Josh said. "The kitchen does not speak well for my managerial talents."

"I'd be glad to help," she said. "Just let me warm the paella for a few minutes in the oven." Her dark, black-lashed eyes shone, and even Scruff was smitten, falling at her feet with a low moan. When she merely gave him a quick chest rub and went into the kitchen with Josh, Scruff heaved a sigh, stretched, and trotted down the hall and up the stairs. He was hearing a strange scratching noise in Emily's room that might, if he got lucky, prove to be that pesky blue mouse.

"And I hoped your opinion of me would improve," Josh smiled down at her. "Now that you've seen this kitchen, I'm ruined."

Once Carmen had taken over, the counters were cleaned, the floor was no longer sticky, and the hot paella was served on a polished table, with candles lit at either end. Emily sat dazed, wondering what kind of strange alchemy made a girl into a woman so that she could turn a mess into a meal. Whatever it was, it had not happened to her yet. She had to admire Carmen and gave the nurse a slight smile as they all dug into the paella, everyone calling out questions about the odd bits they were discovering as they plowed through the yellow rice.

"Mushroom?" Dan called out, holding up a small dark item.

"No, truffle," Carmen said. "Pigs find them under oak trees in Europe. They're to die for."

Dan ate his truffle and then pretended to faint with pleasure, sliding down in his chair with his eyes closed.

"What I like best is this olive with a white thing in it," Jamie said, wanting to distract Carmen's attention from Dan.

"That's garlic, dork," Dan said, rising up again to hunt for another truffle. "You hate garlic, remember?"

"And only pigs hunt truffles," Emily said, jabbing Dan with her fork. "Jamie's allowed to change his mind."

Josh sighed and rolled his eyes at Carmen, who just laughed and gave Jamie some help opening his clamshells.

"What else is life about than changing our minds?" she said, glancing at Josh. "Nothing stays the same, right?"

Emily thought of her mother and the other three Lilliputians sitting on the shelf upstairs. She used to think that only when you were dead did things stop changing. Now she wondered if mysterious things went on even then. If the quantum physicists were right, and Jake said they were, then nothing ever ended. It was only transformed, mostly for the better. Vigorously attacking her own clamshells, Emily chose not to think anymore. Thinking interfered with enjoyment of the best meal she'd had in months.

"So Carmen," Josh said around a mouthful of rice, "what did I do right that rated this fantastic food?"

Carmen put down her fork, her smile fading. "You told me about the military being after you," she said. "And I said I didn't believe it. After my chat with Colonel Sharpe, I'd believe you were hiding extra-terrestrials in the garage." She looked keenly at all of them. "Let's talk about what's going on, okay?"

Chapter 9

When Briglia met Colonel Sharpe at his office, he did not find his boss in the best of moods. It was dinnertime and being called away from his table because his subordinate had discovered some Lilliputians was not the Colonel's idea of joke. He sat down at his desk and glared at Briglia, who was nervously wiping sweat off his thin mustache.

"So you found some little people at Joshua Ross's house," he said. "This had better be good, Briglia."

The lieutenant laid out his photos proudly. "Six inches high, tops," he said. "Honest. Here's the proof."

Unimpressed, Sharpe pushed away the pictures. He was hungry and remembered that his pork chops were getting cold back at his apartment. At least he had no wife to scold him for being late to dinner. His wife and children had abandoned him long ago, and he couldn't care less.

"Might have been photo-shopped," Sharpe said, crossly. "Contrary to the media, lieutenant, the military mind has its moments of rationality. Why should I believe your fantasies, Briglia? Give me one good reason."

"They're for real, Colonel, I swear." Briglia's sweat began to interfere with his eyesight, and he blinked rapidly.

"Just this morning, some people were knocking down my door saying they'd seen a UFO. Now it's you with your miniature people. You're making me crazy, Briglia, and you don't want to see me when I'm crazy." He fixed his lieutenant with a hard, unfriendly stare.

"You gotta believe me, Colonel," Briglia said desperately. "I saw 'em. So did Ross's next-door neighbor. Maybe Josh Ross shrunk somebody. Maybe they're robots. I couldn't get close enough to tell."

At the word 'robots,' the colonel stopped fiddling with his watch and looked up. Briglia pulled out the tiny sword he had wrapped in a used paper napkin and laid it on the colonel's desk.

"I picked this up in the doc's study." He didn't bother to mention that he hadn't actually been inside the study or that he had driven off the small people by his howls when his finger got stuck in a mousetrap.

Sharpe examined the sword with growing interest. The sword handle was filigreed like lace and set with tiny amethysts. He laid his finger against the tip and exclaimed as the point bit into his skin. This weapon was not something Briglia had gotten out of a cereal box.

"A toy, perhaps," he said noncommittally, "but what workmanship. I'll have it checked out in the morning."

Scruff wandered into Emily's room, shook himself with a noisy flapping of ears and hair, then went to the shelf. It was too high for the mouse to have climbed up, he thought, but the scratching had come from here, or his ears were not doing their job. He sniffed and paced, looking up at the shelf, wondering how he could tempt the mouse to come down. Suddenly he heard a high, small, but vaguely familiar voice.

"Come Scruff, come boy," Becky coaxed. "A little closer and we can jump on your back."

Molly held back, murmuring. "I don't trust that beast, Becky. We'd best wait for Emily to come get us."

"Emily has her own agenda," Becky said. "Always has, always will. Follow me, everyone."

She hung onto a torn piece of the guitar player poster, then let it rip as she rode the shred of cardboard down, landing on Scruff's back.

"Go," she cried, "Everybody grab a handful of twenty-first century sleaze and come on down."

One after another, they slid down the same way Becky had, ripping the poster to shreds. Molly was last, modestly hanging onto her full skirts, trying to keep them from flying in her face. Each Lilliputian climbed onto the dog's back and clung to hunks of heavy brown fur so tightly that Scruff growled in protest. Becky crawled up to his ear and started hollering directions into it. The dog obediently turned and trotted out. Becky sat on his head, smiling, looking sure that her moment had come.

Downstairs, her family was having a conference, with no idea who else was coming to dinner. While Carmen and Josh talked about Colonel Sharpe's possible plans, Emily chimed in whenever she had a tidbit of information. Jamie sighed, and looked for another olive. He had given up trying to be Carmen's favorite, feeling totally outclassed by his family. When Scruff came in and nudged his knee, Jamie barely noticed. Scruff pushed again, harder, and whimpered.

Jamie searched his food and came up with a juicy piece of fish. Leaning under the table, he offered it to Scruff, then froze. He couldn't believe what it was he saw. Riding behind his mother were all three Lilliputians hanging onto Scruff's neck fur.

"Mom," he whispered frantically, "Dad's going to see you! Scruff, take 'em back. Go on."

Kicking Dan to get his attention off Carmen, Jamie whispered behind one hand, "It's Scruff carrying Mom and the other guys. Do something." He left the table without excusing himself and ran to the tape player, turning on some rock music loud enough to drown out the high whines of Lilliputian voices.

Dan pretended to drop his fork and peered under the table. "Oh, man!" his voice lilted up into a question. "I can't believe you'd do this to us, Mom. We're dead."

Becky did not answer but flung herself at a fold of the tablecloth, then climbed onto the table before Dan's flailing hands could grab her. "Better you than me," she said, kicking over a saltshaker near her husband's elbow. She cupped her hands around her mouth, screaming at Josh, but he was too deep in conversation with Carmen to hear. They were so into talking, they wouldn't have noticed if Briglia and the entire Pasadena Army Reserve had come charging through the dining room.

"You said you came from hard times," Josh said, pouring Carmen some more wine. "Tell me where you grew up."

"Tijuana," she said, sipping thoughtfully. "And then, East San Diego, after my mother moved to California. The kids in school used to call me Carmen San Diego all the time in school. They acted like they couldn't see me because I'm so small. Everybody kept saying 'Where in the world is Carmen San Diego?' and cracking up. I hated that. It was like I had no identity, you know?"

Josh, whose family had treated him like the crown prince of the United Arab Emirates, didn't know at all, but he nodded gravely. "I'm sorry to hear it. Now, you light up the room, Carmen. No identity problems anymore, right?"

Her mouth trembling a little, Carmen smiled at him. "You bet," she said. "I don't care what most people think of me." She let Josh put his hand over hers. "Not everybody, though."

"Homewrecker," yelled Becky over thuds of rock and roll. "Keep your hands off my husband, Carmencita." Ignoring the fact that it was Josh who had his hand on Carmen's, Becky kicked at her rival's wine glass until it rocked.

Dan snatched her away from Josh's vicinity and put both his arms on the table, encircling the four Lilliputians so that they were hidden from view, not that Josh and Carmen were looking at anything but each other.

"I think we need to get the dessert," Carmen said softly, her full red mouth in a pout as luscious as a ripe California strawberry. "I'll help," Josh offered. She got up, steadied her rocking wine glass with one hand, and followed Josh toward the kitchen door.

Becky plunged through Dan's fingers and gave a judo-kick in the direction of Carmen's hand. "I've had enough," she cried, before Dan caught her in mid-air. "You're history, Carmencita."

Jamie turned up the sound, drowning his mother out, as Josh and Carmen left for the kitchen.

"At least I have a dessert," Josh bent over so his lips were near her ear. "Mocha cream pie. Some things this family does right."

As they disappeared through the swinging door, Becky jumped away from Dan's hand and aimed another vicious kick at Carmen's wineglass, knocking it to the floor. "Like getting a new mom, maybe?"

Sam peered over the table onto the floor, where the red wine was soaking into the cream-colored carpet. "Joshua is a widower, my sweet. What do you expect?" Sam took a bite of the saffron-colored rice and made a face. "A good enough dinner, to be sure, but not a dinner to invite a man to."

Henry swiped a bay scallop from Josh's plate and wolfed it down. "Emily, me luv," he called up seductively, "'Ow about some more of that cold chocolate slop Jamie gave us earlier? It sticks to a man's ribs better than this yellow stuff."

Putting his face close to Henry's, Jamie spoke in as genteel a voice as he could muster. "If you guys will just go upstairs with Scruff, right now, I'll bring you chocolate ripple. As much as you want."

Becky stared at the swinging door, her mouth turning down in an angry scowl. "Thanks a whole lot," she said to Jamie. "Obviously we're going to have to help ourselves, if ice cream is all we can depend on you for."

Sighing, Molly put a hand on Becky's arm. "Can we not take a giant step toward civilization and help each other? Like a family? God love ye, Becky, ye talk to yer children like they're the enemy."

"Yeah, Mom," Emily said, picking Becky up and holding her eye to eye. "Get a grip. We're trying to help you."

"Not hard enough," Becky said, tears sparkling on her lashes. "I need Josh, Emily. I need your father. And he's in the kitchen eating mocha cream pie with Carmencita. Do something, Em. We're dying, here. I used to be an optimist, but there's a limit."

It was true. Emily could almost look through her mother's hands. The Lilliputians might really be disintegrating, just as Dan and Jake had said they would. Brushing a finger over her wet eyes, Emily put her mother down. Seeing Becky fall apart was like dropping the watermelon all over again. She set her lips firmly together. This time, she would not let her mother down.

Handing Becky to Dan, she opened the swinging door to the kitchen a few inches and peeked in to check on Josh and Carmen. They were helping each other slice the pie and licking whipped cream off the same knife. Yuck, thought Emily. I'd never lick the same thing as somebody else. Not even if the somebody was Jake. She pushed her head in a little farther, so she could hear what they were saying.

"I dreamed about you the other night," Josh said, watching her lick the knife. "We were talking."

Carmen cut another piece, and held the creamy knife up for him. "So, what did we talk about?" She was warming to him, Emily could tell, but cautiously.

"About Jamie and you. About us maybe having dinner together."

"Guess I got your message," Carmen said, setting down the knife and looking directly up at him.

"Not the whole thing. I haven't told you what else was going on."

"I don't want to hear it," she said. "Look, I'd better go now. I know better than to get mixed up with a guy who's just lost his wife."

Josh picked up the plates. "You're right," he said. "I'm not anybody's idea of a catch just now."

"Maybe someday, though," Carmen said softly, gathering the forks. "We've got time."

"Don't bet on it," muttered Josh trailing her out the door.

Emily was back at the dining room table when they came in. She pretended to clear the table and didn't look at her father and Carmen when they returned with the fresh plates and forks. Why didn't Carmen think Josh was a catch, she wondered. And why was Josh so down on himself? Maybe she'd inherited this lack of self-confidence from him, along with his computer genes.

"The pie's cut in the kitchen, kids," Josh said. "I'm taking Carmen home. Can you handle clean-up?"

Emily sat down at the table and clutched Scruff's wiggling body between her knees, having put the four Lilliputians again on his back. "Take your time, Dad," she said. "We've got everything under control."

"Yeah, yeah," she heard Becky yell in her tiny voice from under the table. "Sure you have. Sam is already missing his buttons and the fringe has disappeared from my jacket. We're on our way out, Emily, you hear me?"

Emily laid her hand down on the dog where she thought the Lilliputians might be, hoping to keep her mother's voice down. She need not have worried, since Josh and Carmen were already out the door and couldn't have heard Becky's pathetic little cries.

Jamie ran after the two, catching them at the front door. "Don't I get a goodnight hug?" He reached out to Carmen first.

She bent over and held him tightly. "Sure, querido, Anytime."

Jamie walked back into the dining room, his face dazed with pleasure. "Anyone know what querido means? That's what she said I am, her querido."

Going to the front door to check that Josh and Carmen were gone, Dan called over his shoulder, "It means queer dodo."

"Does not," Emily said, as Jamie's eyes started filling up, "it means beloved." She was very proud of having had two years of Spanish already, which Dan had passed up in favor of an extra math class. Jamie smiled and began to dance around the room, singing the word to himself as he swung his arms in extravagant martial arts gestures.

Dan was still looking out the door, beckoning to someone. After a moment, Jake Cohen bounded onto the porch, looking both ways before he came in. Emily observed that Jake was not wearing the dirty football jersey from that afternoon, and that he had washed his hair until it shone. He was trying to impress someone, Emily guessed, hoping it was her.

"Coast clear?" Jake asked, smiling at Emily. "The last place I want to be is in the middle of somebody else's family feud. It's bad enough at home."

Scruff came out from under the table, the four Lilliputians hanging from his long sable ruff. Becky was trying to climb up on the dog's head, the better to control him, Emily figured. Her mother was shouting at all of them in her absurdly tiny voice. Scruff was about to roll on his back for a belly rub, when Dan righted him, barely preventing the little people from being crushed.

"Listen to me," Becky cried, and Emily worried that her mother sounded even weaker than before. "You've got to let me talk to your father tonight. The four of us won't be here much longer if we lose any more of ourselves. Josh can fix us so we won't fall apart. And by the way, that guy at the window was the type who'd be armed with more than a camera."

"Truth to tell," Samuel put in, "I'd feel better if I were armed myself. My scabbard sadly misses its sword."

"Emily, my girl," Henry said in the same voice he used when wanting more chocolate ripple, "conjure us up some weapons out of that there thinkin' machine, there's a good wench."

Setting off for the study, Emily felt proud of herself, knowing that at least somebody respected her talents. "Consider it done," she called over her shoulder.

While Jake and Dan pulled the drapes closed so no more peeping toms could spy on them, Jamie carefully lifted each of the Lilliputians onto the computer desk, where Emily was already at work getting the VR program up. It was only a matter of minutes for her to pull out two tiny swords from the pub room program and present them to Samuel and Henry.

"Ho, guard yourself, scholar," Henry said with a flourish of his new weapon. "I will fight ye for me woman, me Molly."

Sam looked his sword over and shook his head at its lack of amethysts. "But I don't want your Molly," he said mildly. "It's Becky I have a fondness for."

"Well then, let's fight for the 'ell of it," Henry said, stamping his forward foot and waving his blade around his head.

"What other reason does fighting ever have?" Samuel murmured. "Just mind my jacket. It flaps a bit since my buttons have disintegrated. I'd as soon not lose it altogether."

The two were happily stomping and stabbing when Dan interrupted them, wanting to get into the fun. He had grabbed one of Josh's little foil-wrapped chocolate footballs and tossed it to Henry, interrupting the fencing match.

Samuel spoke with dignity and a bit of resentment. "Henry and I were attempting to have a bit of swordplay, a sport with which we are more familiar than football."

"Oh come on," Jake urged, "Just let us teach you how to pass."

Samuel wedged the point of his sword into Josh's computer desk and leaned on it. "No, Sir, I won't learn it. You shall retain your superiority over me by my not learning it."

Henry, who wasn't especially skilled with his sword, didn't mind passing the tiny football back and forth with Dan. He was surprisingly good at throwing, Emily noticed, as she waited for the Lilliput program to come up on the screen.

Samuel, disgusted that the fencing had been interrupted just as he was about to win a point, had wandered over to Josh's papers and begun to rifle through them. He made a sudden surprised gurgle in his throat, then leaned closer, his mouth moving as he repeated a formula over and over.

Speaking softly to Henry, Becky gestured toward the computer. "See if you can get Emily to help us learn how to use this machine. Samuel's off in a haze of theoretical physics. I know the signs. He's Josh all over again."

Nodding, Henry approached Emily, using his most seductive tones. "Emily, luv, would we be strong enough to 'it those keys for you?"

"You can try." Emily leaned back in her chair, noticing that Jake had come around close behind her and was looking over her shoulder. "Here's CONTROL. Hold that one down while Molly jumps on L, for Lilliput. Then step hard on F4 and F7. That opens up your program."

"Like this?" Henry did some keyboard acrobatics and landed with one foot on CTRL, one on F4 and a hand on F7.

"Watch it," Jake cautioned. "If you hit CONTROL and SAVE at the same time, you'll save the program onto Dr. Ross's hard disk. He'll know what you're doing."

Henry exchanged glances with Becky. "Can't 'ave that, can we? Then your 'usband would have to send us back 'imself."

Catching the conspiratorial glance, Dan hurried to say, "We're trying to get you home. Why won't you believe us?"

Becky stood as tall as she could, staring her son down. "Because you're children, and you'd do anything to keep your toys."

Putting her hand on Becky's arm, Molly quieted her friend. "Is that not so?" she said in a firm but kind voice. "Come, admit it. We will not love you less."

Samuel finished repeating his formula to himself and came forward to stand beside Becky. "We may even have reason to love you more, if you can determine that we have a real

Lilliput to go back to. Emily, can you be sure? Would we be less real than we are now, if we return home?"

"Sam has a point," Emily screened through the program, wincing when she saw some of the half-baked graphics. "Dan, let's have another look at your *Gulliver's Travels*."

Emily and Jake took the book out of Dan's hands, their heads close together. She forgot about watching the little people, forgot about everything. Just as she had daydreamed, Jake was beside her, his breath warming her cheek. Her knees knocked together, and she hoped she didn't smell as sweaty as she felt. Dan leaned over her other shoulder, and Jamie squirmed his way into Jake's lap, wanting to see the book too. Nobody was watching the prisoners, as they called themselves when the children weren't listening.

"If Emily can't get us back, we need an alternative strategy," Samuel said to Henry. "Her father has to find us if we can't find him."

"My feelin's exactly," said Henry, climbing onto the keyboard.

"Now, Henry," Samuel said, tapping his sword on the key where Henry was supposed to stamp one foot. "You hit Control, and I'll hit Save. Now!"

The two tiny men hit the keys with all their strength, and a click let them know they had just saved the program to Josh's hard drive, whatever that meant. After their exploit, all four Lilliputians milled around on Josh's papers, pretending they were absorbed in scientific calculations. Only Molly noticed that Scruff dashed out the study door, his tail twitching.

"Where's that beast going?" Molly called to Henry.

"Probably to satisfy some natural urge," Henry called back.

Molly shuddered. "I don't even want to think about that, given the size of 'im. Emily, see if you can program some coffee into me Lilliput pub, dear girl. Me customers will love you for it."

With Jake's help, Emily was adding as many details as she could to the program. When she was finished, she sat back in her chair, exhausted. Jamie was leaning over his mother protectively, his mouth screwed up as if he was about to cry. Saying good-by would be hard for him, Emily thought. He would cry himself to sleep every night, just as he had after their mother had died. Dan called him the local waterworks and said southern California would never run dry so long as Jamie was around. Now Emily would have to give the poor kid even more of her time, when all she wanted was to spend every free minute with Jake Cohen. She glanced up at Jake, who was looking at her as if she was something good to eat. Emily blushed and looked at her lap, where her damp fingers twisted together. She was not used to being looked at like she was dessert.

The glowing holographic square appeared in front of the computer, spilling over onto the floor. As it expanded, the area blazed yellow.

"Okay," she said. "Who wants to try it?"

"Me," Dan cried. "I'm the one who read the book. I'll check out the new details we added."

Becky hung anxiously over Emily's arm. "You'll find a large black metal pot in the town square, Em," she said. "Get it out for me."

Seeing Emily hesitate, Molly said, "Please, luv, there's a good lass."

"You could learn some communication skills from Molly, Mom," Emily said. She studied the computer screen as the program worked, then called out to Dan, "Here it comes. Think of it as our secret weapon," she said, "in case those creeps show up again."

Dan opened the glove and they saw a thimble-sized kettle of black liquid in it. He dipped his finger in and Becky slapped it before he could lift it to his tongue.

"It's poison for our arrow tips," she cried. "We got it from mushrooms. Don't put it in your mouth or you'll trip out."

"Wow, cool," said Jamie, his eyes big and round. "Drugs!" He reached toward the kettle.

"Hands off, dork. What have I told you about drugs?" Dan cried. "Your brains are scrambled enough already." He moved the pot out of Jamie's grasp.

"Okay, everybody, into the light square," Emily whispered, wiping her damp hand on her jeans. She stabbed a few keys. "Now!"

Samuel held out his hand to Becky, wanting her to join them, but she stood to the side, letting the others get into the square without her. Her arms were folded across her chest and she had a determined look. Clearly, Becky was going nowhere. Emily hit a few more keys. Samuel looked resigned, and closed his eyes, waiting.

"Now," Emily said again, hitting the keyboard in frustration, "Now!"

Nothing happened. A little red light went on and blinked rapidly. Then the computer gave a low groan and crashed.

"Now why did that red light go on?" Emily muttered, staring miserably at the machine. "It never did before."

"Maybe the little red light's telling the computer to crash," Jamie said innocently.

"Oh, that's so lame, I won't even speak to it," Emily said, her voice beginning to shake. "And I didn't save the program before the light went on. Now they'll never get home, because there's no home to get to." She put both hands over her face and sat very still.

Laying his hand consolingly on her shoulder, Jake turned off the computer, waited a minute, then booted it up again. "So now we know we can get stuff out but not in," he said. Great." He played with the keys, trying to resurrect the program, but nothing worked. "It'll have to wait for your father, but hey, I'm not going to, guys. I value my life. See you, tomorrow, Emily."

Dan went with him, both boys murmuring gloomily about fathers and likely retribution for sins against paternal property.

Becky said to her daughter, "Emily, I love you, but God, you're stubborn."

"It's inherited." Emily couldn't help smiling at Becky.

Henry started feeling his chest, then his arms. "Y'know mates," he said, "I'm getting the funny feeling that some of me's 'ere and some's not. It's just a feeling. Comes and goes like the feeling I'm going to puke, know what I mean?"

Looking at him soberly, Samuel nodded. "I sense it, too. We may have less time than we think."

"Emily, see if Dad locked the front door when he took Carmen home," Dan said uneasily.

"And Jamie, fetch our weapons. There's a good lad. I think I heard something outside a bit ago," Molly said, clutching Henry's hand. "Maybe it was that fiendish beast of theirs, and maybe not."

Chapter 10

Carmen opened the door of her apartment, pausing before she went in. She was not sure if she should let Josh come in with her, but didn't want him to leave, either. The last man in her life had been Dick Briglia, and she had learned from him to be afraid, something she had never been before. Josh surprised her by waiting to be invited in, after she had crossed the threshold. That, at least, was a lot different from Briglia's style.

"I really thank you for that dinner," Josh said. "It was the best. My turn, next time."

He was still standing there, making no move to walk away, and Carmen sighed. They had not yet talked about Colonel Sharpe's visit to her office, and now was as good a time as any.

"Come on in," She said. "We need to talk."

After sitting down on the couch, Josh patted the cushion beside him, looking at Carmen hopefully, but she sat opposite him on a hassock.

"What do you know about this colonel?" Carmen said, folding her arms around her knees, which she had drawn up to her chin. "Has he threatened you?"

"Not anything specific. He's just a blowhard," Josh said.

She shook her head, thinking that Josh must have lived a charmed life indeed, to be so innocent. "You don't understand these guys. I know their type. They could kidnap your kids or something." She got up quickly and paced back and forth. "Hasn't that occurred to you?"

"They've hinted at it, yes. But I don't think they'd actually try. Sharpe's a careful guy. Plays by the rules."

"So far. But he seemed to me the kind who'd kill, if he thought he could get away with it. Please, Josh," she said, sitting down beside him. "Whatever they want, give it to them. Your kids are what's important."

Josh put his head in his hands. "You don't know what Sharpe's asking for."

"Hey, Josh, they already have the hydrogen bomb. How much worse can it get?"

"I wish I knew." Josh wiped his forehead with the back of his hand.

"It's nearly midnight," Carmen said firmly, getting up. "Time to go. You have kids at home."

"So I have." Josh Ross reluctantly and walked beside her down the hall. "And a computer full of little people wanted by the army. At least the colonel doesn't know they're in there."

"I'll help any way I can," Carmen said. "Anybody the military is after is a friend of mine."

She gave him a businesslike kiss on the cheek and pushed him into the hall. When Carmen had closed and locked the door, she stood for a while, leaning with her back against it, smiling. Her smile faded as she thought of the colonel's cold, penetrating glare, and she shivered. It crossed her mind that Josh might be right not to let this man get hold of whatever new weapon was shaping up on his computer. What would such a cold-blooded shark do with it? Before she went to bed, Carmen checked to be sure her door was double-bolted and her windows were locked.

Andriette Hale was feeling pretty good. Briglia's colonel had come to see her that afternoon, bringing her flowers and a proposition. He wanted her to spy for him on her neighbor, Josh Ross. In return, he hinted, she would become an important part of his government agency. Maybe an important part of his life, Andriette thought. Briglia offered nothing compared to this colonel. She was dazed to the point of sappiness by her good luck in snaring two men at once. Josh Ross could go hang himself.

That evening, she put on her black sweatsuit and pulled a black cap over her dyed blond hair. The idea was to blend into the night like a cat burglar. After seeing so many thriller movies, she knew just how to avoid detection. Andriette tucked her video camera under one arm and went out her back door, carrying a piece of tri-tip for Scruff, in case the dog tried to blow her cover.

Andriette had seen Josh drive away with his small, slinky brunette, and figured she had at least half an hour to get the little people on her video camera before he got back. The key Josh had entrusted to her turned out to be good for the back door as well as the front, as she had suspected. Easing the back door open just enough to slip through, Andriette avoided the squeak she knew would alert the household, if the door was pushed open too far.

Scruff came running toward her as she stepped into the hall. When the dog opened his mouth to bark a welcome, she stuffed the meat into it. Sinking down on the floor, his knees weak with pleasure, Scruff began to gnaw his treat, forgetting all about his role as household guard. He had his priorities, and steak was right up there at the top. As with all dogs, his only defect was that he could not imagine what was going to happen next.

Since she knew the layout of the house, Andriette was aware of the dog flap into the study. With luck, the study door would be closed, and she could nose the camera into the corner of the plastic flap without being seen by those inside. Tiptoeing down the hall, Andriette froze when she heard cries of distress coming from the study. Something about the computer crashing and a little red light. She stepped quickly into the hall closet when the door of the study opened. Two boys hurried out, Dan and someone she had seen before but whose name she didn't know. Shutting the study door behind them, the boys left the house, and she could hear their worried voices as they went down the front walk, talking about death by grounding, once Josh discovered what they had done.

Andriette was pleased that she had learned something Colonel Sharpe couldn't have known. Josh Ross might not aware of the Lilliputians, making it easier for her to steal the little people. The theft, however, would have to wait until she had reinforcements. Josh might be back at any moment, and all she could do for the time being was to get a snippet of the tiny people in action onto a memory card. The colonel could hardly ask for more proof than that.

She got down awkwardly on her knees and elbows, shoving the camera lens through the bottom of the door flap, and peering through it. Emily and Jamie had their backs to her, both hovering over the dark, lifeless computer screen. The little people were in clear view, walking around on Josh's papers. The camera whirred for a few minutes, then suddenly Andriette was knocked over by an enthusiastic nudge from Scruff, who tried to lick her hands to get the last bit of meat juice off them.

"Bad dog!" she hissed at him, slapping Scruff away and getting to her feet.

The noise would surely bring the children into the hall, so Andriette tucked her camera under her arm and fled out the front door, followed by a barking, deliriously grateful Scruff. He obviously intended to follow her right back to the source of the tri-tip and was not about to take no for an answer. Andriette barely got in her door and shuddered as Scruff threw his weight against it. At last, getting no response, the dog whimpered a few times, and went sadly home.

Andriette waited awhile, not sure if the children had followed the dog to her place and learned that she was the intruder. When a quarter of an hour had passed with no knock at the door, she went to the phone and dialed the number Colonel Sharpe had given her. Waiting for him to answer the phone, Andriette examined her long, brilliantly polished red nails and smiled. Being an army officer's wife, she daydreamed, would suit her just fine.

The next day, groggy from his sleepless night, Josh stumbled into his study and booted up the computer. The kids were already in the kitchen making their breakfast, and he was glad to have a few minutes to himself. Rubbing his bristly jaw, then his eyes, Josh stared at the dialogue box on the screen. The software had been wiped. Stabbing his fingers at the keyboard, Josh brought up the hard drive menu and sank back in relief. There was the Lilliput program, safe and whole. But how had it gotten on the hard drive? He wiped his suddenly cold hands across his forehead. Feeling a constriction in his throat, Josh jumped up, and rage roared out of him.

"Okay, you guys. In here right now," he shouted, running into the hall. "I got the goods on you."

The three children, pop-tarts in hand, came out of the kitchen and stood shamefaced before him. Emily's heart was beating so hard that her hand shook, and strawberry goo fell out of the tart onto her brand-new white cashmere sweater. The jig was up, she knew. Time to let the little people speak for themselves. Her father would not trust her for the rest of her life. She would never be allowed to date. No way Jake would ever be allowed into the house again. Doomsday scenarios rushed before her eyes, like your life was supposed to do when you were on the verge of death.

"Answer me, and you better make it good." Josh pointed at the computer and then at them. "How did you get Lilliput onto my hard drive?"

"The hard way?" Jamie said, pulling his innocent routine.

"Don't be smart," Josh growled at him. "I mean, who did it?"

"All of us, Dad," Dan said in his grown-up deep new voice, speaking slowly to keep it steady. "We had a reason. . . ."

Emily butted in, pushing in front of her brother. "I just wanted to make this particular scene, Dad. A Gulliver scene for my graphics project at school."

Dan caught on and followed her lead. "And I wanted to do *Gulliver's Travels* on the computer, so I could get some special effects for my book report."

"Okay," Josh said, caving into resignation. "I see I'm getting nowhere. You're going to be late unless I drive you to school." He turned as he started out the door, looking back hesitantly. "Uh, look, if anybody tries to pick you up at three o'clock, don't go with them. I'll be there."

When Briglia banged on her door, Andriette was just unwinding her hair from curlers so big her head looked like a stuffed laundry bag. She peeked out the window and said she was busy. He banged again, shouting to her that he would bust down the door if she didn't open it. Sighing, Andriette ran a brush quickly through her puffy hairdo and opened the door.

"And what would you be wanting at this hour," she said coldly.

"How come you called Colonel Sharpe without telling me?" Briglia demanded, stomping into her house and slamming the door behind him. "I thought we had a deal."

"My deal is with him, now," Andriette said, brushing his hand away when he tried to grab her by the shoulder. "He was here yesterday."

"Yeah, I got that much out of him," Briglia muttered. "When he talked about you, he looked like he was about to sit down to a steak dinner."

"Better him than you, loser," Andriette said, turning her back to him. "He's gonna retire soon with a fat pension and a triple dip. That's what he told me."

Briglia barred her way as she started back into the hall. "Just remember, babe, it's me that's agreed to split the money we get for the little people. You think the colonel's going to give you even a cow pattie? Lotsa luck."

He stomped out, leaving mud tracks all over Andriette's pink rug, then stood on her front steps muttering. "It was my deal first. And you can bet I'm going to get those little people before you and the colonel do."

Whistling tunelessly, Briglia hurried to his car, not seeing Andriette sneak out the back door with her video camera. Andriette was on her way to Sharpe's office, ready to prove to him that the little people existed and that she was primo wife material.

She found Colonel Sharpe still in his office, a few empty boxes of k-rations on his desk and some crumbs dangling from his otherwise impeccable mustache. The colonel was not in the best of moods, she could tell, since his smile looked like it had been slapped on with a trowel. It was the kind of smile that didn't reach his steel gray eyes, and his voice was carefully neutral. Andriette figured he didn't want to let on how much he was attracted to her, and simpered invitingly.

"You wanted proof about the little people we saw at Josh Ross's," she said, sashaying past the colonel and flopping down on his leather chair. "I got it."

"I hope you're not bringing me another toy sword," Colonel Sharpe said in an even voice. "As proof, your mini weapons don't quite cut it."

Andriette pulled her video camera out of her purse, pushed a few buttons, and handed it to the colonel. "Look in the little screen on the side," she said. "That's them. Six inches high, sure as shootin'."

"I can't see anything but the microwave," the colonel growled.

"Keep lookin'," she said, her voice soft and slow. "You'll see 'em, I swear on my grandma's Bible."

The colonel sat on his desk and put his foot on her chair. He held the camcorder out a bit, then pulled it back toward his eye. "Yes, yes, I see them now."

The colonel was breathing hard, all of a sudden. "A woman, no, two women, and two men. Just the size I've been looking for. No bigger than a ballpoint pen. How about that?" He put the camera down and smiled at her, as if she had suddenly turned into Glinda the Good

"I thought they'd grab you," Andriette said in a throaty voice. "No tellin' what they're worth."

"I know what they're worth to me." The colonel turned away and dialed a number. "Briglia, I have a job for you. Be here in half an hour."

Putting aside his cell phone, he leaned toward Andriette. "Are you ready for a big assignment, sweetheart?" he murmured, sounding to Andriette just like men in the movies talked to their women.

"Anything you say," Andriette sighed, batting her eyes until one eyelash broke loose and flapped around like a bat's wing. In alarm, she reached up and slapped the eyelash into place again, hoping the colonel's mind was on some other part of her anatomy.

"Then here's what I want you to do," he muttered out of the corner of his mouth, as if anyone was near enough to overhear. "You and Briglia are going to break into the Ross house tonight and take those little people with you."

"Briglia?" Furious, Andriette stood up. "Why should he be in on the deal? I told him off. I can handle this job better by myself. The kids will think I'll be babysitting them. Briglia will only make them suspicious."

"We can't take any chances," Colonel Sharpe said, escorting her to the door and giving her back the video camera. "Briglia has a gun. Your job is to get him in the house and help him grab the goods." He smiled again, his painted on, cartoon-shark smile. "Go on now, that's my girl."

It was only the last few words Andriette thought about as she left the building. He thought of her as his girl. He trusted her. Life was looking up, she said to herself, as she listened to the reassuring sound of her sexy high heels tapping on the metal steps. Briglia would have to be told she was the one in charge of the operation. Andriette wouldn't take any bull from an army reservist, not when she had just about arrived at the status of girlfriend to a colonel.

Chapter 11

Carmen and Josh were leaving to pick up a takeout Chinese dinner and arguing with each other about whether or not they should leave the kids for an hour. They stood on the front steps, leaving the door ajar, and Emily could hear their raised voices.

"Are you sure they'll be okay?" Carmen's voice was low and nervous.

"They're a lot more okay than I was at their age," Josh replied. "Me, at that age, I was just a nerd. They know kung-fu. Besides, Scruff's on guard."

"I've got a bad feeling," Carmen said, letting him guide her toward the car. "Something tells me we ought not to leave the house."

"Something tells me we need to eat. It's my turn to provide," Josh said firmly "I've told the next-door neighbor to look in on them while we're gone. They'll be fine."

Emily slammed the door a little harder than she meant to. Babysitters, at her age. Josh had totally lost his mind, in her opinion. She waited by the front door, hoping that Jake would show up. Dan had called him the minute Josh and Carmen were out the door. Emily had washed her hair for the occasion, tying a few beads and feathers into one long, thin, mini-braid, which hung way below the rest of her hair.

"Okay, Scruff, come. You can bring the little guys in with you," Emily called when she was ready to set up in the study. "We're on."

She had just managed to open the hard drive and bring up the Lilliput program, when Jake came in. He leaned over her shoulder and examined the screen. "You have to be sure the program won't disappear again," he said. "How about making a copy on your flashdrive?"

"Good idea," Dan said. "Do it, Em."

She waited till Scruff had brought in the four Lilliputians, not wanting the boys to think she was going to do anything just because they told her to. Emily hated being told what to do, especially when Jake was around. After all, it was her program, she told herself, trying to forget about how angry Josh had been. She had been the one to create the figures and scenery, but Josh was acting like the program was all his. And now he was leaving her with that witch next door as a baby-sitter. Her father's unfairness made Emily grind her teeth. It was time to show him that this program was as much hers as it was his. Having convinced herself that she was doing the right thing, she copied the program onto her flash drive, then hid it under Josh's dusty, little-used book case.

"I say, Jamie." Henry made a lunge for the boy's sleeve and hung onto it until Jamie picked him off the dog and set him on the computer desk. "Let's 'ave something to eat. Maybe some of that cockroach bran?"

"Ripple coming up," Jamie called over his shoulder. "Nobody wants bran when they can have ripple." It gave him a great sense of power to decide what someone else was going to eat. Jamie thought it would be a fine thing to be a dad and tell everybody they could have junk food, the way Josh did.

He came back with a large container of ice cream, opened it, and set it on the hall table while he went to get some doll spoons for the little people to eat out of. On his way to the kitchen, Jamie stopped, startled. He saw someone in the yard, or at least he thought he did. Maybe it was a person and maybe just a shadow thrown by the moon's glow. Jamie looked out the dining room window and gasped. It was somebody with a flashlight, and the somebody was coming closer. At first, he thought it was only one person, but then he saw the shadow of another. Jamie took a deep breath, then called to the others, his voice high and thin.

"Hey, looky," he cried, running out to the hall and grabbing Dan by the arm. "Somebody's out there with a flashlight."

"Come on, dork," Dan said, cuffing Jamie lightly on the back of the head. "It's just a car going by."

Samuel frowned. "Daniel, show a bit of respect. A man will not continue to tell you the truth, if you make fun of him for it. As a matter of fact," Sam continued, "I saw the lights myself, and they were too close to the house to be from a car, if I rightly understand what you mean by one."

Shamefaced, Dan looked at Jake, wishing his friend had not seen him put down by somebody six inches high, then went to the dining room window. "I don't see anything now," he said, "but you could be right, Jamie. I wasn't looking before."

Dan had a quality Emily had often observed with surprise, since she entirely lacked it, and that was humility. Once he had been shown that what he did was stupid or wrong, Dan was usually able to stand back and look at himself honestly, making no excuses for his behavior. Emily had puzzled over this trait before and she puzzled over it now. She herself, when criticized, just about went crazy, maybe because she criticized herself so much. Whatever was not approval was taken as a life-threatening attack. People were supposed to love her unconditionally. If they criticized her, that meant she wasn't being loved, which was totally not okay.

That was why she had always battled with her mother, Emily realized suddenly. Becky's job was to correct her daughter's mistakes, and Emily wouldn't let her do it without a fight. She looked at Becky with appraising eyes, for the first time feeling sympathy for her mother. If Emily had had a daughter like herself, she would have slapped her upside the head a dozen times a day. Maybe, Emily thought, just maybe, all these years she had been giving Becky a bad rap.

"Look sharp," Henry cried, "there it is again. Close, this time." He clutched Molly protectively around the waist.

The little woman clung to him and buried her face in his broad shoulder. Though in the past Molly had made fun of Henry's clumsy manners, Emily could see that the little barmaid was noticing how good it felt to have a strong man around, running interference. Maybe she would marry him, after all, when the two went back to Lilliput. If they ever got back. Hands trembling slightly, Emily watched the Lilliput program come up on the computer and the golden holographic haze spreading on the table like a Kansas wheatfield. Molly and her man deserved to have a life, Emily said to herself, and it was up to her to give them one. She would get these little people back home before it was too late, or give up computer games forever, as a penance. This time, nobody would die because of her mistake.

The light from outside swept by again, and Emily stood still, thinking that Josh and Carmen had returned and would catch them at the computer. She held her breath, her hand hovering above the keyboard. But why would Josh approach the house with a flashlight, she wondered. Maybe he was trying to catch them at the computer, in which case she should turn it off fast and get out of the study.

"It might be Dad, Jake," she whispered. "I'll go check, and you shut everything down. "If you hear me say 'Josh,' you and Dan grab the little guys and get out of the study fast." She started out the door. "Jamie, you're with me."

The two of them had no sooner left the study when they both froze. Someone was fiddling with the door key as if they didn't know they had to twist it to the right before shoving it in. If the intruder was Andriette, they would have to be careful, since the Lilliputians were in plain sight. The woman was perfectly capable of grabbing the little people, Emily knew, and selling them on e-bay, making herself enough money to buy a husband. She hadn't trusted Andriette ever since seeing her dress up for Josh and all but drool as she watched him from her front window. Those okra casseroles didn't fool Emily. She knew what Andriette was really after, and it wasn't a babysitting job.

Scruff began barking as if he'd lost his tiny mind, and was loping so fast down the hall that his ears flopped around like propellers. He skidded to a stop in front of the front door and growled. All four Lilliputians slid down his leg, hanging on his fur, then hid under the side table by the entrance. Jamie followed the dog, once or twice he leaping into the air, practicing his side-kick and grunting 'ho!' in his deepest voice.

"We do kung fu," Jamie yelled to whoever was outside. "It's our duty to warn you that we are living weapons. So go away already, whoever you are."

Emily was right behind him, waiting to hear her father's voice. When she heard nothing but a key rattling in the lock. "Dan, Jake," she hollered. "Dial 911 fast."

Dan shouted from the other end of the hall, "I just tried to. The burglars must have cut the wires. And my cell's upstairs in my backpack."

"Emily, hide," Jake said, catching up with her and pulling her behind him. "They're coming in. Jamie, get in the closet. Go, go."

Jamie accepted the wisdom of keeping the living weapon in reserve. With Scruff right next to him, determined to protect anyone who would let him, Jamie leaped deep into the hall closet, shutting the door. He and the dog huddled amid the coats and dirty boots, wondering when they might come out and spring a surprise attack.

Dick Briglia broke in through the front, his revolver in one hand and a Have-a-Heart trap in the other. He bared his teeth and made strange growling noises in his throat, as if he was working himself up for a fight. Emily was suddenly afraid. Jamie had told her the gym teacher was mean, and until now she had always thought her little brother was just whining. Now she figured Briglia intended more than ordering them to do a hundred push-ups. He looked like a shark that had tasted blood and liked it.

Andriette was close behind him, pulling at his army jacket. "Jackass," she cried, "These kids know me. Let me talk to them before you screw everything up."

She was trying to smile at the kids and scowl at Briglia simultaneously. Emily thought Andriette needed at least two faces, just to get through the day. Here was a woman you would not trust to park your car, let alone to babysit your kids. What was Josh thinking, letting her look after them? Carmen must have addled his brains just the way Jake had addled hers.

Briglia shook Andriette's hand off and aimed his revolver at the children. "Gotcha," he snarled. "Give us the little people and you're home free."

"Oh come on," Jake said, with withering contempt. "You're just the gym teacher. You're not going to shoot anybody. Put that gun down before you hurt yourself."

"Yeah," Emily said, stepping out bravely from behind Jake, then pointing at Andriette. "And all you want to do is nail our dad, like you've been trying to ever since mom died."

"So, you've been after my husband, have you?" Becky shouted and grabbed for her arrows. "Too bad I didn't have time to use my poison pot."

Becky muttered some swear words Emily couldn't quite make out and went into action. First, she shot one of her arrows at Andriette. But she was so furious that her aim was off, and the arrow wound up in Andriette's puffed hair-do. Then Becky ran around behind the intruders and aimed another arrow upward at Briglia.

"Sam, go for their ankles with your sword," she cried. "We'll have to do whatever damage we can without the mushroom brew."

Sam circled Andriette's feet, barely avoiding her grasping hands.

"Hold, giant wench," he cried, "I have you now."

Briglia shoved his revolver into his pocket, and reached for Molly with both hands. Molly screamed and tried to run farther under the hall table. Stumbling over her long skirts, she fell flat. Briglia grabbed her by the foot and began to pull, just as Henry grabbed her by the arm. The little man hung on with all his might, shouting for help.

"Somebody let go," Molly shrieked, "The two of ye are pulling me apart."

Henry released her arm, afraid she would be hurt if he hung on, but Briglia did not let go. Making more growling noises in his throat, he stood up, dangling Molly upside down, then grabbed at Henry, seizing him by his leather jerkin. Becky shot an arrow smack into his elbow, aiming carefully to avoid hitting the barmaid. Henry slipped out of his jerkin, leaving it in Briglia's hand.

"Right on," Becky shouted, leaping with delight when the arrow hit home. "Keep your hands off my friends. Emily, grab his gun."

Briglia roared with pain and hopped up and down, rubbing his elbow, hardly noticing that Emily had pulled his gun out of his pocket. She ran for the front door and tossed the revolver outside. When she came back, she saw Briglia drop the little barmaid headfirst into Jamie's open container of chocolate ripple.

"*Merde*," Becky cried. "She'll have hypothermia. Dan, Emily, somebody, get her out of there." Her mother had always told Emily that it was okay to say disgusting words, so long as you said them in French. Vulgarity, Becky said, could always be cancelled out by elegance. Since Emily knew no French, her vocabulary of acceptable swear words, at least when her mother was around, was annoyingly limited.

Maybe she was culturally challenged, Emily told herself, but at least she was big enough to save Molly. She ran to the container and rescued the barmaid, feeling a sudden rush of protectiveness toward the tiny woman. Only when Scruff had been a puppy trying to run into the street had Emily felt this urge to risk her life for someone who was helpless. Never mind what Briglia might do to me, Emily said to herself, Molly needs rescuing. Cuddling the little woman against her, Emily realized that she was feeling like a mother must feel, just the way Becky must have felt when trying to protect her. Actually, mom must have loved me, Emily thought, really loved me. And I was such an ungrateful brat. My bad. She looked away from her mother, not wanting to meet Becky's eyes.

To distract Briglia, Sam snatched up a walnut and pulled Henry's slingshot from the blacksmith's pocket. Tucking the walnut into the sling, Sam swung it around him and heaved the nut at the intruder's temple. The walnut hit squarely and Briglia staggered.

"A score for king and country," Samuel cried, picking up his sword and waving it at Andriette's thumb, which had come dangerously close to wrapping around him. "Prepare yourself, Goliath," he said grimly, "for the onslaught of David."

"Ow, you nasty slug," Andriette screamed, sucking her thumb. "You belong in spaghetti sauce, chopped up like a sausage, ya' hear?" She nursed her sore thumb, muttering to herself about various recipes in which ground Sam would be appropriate.

Briglia shook his bruised head. "Get busy," he howled to his accomplice. "Grab one of the little guys. Without 'em, we got nothin'."

Briglia snatched up Becky, determined not to leave without a trophy. "Gotcha, squirt," he snarled. "Think you can fight me? I could squeeze you to a pulp."

Taking a leap prodigious for a man of his girth, Samuel clung to one of Briglia's ankles, stabbing his sword right to the bone. "Let her go, or by my life, felon, I'll see you hamstrung!"

"Forget it, worm-man" Briglia shrieked, leaning down to grab Samuel. "You're dead in the water."

Dan leaped on Briglia's back, pummeling his head, while Jake chased them both through the kitchen waving a bread knife. They were concentrating on the man, ignoring Andriette, who was reaching for Henry. If Emily didn't move fast, the woman would have him in her pocket. She followed Andriette, almost treading on her heels, not able to forget the mental picture of her next-door neighbor trying to sell the little people like puppies.

Andriette ran, ducking away from Emily's pursuit, then abruptly turned around, grabbing Henry, who was tearing after her, waving his sword. The little man was obviously determined to take her down, but he didn't stand a chance. Andriette had him clutched in both hands, holding him so tightly he couldn't swing his sword.

"Leave him alone, Andriette," Emily cried. Her voice caught in her throat and she would have burst into tears, if Jake hadn't been there. She wouldn't let Jake see how much she cared. It might make him think she could be made to care about him. One thing Emily didn't want was to let anyone know she cared. They'd have her by the heart and could cause a world of hurt. Andriette looked back to see if Emily was still following her and ran headlong into the door jamb. She sat down hard and blinked, not noticing that Henry had jumped out of her hands and rolled under a desk.

Just then, the blue mouse streaked through the kitchen, stuffed the walnut in its mouth, and ran between Briglia's feet, knocking Samuel away from Briglia's clutching fingers. The mouse seemed to be made of mylar, gaps between his blue hairs sparkling in the beam of the flashlight. Briglia grasped at the counter to steady himself and spilled the bowl of walnuts onto the floor. The golfball-sized nuts rolling under him, Briglia's feet skittered as if on roller skates, and the man went down, releasing Becky as he fell.

Becky hit the ground and shot another arrow at Briglia, hitting him in the hip, then aimed at Andriette. Riding nimbly on a walnut, her feet dancing to keep her balance, Becky yelled, "Your turn, scum queen." Her arrow hit Andriette, who was already out the door, in her substantial rear. "Chase my man again and you'll be as full of holes as that mouse."

Briglia, crawling as fast as he could behind her, nursing his injuries, managed to be out the door before Becky could shoot again.

Jake quickly slammed the front door shut and locked it. "Okay, let Jamie and Scruff out," he directed the others, "before Scuff claws the closet door to sawdust."

With Scruff roaring his full-throated bark at them as he dashed out of the closet and through his dog door, Andriette and Briglia disappeared into the night, shouting curses at each other and rubbing their wounds. Each one hollered that the other was to blame, and their voices receded like dying sirens as they ran away.

Chapter 12

Quiet reigned in the kitchen. Jake brushed his hands together, as if he was getting rid of Briglia-dust. He had always said to Dan the gym teacher was dog dirt, and now Emily could see how right he was.

"They're gone," he said, wiping the sweat off his upper lip. "Let's get back to the computer."

"Not so fast!" Becky called out as she turned toward the little pot that was miraculously untouched.

"Check the downstairs windows," Jake cried. "Make sure they're all locked. Jamie, Emily, help him." He shoved the heavy antique hall table across the front door and stood panting in front of it.

"Jamie, our weapons please," Sam said, a worried frown creasing his broad forehead. "We are singularly unprotected against intruders."

While Jamie was picking up the swords, which had been scattered among the walnuts on the kitchen floor, Becky dipped her arrows into the poison pot. "Your swords, gentlemen." She nodded at Henry and Samuel, who plunged their weapons into the pot. "Best to be prepared."

"This time we'll be ready, Mom," Emily said gently. "We'll protect you."

"Stay back," Becky called to her daughter. "We'll protect ourselves, thank you very much."

"Civility, my sweet," Samuel murmured to Becky, so softly that Emily could barely hear him. "Civility is the way to tame the young brutes. If you sink to their level of diction, you will teach them nothing but barbarism."

Emily wrapped up the shivering Molly in a dishtowel, and held her close, hoping the cashmere sweater she was wearing would help keep the small woman warm. She felt the urge to croon some tender lullaby to calm Molly's hysteria, but was

afraid Jake would hear her and think she was being a sentimental twit.

Henry was standing on tiptoe, wanting to get closer to
Molly. He trembled all over, barely able to keep his voice
steady.

"Ye saved me Moll, you did," Henry shouted up to Emily.
"Bleedin' good lot these children are, Becky. Ye might say
something nice to 'em for a change."

Becky nodded. "You've got to give them credit for char-
acter," she said proudly. "They're my kids, all right."

Smiling, Emily sat down on the floor and looked closely
at her mother's face. "Hey, mom, that's more like it. Hang
around these little guys long enough and you might even learn
how to motivate me."

Playfully, Becky touched an arrow to her daughter's ankle
and laughed. "You have a point, girl, so you do. Now, how
about getting me that poison pot? We could have finished
them off, if we'd had time to use it before. Hurry! I expect
those two to try again."

As she went back to the study, still carrying Molly, Emily
felt a surge of power. She would bring this rescue off, she told
herself, and she would show Jake that he wasn't the only
computer expert around. She glanced back and saw the other
three Lilliputians right behind her, holding their black-tipped
weapons high.

Jake and Emily set up the computer for another attempt to
return the four little people to Lilliput. Emily was unsure
whether her heart was beating so hard because of their narrow
escape, or because Jake was sharing a chair with her, his body
leaning close to hers. She fanned herself with one of Josh's
reports and prayed that her face hadn't gone all red and shiny.

Scruff was back, growling and whining, nosing Emily's
elbow the way he did when he wanted to be patted. He hoped
Emily had learned a lesson and that when he warned her, she

would notice. It felt good to nuzzle her, and he forgot all about the intruders. A belly rub would suit him just fine.

"No time for rubs now, dog," Emily said, pushing Scruff away. "Go lick yourself or something."

But Scruff continued to jiggle her arm and moan plaintively. His people were dense, he knew, but he couldn't believe Emily didn't hear the voices in the distance and put two and two together. Those large, unfriendly people were coming back, he said to himself. He knew it as surely as he knew there would be kibble in his bowl every morning. Even for a human, Scruff growled to himself, Emily was so dumb she needed a keeper. He nudged her hard enough that she missed a keystroke.

"Shut him in your room, Dan," Emily said. "We're concentrating here."

As Scruff was being led upstairs, he let out a howl of protest and dug into the carpet, stiffening his long legs. Dan smacked him lightly on the head. "You're not in charge, Scruff," he said. "You're just a dog, remember?"

Scruff slumped onto the rug and put his paws on either side of his head. He knew when he was licked. Speaking of licked, he thought suddenly, there was something he could do when all else failed. Forgetting about the intruders, Scruff slapped out his long pink tongue, his best friend next to his nose. Well, maybe next to his humans, though Scruff didn't exactly consider his humans to be friends at the moment. Using patient, lingering licks, he took out his frustration by slathering his front paws with saliva until they were wet enough to leave tracks on the floor. He yawned with a little growl of contentment, then crawled under Dan's bed. For the moment, Scruff had had it with human stupidity and was going to sleep.

"What was that?" Hearing a sound at the door, Jamie, who'd been practicing his kicks again, skidded to a stop and turned around. "It's them! It's the burglars!"

Emily ran for the study and set Molly down on the desk. "Mom, everybody," she cried, opening the desk drawer. "Hide in here!"

"No way," Becky shouted, "We're on it, kids. Dan, give me a lift onto the desk."

Dan scooped his mother up and set her on the computer desk, next to the window and the lamp, hoping she was far enough away from the action not to get hurt. But Becky had a plan. She kicked over the study lamp, knocking off its shade, and shattered the bulb with the point of an arrow, making the room so dark that Emily could see how the little people glowed at their extremities. They're falling apart, she worried, tearing off the tip of a ragged nail with her teeth. She didn't care if Becky hated it when she did that. The situation was out of control, she said to herself, feeling her teeth chatter together. We're running out of time.

Chapter 13

At that moment, Andriette and Briglia charged through the back door and down the hall to the study. Andriette was carrying a fishnet and a barbecue fork. Briglia swung a bucket close to the floor, stooping as he ran. As he entered the room, his flashlight, which he held under one arm, bounced and made shadows tremble around the room, while his revolver waved in the general direction of the enemy.

"Stand back, kids," Briglia shouted. "I got you covered. Give up."

"That's right," said Andriette, fumbling in the dark with her net, trying to remember where everyone had run to before the light went out. "You ain't got a prayer. Let us take the little people, and we'll leave you alone."

"You bet you will," Becky said as she grabbed onto the Venetian blind cord and swung off the desk, kicking her legs to steer herself.

She landed on the floor, next to Briglia, and shot her black-tipped arrow upwards into his thigh, making him gasp and drop his bucket. The man staggered after a moment and began to run in circles. One foot hit the bucket and knocked it under the table. Becky dove into it and with both dancing feet rolled it against the wall.

"Mom, stay in there," Emily cried, pushing Andriette backward into the floor lamp. "We got 'em now."

"You haven't got them, not by a long shot," retorted Becky, racing over to the lamp, which had fallen to the floor, losing both its bulb and shade. "Watch this."

Waving her bow and arrow, she got Andriette's attention. The woman dropped to all fours and angled her fishnet so she could grab the Lilliputian. Standing behind the empty lamp socket, Becky coaxed Andriette toward her, then, at the last minute, dived behind the couch.

"I'm electrocuted!" shrieked Andriette, as her barbecue fork plunged into the socket. "Help, Briglia, I'm cooked!" She twitched all over as the current poured through her, until her hands finally dropped the fork and she rolled free of the lamp.

Leaping into action, Becky aimed a poison-tipped arrow straight into Andriette's hand, which was still trembling from the shock.

"Go after Josh again, bimbo," Becky shouted, "and I'll fry you like a trout."

She was so excited she shot too wide and hit Briglia in the knee, instead. The man jumped in the air and roared, staggering toward the door. Andriette had stopped twitching and was crawling toward Becky, trying to hold her fishnet steady. Seeing Becky's danger, Samuel had rushed to her side, his sword swinging. As Andriette approached, Samuel jumped in front of her, pushing the tiny woman behind him, well out of the way.

"Hide yourself, my sweet," he called over his shoulder to Becky. "The woman's gone off on that drug. No telling what she might do."

Getting up awkwardly and lurching forward, Andriette lifted one sandaled foot to stomp the little man. As the foot descended over him, Samuel lay down on the floor and braced his sword hilt against it, holding on with both hands. The poisoned point went straight into Andriette's bare toe, making her yell and fall backward, sitting down so hard her teeth clacked together.

Eyes crossing as she tried to focus, Andriette examined her bleeding toe and the black goo smeared around the puncture. "Hey, the little finks must have poisoned us."

Holding onto the doorframe, Briglia fumbled in his pocket, looking for his flashlight to find his way out. Instead, he pulled Henry's jerkin out of his pocket and looked puzzled as he held it up. "This thing ain't never gonna fit. Gotta talk to the military tailor," he mumbled, shoving the jerkin back into his pocket. "Did you get one of them little people yet?" he called to Andriette.

"You get one," she yelled back. "My guts are coming up my throat any minute." She stood up, reeled around as if she was drunk, and fell against the wall.

Becky's poison pot had done the job, Emily said to herself clapping her hands with joy. They're going down any minute. Now, if only they could get rid of the two intruders before Josh got back, they might have a prayer of getting the little people home.

"Hey, I'm seeing purple snakes crawling up the walls," said Briglia to no one in particular, his hands snatching vaguely at the air.

"Sam, Henry, Mom," Dan shouted, barreling into the study with Jake, "Run. We can take 'em." Both boys leaped for Briglia, then stood back as the gym teacher reeled around, waving his gun feebly at the ceiling.

"My hands," Briglia moaned, "they're like wet noodles." He wiggled his fingers in front of his face, examining them with vague, unfocused eyes. "They ARE wet noodles. How about that?" His gun dropped to the floor, and Jake grabbed it.

"Okay, mister," Jake said. "We're turning you over to the military police for breaking and entering."

"You can't do that," said Briglia, sticking one finger experimentally between his lips, as if it really had morphed into a noodle, "I AM the military police." Briglia's words were coming out thick and slow, like his tongue had suddenly grown too big for his mouth.

"The mushrooms got to him," Becky exulted, helping Sam get up and pulling him out of the way of Andriette's feet, which were kicking helplessly. "He's long gone for the tall timber. So's the bimbo. Whoa, what's that shiny blue thing?" she cried out, jumping back.

The blue mouse avoided Becky and ran under the bookcase, his fur fading and glowing by turns in the dimness. At least he's still alive, Emily said to herself. That means the little people still have some time to get back. This mouse was the canary in the coalmine. When he exploded into nothingness, they would know they had only a few short hours left to save the four Lilliputians.

Jamie was behind Andriette, threatening her, kung-fu style, with the edge of his stiffened hand. "Just you try getting up, okra-woman," he yelled, "and I'll flatten you like a rug."

Andriette's eyes were vacant, her tongue lolling out like Scruff's after a long run. "I feel funny," she said, giggling. "I feel like my brains just turned to marmalade. Whee! This is some fun!".

The blue mouse ran over her feet and flashed through the open study door, sparkling like he was plastered with sequins Andriette was so far gone that she just pointed at him, then fell flat on her back.

"Pick me up, darling," she said to Briglia, who was staggering around her, barely able to stand up. "I have completely lost control of myself."

"Don't expect nothin' from me," Briglia stuttered, "I'm down for the count." He fell on the floor beside her and stared around him, his eyes ready to pop out of his head. The two of them leaned against each other, back-to-back, cracking their heads together hard as they gawked at the ceiling.

"I spy with my little eye. . ."Andriette began dreamily.

"Stars," Briglia finished for her, chortling to himself. "I see stars when I shake my head."

"Any minute they're going to puke," said Jake, "Let's dump 'em outside before they do."

Emily went toe-to-toe with Andriette, braced herself, then with Dan's help, pulled the woman up. "We've got to get them next door before Dad gets home. You push, Dan. I'll pull."

Jake had just managed to lift Briglia to his feet and started to haul the man down the hall, when outside a car door slammed and Emily heard voices. Startled, Jake let go of Briglia, who fell back against the entry table and used it to hold himself up. Andriette slipped back to the floor and stared at the ceiling.

"Oh terrific," Emily said, "Dad's home. Jake, out the back door. Jamie, take the little people upstairs and shut them in Dan's room. Use the bucket. Go, go."

Jamie scooped up all four Lilliputians and ran for the stairs. Dan stood in the hall shaking, holding the gun Jake had given him before he took off. Just then, Josh and Carmen came in the front door, making a thunderously dramatic entry as they pushed away the heavy, antique hall table that Jake had used to block the way in.

"Okay, kids," Josh hollered, shoving the table back against the wall as he busted in, "What the hell have you been up to now?"

"Burglars, Daddy," Emily said in a trembling voice, suddenly reverting to about six years old. Her legs shook and she was afraid she was going to wet her pants. Good that Jake had disappeared out the back door and she didn't have to be a hero anymore. "We got 'em covered."

Carmen stood in the hall, her fists clenched on her hips. "Briglia," she said, her voice icy. "Hitting on kids now?"

"Better'n hittin' on their dads." Briglia gurgled, leering at her.

"Watch your mouth, mister," Josh warned, "The lady was invited here. Not like you." He peered more closely at Briglia. "What's the matter with him? Rabies?"

"I don't know if he's drunk or loco," Carmen said in disgust. "Both, probably."

"Drugs," Dan said helpfully, clearly hoping to redeem his complicity in the chaos by telling at least part of the truth. "Andriette and him were on something and crashed here. We were just going to get them back to her house. Neighborly-like, you know. . ." His voice trailed off uncertainly.

Emily was about to add that they hadn't even considered touching Josh's computer, when out of the corner of her eye she saw Jamie come down the stairs with Becky on his shoulder, hanging onto his shirt collar. Right behind him, carrying the other three Lilliputians in the bucket dangling from his mouth, was Scruff.

The dog descended with a prancing gait, holding his head high, proud of himself for being right about the burglars. Next time any burglars came along, maybe the kids would pay attention to his warnings. When he got to the bottom step, he shoved himself against Briglia's leg with bared teeth and snarled. It pained him to think that Josh must be assuming Scruff had failed in his canine duty. Not for the first time, the dog wished he could talk and explain that Josh's feckless kids had kept him out of the fight. In fact, if he could have talked, Scruff would have let Josh know that no kids he'd ever seen were as without feck as Emily, Dan, and Jamie. And Jake too, for that matter. It had not escaped Scruff's notice that Jake had kind of slobbered over Emily, a privilege Scruff felt should be reserved for himself.

"Nice doggie," Briglia murmured, too stoned to be impressed by Scruff's snarls, and unconscious of any danger. He made his voice smarmy and high-pitched, addressing the dog like it was a cute baby. "Wantums a little treatkins?"

Pulling a piece of beef jerky out of his pocket, Briglia offered it to Scruff. But the dog sniffed and turned nobly away, wanting everyone to know that some treats come with too high a price, and this jerky was one of them. Bribery would get the intruder nowhere, Scruff communicated with a shake of his head that flapped his long ears noisily and shook the contents of the bucket, causing a buzz of protest. Briglia tried to snatch the bucket, but Scruff growled and backed away, showing large yellow teeth that made him look like the hound from hell.

Becky's voice continued to whine and shriek, making Carmen frown and glance around. Taking a long, desperate leap, Emily landed in front of her little brother. Maybe, she thought, the crime scene would divert Josh sufficiently to keep Becky from being discovered. If only her tiny mother would just shut up and stop waving her hands around. Emily wished Scruff would keep snarling, but the dog, having proved his moral integrity, subsided and stood stiffly on guard beside Jamie, the bucket handle clenched tightly in his jaws.

Josh walked over to Briglia and peered closely into his face, which was turning a sickly color, like rotting lemons. "Okay, soldier," he said. "What's going on here?"

Emily turned slightly, keeping her eyes on her raving mother, praying that neither Carmen nor Josh would notice that Jamie had what looked like a demented elf perched shrieking on his shoulder

"Talk to us, Briglia," Carmen demanded, her voice steely. "Looks like breaking and entering to me. I hope you have a good lawyer."

"I got better than that," Briglia growled. His head was beginning to clear, and he blinked rapidly, trying to get himself together. "I'm the military police," he went on, looking for his gun like he expected it to materialize in his shaking hand. After a moment, he gave up on the gun and snapped his fingers authoritatively. "You're all under arrest."

"Can it, Briglia," Andriette giggled, struggling to stand up. "You got nothing. Let's blow this joint and go to my place." She fell against Briglia and drooled on his shoulder.

"You got a warrant?" Carmen asked, her fists curled up on her hips.

"Don't need one for domestic violets," Andriette tittered. "I mean violence." She backed into Dan, who was still holding the gun. He stumbled when the woman bumped him.

Josh grabbed the gun from Dan's hand and aimed it carefully at the picture hanging over Briglia's head. Having had no experience with guns, he would rather be thumb-screwed to the wall than to shoot somebody by accident. He was being especially careful, since Jamie had stepped away from Emily and was looking like he had just eaten the family's dessert, equally triumphant and sick to his stomach.

And there was someone else, someone that common sense said couldn't be there. Josh shook his head and looked again.

Chapter 14

Becky leaped from Jamie's shoulder to Briglia's and was finally nose to nose with Josh. "Okay, Josh," she said. "Let's hear it. What's this chick doing in my house?"

Josh froze and stared at her, his fingers loosening on the gun. As if he had no muscles at all, his arm dropped to his side, the gun pointing at the floor. Emily took deep breaths, feeling like her lungs would burst. Now her father would know what she had done and would never trust them again. They had stolen the fire of the gods, she thought, remembering the myth of that proud, miserable hero who had done the same thing and been forced to spend eternity chained to a rock, his liver continually nibbled by a greedy bird. She envisioned herself tethered to her desk doing homework every night until she was eighteen, an eternity away.

"Becky," Josh breathed. "My God, it's Becky" He clapped his hand over his eyes and staggered back a step.

Taking advantage of his captor's momentary lapse, Briglia grabbed the gun back. "I'm a cop," he chuckled maniacally, "a military cop, and I got you dead to rights. Possessors of government property, that's what you are." He took a sudden step, startling Becky from her perch on his shoulder. Dropping the gun, Briglia lifted both hands to catch her.

"I got me a little hostage," he said, his eyes finally able to focus. "So, you gotta let me go."

Andriette suddenly turned pale green and retched. "What I gotta do is hurl," she cried, and ran out the door, her hip ricocheting painfully off the doorknob as she stumbled choking into the yard.

"Madre de Dios," Carmen cried, "Jamie's little mother." She grabbed the gun, which had clattered to the floor. "Get your wife, Josh, before Briglia squeezes her to pulp."

"Mom," Jamie yelled, "I'll rescue you." He rushed toward Briglia, then stopped short as Carmen spoke.

"Back off, Jamie. I got him covered," Carmen said, clicking off the safety catch. Jamie stood tensely watching, taking deep breaths, building up a reservoir of energy for an attack.

"Briglia, give her to Josh, before I put you down like the dumb dog you are," Carmen continued.

Scruff growled plaintively, not sure he liked being compared to Briglia, but grumbled into silence when he remembered that Carmen had fed him fish in the kitchen the night before.

"You wouldn't shoot me," Briglia sneered at her. He held Becky up by the neck of her shirt, letting her dangle helplessly. "We used to be pretty good friends, remember?"

"I remember you were one huge pain in the butt," Carmen said. "And that's just where I'll shoot if you don't hand that woman back."

Jamie crept up a few steps, giving himself a little space for height, then leaped forward, his kung-fu kick landing squarely between Briglia's shoulders. "Ho," he shouted. "Let go of my mom, you putz."

Briglia's grip loosened and his arm flew up, sending Becky gracefully into the air. She sailed right into Josh's cupped palms. Briglia, realizing he had no gun and no hostage, ran out the front door, covering his rear with his hands. Carmen might, after all, have meant what she said about where she'd like to shoot him. As the man stumbled out into the dark, Dan slammed the door behind him. Looking at his father anxiously, Dan was clearly wondering when the blow would fall. Since Josh now knew everything, they were all in the deepest possible doo-doo.

Carmen opened the clip of Briglia's weapon, poured out all the bullets on the floor, and flung the gun out the window after him.

"Yo, cop," she called. "Here's your gun. Like you'll ever figure out how to use it."

They couldn't hear Briglia muttering into his cell phone. "Tell the colonel he'd better get over here before Dr. Einstein sends the mini-people back where they came from. And tell him they've got a secret weapon that sends you into orbit." His voice trailed off, and a fizzing electronic thud could be heard as he fell onto his phone.

"Why'd you give him back his gun?" Dan asked, looking between Carmen and his father, not sure which of them was more dangerous.

"He would have come back and busted me for stealing it," Carmen said grimly. "Trust me. I know the type."

"Josh?" Emily ventured a weak smile and approached her father with small, reluctant steps. "We gotta talk."

"Confession time?" Carmen put her hand on Emily's shoulder, and gave it a reassuring squeeze. "We're listening."

But Josh had nothing on his mind except his minuscule wife.

"Becky, honey," Josh said, "where'd you come from?"

"I know," Jamie said, waving one arm in the air, like he was in school and had the right answer to the teacher's question. "Out of the computer, along with her friends."

Dan frowned and shook his head, while Emily covered Jamie's mouth with both hands.

"And how did they do that?" Josh turned away from Becky and frowned at the children.

"All by theirselves." Jamie smiled charmingly, shaking Emily off him. He spread out his hands as if he hadn't a clue.

Carmen was staring at Becky. "What's the deal, Josh?" she asked, tapping one foot and staring at him. "Isn't this your wife? And didn't you say she was gone?"

"She was gone," explained Jamie in a high, nervous voice, not wanting Carmen to think his dad was a liar. "But now she's back, just like I told you." His innocent smile was lost on Josh and Carmen, who were looking into each other's eyes, confused.

"I think I've missed something," Josh began, clearly not sure what to say to make Carmen understand that he had had no part in Becky's mysterious resurrection.

"Apparently it wasn't me." Becky folded her arms across her chest and tried to keep both her dignity and her balance, no easy task, since Josh's hands were trembling under her. "I asked you before, Josh. Who's the girlfriend?"

"My name is Carmen Rochas," Carmen said with a dazed kind of dignity. "But I think the question is, who are you?"

"I'm his bloody wife," Becky shouted, "that's who. And I'm back. So flake off, Carmencita."

Carmen started backing toward the door, grabbing her purse off the hall table. "Look, lady. I'm no home-wrecker. Where I come from, home's all there is, *comprende*?"

She tucked her purse under her arm, and gave Josh a hard look. "Hey, Josh, if you get your marital status figured out, let me know."

"Carmen, wait." Josh held Becky gently in one hand and reached the other out to Carmen. "All I need is a chance to. . ."

"I don't compete with Barbie dolls," Carmen interrupted and slammed the door behind her as she left.

Covering her mouth with one hand, Emily suppressed a nervous giggle. It was true, her mother looked just like a Barbie doll, with her waist-length blond braid, long legs, and tiny waist. She wished she had noticed the resemblance before, since it would have been great ammunition against Becky in one of their verbal duels. Becky had always hated Barbie dolls, and wouldn't let Emily have one. They looked like common tarts, Becky had said, not like real women. So last Christmas, Emily had received a Skipper doll with a flat chest and babyish outfits, instead of the Ski Barbie she wanted. It occurred to her now that her mother might have been trying to keep her from growing up too fast. Maybe Becky was just trying to keep her safe, Emily thought, just as she herself was trying now to keep Becky safe. She could relate to that urge, worried as she was that all her little captives were about to dis-integrate.

Josh was running down the hall. "Carmen," he cried. "Becky!" Then he stopped and looked down into his hand at the face of his wife. "I can't handle this."

"You'd better," Emily said, "since we sure can't."

Josh stood still frowning the way he always did when computing a problem. He thought out loud, his eyes fixed on Becky. "Like the beer bottle," he said, stroking his bristly chin with one hand, making a scratchy noise. "You figured out how to precipitate Becky out of the VR hologram," he said with a jolt that made Becky sit down hard on his palm. "That's why Colonel Sharpe is after her!"

"Andriette and Briglia must be working with him," Dan added importantly.

Emily was annoyed, figuring that Dan was trying to un-stick himself from the schemes they had plotted for the past two days.

"We were trying to get them back into the computer, Dad," she said with as much dignity as she could rescue from Josh's humiliating discovery of her computer hacking. The last thing Emily wanted was for Josh to think that Dan was some kind of hero. If any medals were to be handed out, she should get them, since she was the one trying to put the Lilliputians back where they belonged. She glared at her older brother with her coldest glare and thought fast.

"Dan was a big help," she said ingenuously. "He helped me break into the computer." When Dan furiously sucked in his breath, Emily gave him the sweetest of smiles. "I couldn't have done it without him. Now we have to get them back into the computer fast, before Colonel Sharpe steals them."

"Stop right there. You're trying to manipulate me." Josh ordered. "You know how I hate that. What do you mean, 'they'? I thought just Becky had jumped dimensions."

"We got four of them," said Jamie proudly, "but I was the one who rescued mom."

Nudging each other, Dan and Emily tried not to smile. Jamie had just let himself in for a third of the blame, leaving that much less for them.

Becky tugged on his thumb, trying to get his attention. "Josh, who'd want to steal us. Why?"

Josh held her up close to his face, which was crumpled with worry. "The colonel might want you for his cybernaut program. He's had no luck with his bio-mimetic robots. We have to get you back to Lilliput before. . ."

Becky made her stand, arms folded like Mr. Clean. "I'm not going back, Josh. No way am I going back. This family needs a mother, and I'm it."

Jamie snatched her out of his father's hands and cuddled her in his own. "You heard her, Dad. She's here to stay. She's mine."

"If she's anybody's, Jamie, she's mine," Josh said dryly. "We'll argue ownership rights later. Right now, we've got to put them back into the program before they fall apart. Can't you see they're only half here, disintegrating as we speak?"

Scruff chose this dramatic moment to tip his bucket on its side and spill out the other Lilliputians at Josh's feet, proud to be the one to let his master know how clever and important he was.

Getting up and brushing off his waistcoat, Samuel said. "We are indeed falling apart, Sir. The sooner you can put us back where we belong, the better."

"I think you must be Dr. Johnson," Josh said, making an awkward bow. "I regret that I've endangered you and your friends."

"Think nothing of it, Sir," Sam said, returning the bow, with an elegant turn of his ankle. "Were it not for your work, I would never have met your wife."

Josh straightened up and stared at Sam. "I take it, then, that you are fond of her?"

"Immensely so, Sir, begging your pardon," Sam said politely. "Since you are her husband, my attachment might be considered an affront to your honor. I am happy to see that our unequal size makes a duel quite impossible."

"So you don't want her to stay with me?" Josh fingered his bristling beard, trying to make sense of what he was hearing.

"She cannot survive here," Sam replied. "I urge you to ignore her pleas against repatriation to the gulliver world. Already I can see light sparkling through her arms. Like all of us, she has little time left."

"Don't listen to him, Josh," shrieked Becky, trying to stand upright in Jamie's hands. "You can re-program me. You can make me permanently part of your life again. Just do it"

"Dad, can you?" Jamie's eyes were wide and wet. "I want her back."

"You've got a thing for that Carmencita," Becky said, her voice rising into a wail. "That's why you don't want me back."

Josh wiped his forehead. "Becky, it's over. There's no way I can bring you back to life. I'm a computer scientist, not God."

Emily tugged at his sleeve. "Dad, if you're ever going to put them into that program again, it'll have to be now, while they've still got bodies."

"You're right," Josh said, leading the way into his study. "I'd guess we have twenty-four hours before they've totally disintegrated, maybe less. Let's get at it."

Andriette had come to, thoroughly cleaned out after leaving a noxious puddle of puke on the lawn. She rolled her wheelbarrow over to Briglia's Porsche and dragged him into it, cursing him up and down for losing his grip on both the gun and the tiny woman. She was fed up with Briglia. If she had had it to do over again, she would have accepted this assignment with no one but the steely-eyed Colonel Sharpe. Since her useless partner was unconscious and lay sprawled on the front seat of his car, Andriette figured she could handle the problem. The colonel had told her he didn't want to be called in the middle of the night, but he also wanted immediate news of the Lilliputians. Catch-22. Andriette decided she would risk a call.

"Colonel, sweetie," she said over the cell phone in her most honey-lathered southern voice. "Guess who's out cold? And guess who has the goods on Josh Ross?"

Briglia half woke up and moaned in the direction of the cell phone, "Tell the colonel he'd better get over here. Dr. Josh Einstein is gonna send those mini-people back where they came from…." He took a breath, looking confused, then remembered. "Oh yeah, and tell him they have a secret weapon. . ."

Before Briglia could finish his sentence, he slumped over in the front seat, banging his forehead on the steering wheel. The horn blared, and Andriette roughly pushed him off it, afraid that Briglia would wake the whole neighborhood.

As it turned out, Andriette hadn't gotten the colonel on the phone after all, but his subaltern, an ex-con who would die for the colonel, given that Sharpe had helped him beat a murder charge.

"Colonel, you got a call from that woman with the neon hair," The man said, covering the phone with one hand. "Her and that guy with the lit-up gym shoes. They want you over at Dr. Ross's, like yesterday. Claims they've been drugged. . ."

Sharpe rolled his eyes to the ceiling and polished his nails vigorously. "And they're seeing little people again, I suppose." He looked at his watch and turned out the lights. "Check him out in the morning," Sharpe said. "When he's sobered up. I'm going home to bed, if these whacked-out pests will let me alone."

The colonel slammed the door behind him, knowing that he wouldn't sleep without a handful of Valium. Even the luxury of bad dreams was lost to him. Nothing was in his head but a scheme that wouldn't let him sleep. And the more he thought about it, the more possible it seemed. Colonel Sharpe's plan was to hold the world hostage to nuclear bombs controlled by little people who were controlled by him. Now neither God nor conscience would let him off the hook he had twisted for himself.

"So, how do we get these little guys back to where they came from?" Josh was talking half to himself, half to them, as he puzzled over the computer. The kids had gone upstairs to get ready for bed, while Josh and the Lilliputians considered next steps.

Samuel stood by the keyboard. "Those scoundrels will be back to fetch us, mark me, Joshua. Society has come to a sad pass when the constabulary tries to make off with one's guests."

"Can't we go to the Attorney General or something?" Standing close to Samuel, Becky put her braid in her mouth and chewed it, exactly what she had told Emily never to do. "This colonel is way beyond his rights," she said, her voice trembling. "There's got to be somebody in the government who can put him down."

"Nobody I know." Josh bent over his computer keyboard. "All we can do is get you folks back to Lilliput before you turn into pixels. Or Sharpe turns you into cybernauts for use against North Korea."

"How many ways do I have to say it before you hear 'No,'" Becky said, standing right under her husband's elbow. "Get this. I'm not going back."

"Come on, Mom," Emily said as she entered the study. "We've been through it all before. You have to go, if you want to live." She turned to her father. "We made them, so they're not even real."

She had just come back from taking a quick shower and had put on her most unfavorite sweater. Becky had picked it out just before the accident, and it hung all the way to her daughter's pitifully small hips. The thought had flashed through her mind that before Becky left for good, she should see Emily wearing this last gift. Maybe it would serve as an unspoken apology for all the times she had not thanked her mother in the past.

"After a fashion, they are," said Josh soberly, pulling on his VR glove. "I was the one who programmed Becky to be a piece of me. She IS a piece of me."

"Damn straight," Becky said, tucking her bow over her shoulder. "Has Carmencita got that?"

"I'm afraid so." Josh's head was bent over the keyboard, so no one could see his face.

"Look, these kids need a mother," Becky said, climbing onto his fingers as he tried to key in information. "They're dying on the vine, just like us Lilliputians. I belong here with my kids. With you."

Samuel stepped up behind her, his arm draped over her shoulder. "Where you belong, my sweet," he said, "is in our story, not theirs."

"Sam, I see why you love Becky," Josh said, as if a light had suddenly gone on in his head. Being a scientist, his wife had always said, Josh had always been slow in the area of feelings. "Because I programmed myself into you, along with all my cybertronic information."

With a courtly bow toward Becky, Samuel explained, "I've loved her ever since she dropped into Molly's pub with her longbow, tights, and perfect mastery of dactylic hexameters."

Becky couldn't seem to help smiling at him, despite her losing battle with Josh. As always, Emily thought, her mother was pleased to be admired. "And you haven't even seen my tennis game!"

"At this rate, my sweet, no one ever will," Sam sighed. "Joshua, shall we have a go at your computer before the four of dissolve into… what was it you said? Pixie-dust?"

"Right behind you, Dr. Johnson," Josh said, grabbing his computer mouse and clicking on screen icons.

"I fear those blockheads will attack again," Sam worried, unrolling a paper on Josh's computer table. "We have to be quick. Have you considered using parallax theory applications?"

Josh picked up the paper and held it close to one eye, reading carefully. "Damn, you're good. No, I hadn't. Let's give it a try."

"I haven't had a chance to work to work the calculations out thoroughly," Sam apologized. "Rather a lot of interruptions, you know."

Emily curled up with Jamie on the study couch, where they went to sleep like a heap of puppies. Lying down on the rug in front of the couch, with his arm around Scruff, Dan kept his eyes on his father until they began to drift closed. All of them woke up with a start when they heard the computer chimes ring as their father finished working.

"That's all for tonight, Sam," Josh said with a yawn. "My last cerebral synapse just shut down. I'll grab a few hours sleep and get back on the job."

"I'll just stay on and work a bit while you rest, Joshua," Sam said. "We cyber-creatures may be subject to disintegration, but not to the need for sleep."

Jamie rose up in a panic and fell on top of Dan. "Where is she?" he cried. "Where's Mom? Did you send her back without giving me a chance to say goodby?"

"Hey, dork," Dan grumbled, "get your freakin' elbow out of my eye."

Sam stood tall and spoke in his loudest, deepest voice. "Sir, a man has no more right to be rude to another fellow than to knock him down. You must be more civil to your brother, unless you want to train him up to speak and act like a guttersnipe."

Dan sat up and hung his head. "Sorry, Jamie. I forgot."

Rubbing her eyes and getting off the couch, Emily felt a sudden solidarity with Dan. Both of them had pretty much treated Jamie like an infestation of fleas. "Me, too," she said. "I got a big mouth, and that's the truth."

"It's inherited," said Becky, looking at her daughter fondly.

"Along with a big brain." Molly beamed at them all. "Ye show signs of learning, me bairns," she said. "There's hope for ye yet."

Chapter 15

Colonel Sharpe had changed his mind about going home that evening. He had begun to hope that Andriette and Briglia might yet bring in the little people they claimed had come out of Josh Ross's computer. The toy sword and the videotape had impressed him more than he had let on to his underlings. All he needed was to see one more piece of evidence, and he would be sure that the little people were his to command.

He wasn't surprised when the phone rang. Hewitt answered it and was noncommittal. When he had hung up, Hewitt said, "It was that babe with the fake eyelashes. She wants you to come over to her house ASAP. Somebody drugged her, she says."

"Wouldn't surprise me if she's been drugged all along," the colonel said, pushing Cuban tobacco into his pipe and lighting it. "Check her out in the morning and let me know what she and Briglia are up to." He looked at his watch, yawned, and settled back in his easy chair, eyes closed.

At three in the morning, Briglia staggered into Sharpe's office holding Henry's tiny jerkin in his hand, gibbering incoherently. "I almost had the goods," he said, trying to control his chattering teeth, "but they drugged me and Andriette. She's still sleeping it off. But I wanted you to see what I got." Briglia leered hopefully at the colonel and laid Henry's jerkin on the desk. He was clearly pumped at having gotten there before Andriette.

Sharpe held it up and sized the item up like he was the judge of the Antiques Roadshow. "Eighteenth-century style." He held the jerkin to his nose, sniffing, then dropped it. "Eighteenth-century stink, too."

"I been tracking Carmen and Einstein, like you said," Briglia muttered, trying to keep his flapping lips around the words. "They're a number, all right. You can't count on her for help." He cracked his large knuckles menacingly. "I'd like to take that nerdy Einstein apart. She was all mine until he..."

Sharpe looked at his watch and pushed the jerkin to the side of his desk. "Stuff it, Briglia. Report to me at 10 hundred hours. I got a job for you. You'll like it."

When Briglia had reeled out the door, the colonel got on his cell phone and called to check the progress of Plummer, the assistant in charge of miniaturized robot operations. The man had begged his boss to come to the lab for a demonstration by his prize performer. The little Slugger had bombed out a few days ago, and Plummer wanted to prove that it was time Colonel Sharpe made him, not Hewitt, assistant chief. Sharpe was inclined to agree; Hewitt deserved to be demoted, given his failure to produce a robot that had the right stuff.

Plummer's robot was lean and mean, as skilled at combat as any veteran soldier. The only trouble was, he was in a computer program. Plummer wondered how the colonel would react when he realized that Fat Boy, as he jokingly called his slim killer, in honor of the bomb dropped on Hiroshima, was the product of better software and was more reliable than the ill-fated Slugger. To his surprise, the colonel was not critical, not critical at all. He seemed to think he could free Fat Boy from the computer and get a lot better results than Slugger ever could.

"You say Fat Boy is ready to go?" he murmured, polishing his fingernails nonchalantly to show he didn't care much. "Let's see him in action. I got a feeling he won't be stuck in the computer forever, not if I can get Josh Ross to use his formula."

Settling down in his leather chair, the colonel watched Fat Boy knock out every attacker and turn the last one to a heap of twisted metal parts. "I think he'll do just fine," Colonel Sharpe told Plummer. "I'd like to see him with some rotating steel blades instead of a left hand, but otherwise he's good to go. Work on it. Now all we need to do is to find Josh Ross and bring him here. Call Hewitt and tell him to bring my car to the sentry post."

The Lilliputians woke Josh up before dawn the next morning by jumping all over his head. Scruff had delivered them as Becky directed, and now stood by the bed, wagging his tail over Josh's face like an insistent, hairy fan. The dog could never understand why people couldn't be wide awake at a moment's notice, the way he was. They seemed to have no sixth sense that enemies were lurking nearby. Instead, his humans just lay there for eight hours at a time, totally useless.

"Up and at 'em, Josh," Becky ordered. "That colonel could be here any minute."

"I'm not awake," Josh muttered, sticking his head under the pillow. "Have mercy."

"No time for sleep, mate," said Henry, leaping for Scruff's tail and swinging back and forth, kicking his sharp, pointed boots against Josh's exposed neck. "Ye got work to do."

"Where are the kids?" Josh rolled to the other side of the bed and got up, stretching and yawning. "Are they okay?"

"They're at the computer in your study," Becky said sweetly, knowing how that news would grab her husband.

Swearing, Josh threw on a sweat suit and tore off downstairs, followed by the dog and his four riders. "That's where all the trouble started," he called over his shoulder. "You shouldn't have let them, Becky."

"And what do you expect me to do? They are twelve times my size," Becky hollered to him, as she bounced down the steps on Scruff's back. "I couldn't get Emily to mind me even when I was bigger than she was. Now it's hopeless."

She raised her voice to a soprano shriek, angry that Josh had escaped her. "You want them disciplined? Your turn."

The doorbell rang and Josh veered from his trajectory toward the study in order to answer it. Carmen stood in the doorway in her Sunday best, carrying a tray of sweet-smelling

Mexican cornbread. Her dark eyebrows were drawn together, and her lips were pressed into a line. She looked like she had slept on tacks all night.

"I was on the way home from church," she said, her words all in a rush, and her voice husky. "Your phone was dead when I called last night, but I got the repairmen on it. Just thought you should know."

"Thanks, Carmen." Josh gave her a quick hug. "I thought you were through with me."

"I tried to be, but it didn't work." Carmen gave him a shaky little smile. "I can't stay. Call me sometime." She handed him the pan of cornbread and ran down the walk.

When Josh stood still, looking after her, Becky stood up and furiously waved her bow in the air. "Hel-lo-o! Remember us, Josh?"

"I'm on it, Becky," Josh said hastily. He ran his hands through his pepper gray hair, which was standing straight up like a scared cat's. "Jamie, serve up the cornbread. Scruff, bring the little guys to the desk. I need Dr. Sam."

Samuel hung onto Josh's hand as the scientist lifted him onto the computer table. "I say, Joshua, it's a bit unsettling to think of being returned to the video game. Won't it just disappear entirely, taking us with it, once we're back in there?"

"Good question." Josh booted up the apparatus. "It bothered me, too. But I've installed a looped subroutine that allows the scenario to keep unfolding continuously in cybertime. You'll be virtually immortal, no matter what happens to the main program. Here, Dr. Sam, help me flesh out these parallax applications."

Becky and Henry patrolled the windowsill, peering out anxiously whenever they heard a car pass. The older two children hung over Josh's shoulder, while Jamie, followed by Scruff, carried Carmen's cornbread into the kitchen, grabbing hunks of it out of the middle. To his credit, Jamie had first given some to Molly, knowing the little people hadn't eaten since the night before.

Meanwhile, Sam had picked up a small magnifying glass and lugged it over to the keyboard. He stood patiently, waiting until Josh had gone through his manipulations.

Slapping his hand on the table in frustration, Josh shook his head. "I tried the old combination. I tried parallax applications. Nothing." He started to heat himself a cup of coffee in the microwave, but left the cup untouched and the door open when Sam called to him.

"You spilled something called pizza on certain keys. Emily told me," Sam said holding up the magnifier and balancing on the edge of the keyboard.

"Yeah, but I wiped it off." Josh lowered his head, staring closely at the keys. "You won't find anything now."

"Not anything you can see, Sir," Sam replied, peering through the glass. "But my eyes have a focal advantage, being so small."

"So, what do you see?" Dan craned his neck. "Any stains?"

"A bit, here and there." Sam began reading off letter and number combinations, hopping around on the keyboard awkwardly, pushing the magnifying glass in front of him.

"There you have it, Sir," he said finally, standing straight. "Now, we apply the parallax applications to these elements, using the computer, and we will find out which combination works."

"Right." Josh's fingers moved fast. "No, no, yes! Got it."

Suddenly the phone rang, and Emily ran to pick it up. "Carmen? You OK?"

Carmen's words came fast and frightened. "Get Josh. I'm in deep bazu here. Some guys in uniform are sitting outside my apartment building in a black van. . ."

"Okay, I'll get him." Emily held her hand over the phone. "Dad, you gotta take the call. It's Carmen. She's in trouble. . ."

Josh nearly knocked over his chair in his hurry to get to the phone. "Carmen! What's up?"

Her voice was small and high. "Some guys in a uniform are guarding the front of my place. One's on his way into the building. What should I do?"

"Wait for me. I'll come." Josh started down the hall, carrying the cordless phone with him in his haste.

"Come around back. I'll be waiting in the alley." She hung up.

"Josh, you're not leaving us for her," Becky insisted. "We need you more than she does."

"We're into the program," Josh said, dropping the phone as he left. "Emily, you and Sam can take it from here. I'll be back with Carmen in a few minutes. Don't unlock the door, kids. Not for anybody."

He was gone before they could answer and they heard his car zoom off with the growling sound it had developed because Josh couldn't remember to have the muffler fixed. Scruff howled and pawed the carpet, not happy that any machine could make a noise more ferocious than his.

The blue mouse, sparkling as if Scotty was beaming him up, suddenly rushed across the floor, then ran in circles, flinging sparks off like a firecracker. Emily jumped back, scared the mouse had some exotic variety of rabies, and Dan grabbed a wastebasket.

"I entreat you to drop the rubbish basket over his head, Daniel," Sam said. "We need a laboratory animal."

Dan hung onto Scruff's collar with one hand, and lowered the basket to the floor. "Okay, Scruff," he ordered, "Chase that mouse into my basket, and you'll get Beggin' Strips every day for the rest of your life."

The mouse squeaked and reared back on its hind legs at the double trauma of Scruff's growl and the descent of the basket over its body.

"Now, Dan my boy, take the virtual reality glove and seize that mouse by his tail." Samuel tapped his fingers on the keys, and shook like a hula dancer in his excitement.

Emily remembered that the good doctor had a medical history of tics, and moved her fingers toward the keyboard. "Sam, relax. I'm on it. Just read off the combination." Emily flexed her fingers, getting ready to type, and cast a glance at Sam. He had finished writing down the combination on the back of a grocery receipt and was waving it in the air.

"Some of that sherry, Henry," Sam called, triumphantly. "A celebration is in order."

Henry was so overjoyed that he spilled drops of sherry all over Sam's hand. Together, he and Sam lifted the glass, first to one's lips, then to the other's.

"I know how it's done," Sam shouted triumphantly. "We're as good as in." With the tip of his finger, he tapped in his figures, leaving a drop of sherry on every relevant key. The crumpled paper on which he had written the combination and left a sherry stain, fell unnoticed to the floor.

Chapter 16

Andriette Hale was a wreck. Her hair was straggling out of its puff ball around her head and hung like snakes down her cheeks. She was sick to her stomach and angry at every man in sight. Since Colonel Sharpe had just barged in with Hewitt, and Briglia was draped like a sick python over her armchair, she had a lot to be angry at. Her makeup was smeared, Andriette was sure, and she grabbed a handful of tissues to wipe her face clean. Since her aim was off, she left a dribble of black mascara on one cheek, and a flyaway lash hanging down into one eye. She had looked better and hoped Colonel Sharpe remembered that.

"So, they came over here and attacked you, is that it?" Sharpe stood in the middle of her living room, his fists on his narrow khaki hips.

"Not exactly." Andriette sat down on top of Briglia, ignoring his gurgle of protest. "We were over at Josh's house, trying to grab one. To show you, Colonel Pete." She smiled up at him ingratiatingly, unaware that her front teeth were covered with lipstick.

Briglia's head rose slightly, then sank again. "They got poisoned arrows. I don't feel so good." He bucked Andriette off him and fled to the bathroom, making urping noises as he went.

Colonel Sharpe was not sympathetic. With one toe, he nudged Andriette, who had fallen to the rug.

"You mean both of you, two armed, functioning adults, couldn't handle three kids and a couple of six-inch-high people?"

"They shot us full of drugs," Andriette moaned. "I keep telling you, Colonel Petie, sweetie." Her shoulders hunched over and she coughed. "Sorry. I gotta toss my cookies again." She rushed into the kitchen, flailing her arms and gagging.

"Hurry up in there," Sharpe called to them both. "We have no time to waste." He looked at his watch, tapped his foot, and nodded to Hewitt. "Get the neighbor kid down the street. We're going in."

Emily pulled the blue mouse out of the trash basket and held it up. "Okay, Sam," she said. "We got our guinea pig. What now?" She patted the animal's soft blue fur reassuringly with one hand and pushed the curious Scruff away with the other.

"We'll try to send him to Molly's pub," Samuel said, "before he goes up in a puff of indigo smoke." Tersely, he added under his breath, "As I fear we are about to do."

"Not me, Sam," Becky said, keeping her voice desperately upbeat. "I'm doing just fine."

"You're not," Emily answered, her voice soft with sympathy. "You're as full of holes as an old sock. What's the problem, Scruff?"

She turned to the dog, afraid to guess what he might be hearing or smelling. Last time he had growled like that, they were about to be attacked by Andriette and Briglia. Suddenly she found it hard to breathe, as if her pounding heart was occupying too much space in her chest.

Scruff ran to the front door and back to the children, barking his brains out, his tongue flopping in his mouth like a red flag. He could smell the enemy approaching and hear their feet on the driveway between the houses. Scruff paused, then barked four times, to indicate that four people were coming. That seemed like a clever move to him, but at once he saw it was lost on his dense humans. Then he barked again, two loud barks and two small barks. He was trying to suggest to his hopelessly out-of-touch people that two strong bad humans and two weak bad ones were on their way, but still, nobody got it. They were busy with that stupid blue mouse and were paying no attention to their guardian angel dog. Scruff thought he might as well take off and join a pack of wandering wolves, for all the good he was doing in the Ross household. With a last, hopeless howl, Scruff collapsed moaning, with his head on Emily's lap, ready to share whatever dreadful fate the four intruders had in store for his human children.

"Jamie, take Scruff upstairs into my room, and shut him in there," Emily ordered. "We got work to do."

"We do indeed," Sam said. "Dan, put that mouse into the lighted square before he explodes into pixie-dust. Do it, man."

Dan's voice went all high and squeaky, and he put his hands behind him. "I wouldn't touch that weird thing with a fly rod."

Shoving her hand into the glove, Emily grabbed the mouse by the tail. "Move over, bro. Sam, whenever you're ready."

Sam pointed to the keys. "Here, Henry, jump. And here. Over there, on the W, Molly, jump hard. Now, Emily, hit alt control insert and drop the mouse into the holographic square in front of the computer."

Emily tucked her tongue tightly between her teeth, concentrating. On the table where Sam pointed, she could see first a blur, then a whirling, spiral twist of gold light that slowly spread to a square. "Okay, mouse," she murmured, pushing him into the center of the square. "On your way. Live long and prosper."

They all stopped breathing for a moment and stared at the screen. There was the mouse, scampering under the Molly's bar, kicking up his heels as he disappeared. The Lilliputians cheered, and Emily sat back on Josh's computer chair, breathing fast to quiet her out-of-control heart. Now, it would be only a matter of minutes before they could put the others back in, and all things would be as they had been.

If only time could go backward, she said sadly to herself, which probably it couldn't unless you could travel through a wormhole, faster than the speed of light. If such magic was possible, Emily thought, then on that awful day of the car crash, she would have put the fall of the watermelon into slow motion rewind and bring her mother back to real life, not just virtual life. As it was, all that could be hoped was to get her and the other Lilliputians home before she died again. Maybe someday, a scientist as smart as Josh would figure out how to pull people out of an alternate universe and Becky could come back to life. But for now, Lilliput was the best place for her mother.

"It's safe to go," Emily said. "Who wants to be first?"

Sam scratched under his wig, leaving it askew. "In the event this procedure fails to work, I'd like to be sure you children are protected," he said. "Emily, could you go into that video game you talked about and get us some modern weapons?"

"Good idea," Dan said. "Here's the Space Marauder game, Emily. How about materializing some tiny stun guns and a plasma beam cannon?"

Emily nodded and went to work. It didn't take long before the weapons had materialized in the golden square. Jamie put the cannon in his pocket before the others could stop him

"It's okay," said Emily. "Jamie's the youngest. He should have the most protection."

"Right ye are, dearie," Molly said, clapping her approval. "I'm that proud of ye."

Sam took one of the stun guns and gave Dan the other. "I gather these require little more skill than aiming and pulling the trigger?" He studied his gun cautiously, then tucked it in his belt, under his waistcoat.

"They're heat-seeking," Emily said. "All you have to do is pick your target and the electronic program does the rest. Now, is everybody ready to go?"

Dan bent his head down close to the little people. "We'll miss you guys. And mom, I'll miss you most of all."

"I love you, Molly," Emily said, carefully giving the tiny woman a kiss on the top of her pile of yellow curls. "I wish you could stay forever."

Jamie stood silently, holding his mother in his hands, hoping she wouldn't change her mind and decide to leave with the others. He refused to meet Emily's eyes, but just watched Becky, alert to any move she might make.

Molly squeezed Emily's finger and smiled. "You tell that clever papa of yours to make me a little girl just like you, duckie. Then I'd have to marry 'enry, so my baby would have a father. I'd need help with such a wild wench." She smiled sadly, letting go of Emily's finger with reluctance.

"Okay, Molly, just give me a minute." Emily sketched out a baby with her illustrator, installed it in the program, and added some verbal instructions. If Molly was going to have an Emily-baby, it was going to be as real as Emily could make it.

"Done," she cried. "Molly, your baby girl is waiting for you in the pub. Name her after me, okay? Now, we're ready for all of you to make the jump."

"Everyone ready?" Samuel looked at Becky like he was going to cry any minute. "Becky, think again. You cannot survive here. You belong with me."

Becky shook her head and kept her eyes on Josh. "Sam, I love you. I loved you from the time I first read about you, back when I was a kid. But my place is here. God knows what that colonel has in mind for my family."

"I will stay to help you, Becky, if you want me to," Sam said, one foot poised to step into the glowing holographic square. "That's why I insisted on being properly armed."

"No, Sam," Becky said, waving him on. "Take care of the others. Get them home. I've got a daughter to save from terminal punk."

"Mom has me to take care of her," Jamie said, lifting Becky to his shoulder. "She'll be just fine." He frowned at Sam, clearly jealous of the scholar's closeness with his mother.

A sudden crash shook the house, as the front door lock blew apart. Samuel rushed Molly and Sam behind the computer and stood in front of them, his stun gun drawn. Jamie started yelling, and Scruff, upstairs, was barking as if the world was coming to an end, and he was the Fourth Horseman of the Apocalypse.

"Don't go up those stairs," Jamie shouted, handing Becky to Emily. "The demons of the Shaolin Temple await you." He danced up and down, waving his fists in the air.

Stomping feet on the back steps told Emily that the Colonel and his men had swallowed Jamie's bait.

"The goons are here, Dan," Emily muttered. "Go get Jake. Run. They've probably cut the wires again."

"You'll be okay?" Dan paused to try the phone, his face so pale his freckles stood out. "You're right. The line's out again. Em, I shouldn't leave you and Jamie alone."

"You have to. We've been too busy to recharge our cells, so we're on our own. Go!" Emily reached behind the computer and carefully placed Henry and Molly into the glowing holographic square.

"Okay, guys," she whispered. "At least maybe I can get you two back where you belong."

Molly and Henry stepped back and clung to Samuel. "We're a family," Molly cried. "If we don't all go, none of us go. I'm staying, too." She held Henry's hand and they both jumped out of the square.

"They're back!" Jamie yelled. "Enemy ninjas on their way downstairs!"

"Henry! Molly! Hide behind the curtain," Samuel directed as he pulled Becky with him across the table. "Quick! Into the box." He pulled Becky into the open microwave and both crouched down behind Josh's cracked Harvard coffee cup.

"Not the greatest idea you've ever had, Sam," Becky's said. "What if someone closes the door? This machine fries you from the inside out."

Emily peeked in the microwave to be sure they were safe, then was careful to leave the door slightly ajar.

Dan burst in the back door. "Emily," he cried, "you'll never believe what just happened. I made it to Jake's door. Then I saw two guys in army uniforms go in. Jake was talking to them in the front hall. When he saw I was there, he looked at me funny and slammed the door."

"They must have gotten to him. Scared him the way they tried to scare Carmen," Emily said, grabbing Molly and Henry with one hand.

"Except that Jake caved. Finked on us," Dan muttered. "Guess who will never again get help with his trig homework."

"Or go with me to the Homecoming Dance. Not that he's asked me yet." Emily said, handing Molly and Henry to her brother. "The traitor! And I was really getting into him, zits and all." Tears came to her eyes so that she could hardly see the computer screen, but she blinked them back. If he had ratted them out, Jake wasn't worth crying over.

As they heard feet thundering down the stairs, Dan leaned over, putting the two Lilliputians into the lighted square. As he moved, his arm clumsily knocked the microwave door shut. Emily was too intent on her work to notice. She tapped the keyboard, paused, and called out "Now!"

Chapter 17

Just at that moment, Colonel Sharpe charged into the study, followed by Hewitt and Briglia. They all swiveled from side to side, each holding his weapon with both hands. Sharpe's squad looked like they expected an armed ambush, not just a couple of kids and four Lilliputians.

"Pull that plug," the colonel ordered, pointing, and Hewitt dived for the cord. He pulled it so hard the plug almost split from the wire as it left the socket. Sparks flew and the computer made a tired, dying moan. The monitor went blank and the shimmering golden holographic square disappeared, leaving Henry and Molly standing where it had been.

"Now you've done it," cried Emily, her voice tight and angry, the way it got when she was felt like crying, but wasn't about to. "You've probably offed the whole program."

Before Hewitt could lunge to grab them, Molly and Henry jumped behind the flowerpot and worked together to push it over the edge of the table. It landed on Hewitt's toes, and he hopped around in a circle, yelling like a cheerleader.

Henry took the extra moment to get away. Seizing Molly with one arm, he used the other to support them both as they slid down the halogen lamp pole to the floor. They ran under the couch, and clung with both feet and hands to the springs beneath, staying off the floor. When Colonel Sharpe's hand flailed under the couch, it came up with nothing but dust.

"Move the couch, idiot," Sharpe hissed. "Hurry it up."

Briglia pulled the couch out from the wall and the colonel stuck the net under it, shoving it around like a mop.

"Hold it, everybody," Jamie shouted from the study door, with Scruff growling behind him. "Give up or die." He waved the plasma cannon menacingly in their air, while he crouched in his most lethal kung fu stance.

"Never mind us, Jamie, just run," Dan said. "We need Dad. Find him!"

Jamie nodded and stashed the cannon in his pocket again. Before Briglia could get hold of him, Jamie grabbed Emily's skates, and ran out the front door. Scruff decided to make one last, heroic attempt against the intruders and nipped Briglia in the leg. Before the dog left to follow Jamie, he had the satisfaction of seeing Briglia writhing on the floor, howling and holding his calf. What a wimp, the dog sniffed to himself, trotting after Jamie. His nip had hardly broken the skin. Scruff knew better than to seriously bite anyone, having been trained to be a civilized dog, no matter what the provocation. He also knew when his victim was acting, and snorted in disgust at the wimp's phoniness. Surely Emily and Dan could handle these clumsy intruders. Loping after Jamie, who Scruff knew needed the most protection, the dog ran out the open front door. Jamie was sitting on the curb out front, putting on Emily's skates. Sensing a chase, Scruff wagged his tail and crouched in his play posture before Jamie took off at top speed for Carmen's apartment.

Sharpe grabbed Emily around the neck and held a gun to her throat. "You have one nanosecond to come out from under there," he called to the hidden Lilliputians, "or I'm going to blow this kid away."

"Hold, scoundrel," said Henry, peeking out from under the couch. 'We'll surrender. Do not blow the child anywhere." He looked anxiously into the air, like he was expecting to see Emily flying about. For all poor Henry knew, modern technology might be capable even of sending a girl into the air like a soap bubble.

Sharpe's net caught both Molly and Henry as soon as they came out from under the couch. "We can't stop to look for the others," he cried, checking his watch. "Pack up Dr. Ross's equipment. Take it back to my lab."

"Use that stun gun on the colonel," Emily whispered to Dan.

"I can't," Dan replied. "If I hit Molly or Henry by mistake, they'd disintegrate on the spot."

The colonel turned to Briglia. "Stake out the doctor and his girlfriend. When they get here, bring them to the lab, along with the kids. And find the other two Lilliputians. I want them all."

"I'll need back-up," said Briglia, "Andriette and maybe that kid, Jake. They're the only ones that know about us."

Emily sucked her breath in hard. She hadn't wanted to believe that Jake could betray them, but here was the proof. Jake had been so kind, she told herself. So admiring of her great mouth, her excuse for a figure, and her genuine computer smarts. And all this time he was just a snitch. Emily's eyes stung. She would never trust a man again, unless he was six inches high, like sweet Henry and wise Sam. Molly had the right idea. Dear old Henry was worth ten of Jake. Never again, Emily vowed, would she think a guy was cool just because he had a pony-tail and a great line. She would go to graduate school like her mother and become a bookworm. Nobody would ever get to her again. Her heart hurt in her chest, as she blamed herself for her stupid fantasies.

"Hewitt, go get them," Sharpe said, dragging Emily toward the door. "And this little girl will help us with her dad's computer."

"I'd never help you." Emily kicked at Sharpe's shins.

Sharpe grinned and held Molly up between two fingers, beginning to squeeze. "Oh, I think you will."

"Don't hurt her," Emily cried. "She's a real person." When Molly cried out, a pain sliced through Emily's middle. For a moment, she felt as if she was the tiny woman, not just her vain little self. The constant stream of anxiety that flowed through her head suddenly stopped, and Emily was free of it. She felt larger than life, more than the girl she had been only a moment before. So this is what it takes to grow up, Emily thought--just knowing the world doesn't revolve around me alone, just stopping all the focus on me, me, me. All the separation between the two of them, Molly and her, suddenly vanished, and Emily was suddenly more complete than she had ever been in her life. She felt still and calm, able to handle whatever was up for her. And a lot was going to be. Emily was sure of that much.

Sharpe handed Molly to Hewitt and picked Henry up with his other hand, squeezing him until the little man groaned. "So, you'll cooperate?

"Just leave them alone," Dan said. "We'll do whatever you say."

"So will your father, when he knows we have his kids."

Sharpe looked at his watch again. "No time to waste. Let's go."

As Sharpe pushed the two of them along, Emily whispered to Dan, "What's going to happen to Mom and Sam in the microwave? I can't believe you shut that door."

"Why didn't you open it?" Dan hissed in her ear. "It's your fault if they suffocate, genius. You're the only one who knew they were in there."

Hewitt held Molly up next to his face, snapping his jaws like a dog, to tease her, then followed Colonel Sharpe into his military police car. Before they could pull away, Andriette ran across the lawn, and jumped into the car, not waiting to be invited. She didn't give Briglia even a backward glance.

Going around to the back of the house, Briglia muttered, "I'm finally gonna get my chance to kick some butt." He cracked his knuckles and grinned.

Josh was driving too fast, almost hoping a cop would stop him so he could get help. "I still don't think you should go to work today," he said to Carmen. "You should come home with us. If we separate, they can pick us off."

Smiling down at her lap, Carmen said softly, "I can take care of myself. You just take care of that six-inch tall wife of yours." She looked out the window and gasped. "Josh, slow down. It's Jamie."

Surprised, Josh slammed on the brakes. Jamie was skating along the sidewalk, his head down so he could go faster. He was followed by Scruff, who was panting noisily, the way he did while chasing some unfortunate cat.

When the car had come alongside Jamie, Carmen jumped out and grabbed the boy as he skated right into her arms. "Whoa," she cried. "Que pasa?"

"They came busting in the front door," Jamie cried, as Carmen plunked him down beside Josh. "Scruff bit Briglia, and Emily told me to go get you. So I did, and here I am."

"Jump in, Scruff," called Josh, grinding the gears as the car took off. "We're going home."

Scruff leaped onto Carmen's lap, gratified to see that she didn't mind having a dog as big as she was rumpling her white skirt and drooling with excitement on her shoulder.

"Faster, Josh," Carmen said, caressing Scruff's neck, ignoring the slobber. "They may still be there."

"Becky never let me drive fast," Josh smiled at her. He looked at her approvingly and sped up even more.

Josh pulled up in front of the house, coasting slowly and quietly into the driveway. The sound of the motor, he figured, might alert whoever was in the house. If surprised, they would be easier to handle. Of course, Josh had no idea about how to handle intruders. He wished he could be back in his childhood Captain Marvel days when the bad guys could be dispatched by a miraculous figure in a red suit and cape. Those days were long gone, and Josh hadn't even bothered to pick up some of Jamie's kung fu skills. Worse yet, he didn't have a gun in the house, and if he had tried to fire one, would probably have shot off his own big toe by accident.

Not for the first time, Josh wished his life hadn't been one long head trip, with no time spent on how to defend that head against ordinary wear and tear, let alone attack by his own military. Well, maybe it wasn't too late, Josh thought. From now on. he would take vitamins, eat enough spinach to turn him green, and use Becky's exercycle every day. Good intentions had to count for something. Maybe, as Becky had said they might, he could expect them to make him a stronger, better-coordinated body. She had always believed that your thoughts created reality, and practiced her tennis serves in her mind before going to sleep. It must have worked, for she seldom lost a match. Josh wished now that he had followed her advice, but it was a bit late to practice either athleticism or metaphysics. As he crept in the back door, Josh picked up Dan's baseball bat and motioned to Carmen that she should follow him into the kitchen.

When they got to the living room, with Jamie and Scruff behind them, they stopped and looked around, confused. The house was apparently empty. Josh had the sinking feeling that Colonel Sharpe had come and gone, having gotten what he wanted. His stomach turned cold, and he felt like he was going to be sick, the way he had when the police had come to the door and told him Becky was dead. Strange, Josh thought, how just a thought could turn his body off and on. Apparently, his brain and the rest of him were more connected than he had ever believed.

"Dan? Emily?" Josh's voice echoed through the house, but no one answered. "Maybe they left the kids here. Maybe they're upstairs getting ready for school."

Jamie hurried past him into the study. "They're not here. I got psychic powers. I can sense it."

"Forget the psychic powers, querido." Carmen hunkered down beside Jamie. "Can you get to school by yourself? You'd be safe there."

"Sure I can," Jamie said, glad to be her querido, but offended that she thought maybe he was a baby of five instead of a living weapon. "I do it all the time."

"That's right, he does," Josh said, tossing the bat on the living room couch. "Skate fast, Jamie. When you get there, have the principal call the high school. Maybe Dan and Emily are there."

I'm on my way," cried Jamie, puffing out his thin chest with importance. "Scruff, you're with me."

The dog barked sharply to let Josh know he understood his orders and loped down the hall after Jamie, his nails clicking and sliding on the wood floor in his haste to beat Jamie to the back door.

"They wouldn't have left without the little people," Carmen said thoughtfully, going into the study to scout around after Jamie had slammed the door behind him.

Josh followed her. "Holy. . ." he stopped in mid-swear word as he stared at his empty computer table. "It's gone. Lilliput, the little people, everything."

On the floor, he found only a small, crumpled paper marked with yellow stains and a few tiny, faint symbols. "Samuel's writing," Josh said, holding the paper close to his face.

He sniffed it, frowning with concentration. "Sherry," he said. "Sam must have been celebrating. Celebrating what?" Josh waved the paper in the air suddenly and smiled. "Celebrating this! It has to be the combination we need to get the Lilliputians home."

Stuffing the paper in his pocket, Josh turned to the microwave. "What I need is a cup of coffee," he said, punching the "slow cook" button.

Becky, huddling with Sam behind the coffee cup, was the first to notice that the oven felt warm. She passed her hand over her damp forehead, then looked up at Sam, noticing that sweat was dripping down his full, florid cheeks. He pulled off his white wig and slicked back his damp, gray-brown hair with the other hand. For a moment, Becky imagined herself going back with Samuel, into the safety of Molly's pub. They could sit forever in that pub, sipping cups of foaming ale and talking about the great writers and events of the time, make literary jokes that only the two of them could understand, forgetting about the crazy modern world altogether. If it wasn't her duty to stay and help Emily grow up right, she could see herself happily spending the rest of her life with Sam Johnson. Now, she would be lucky if she ever got the chance.

"Sam," she said, "is it my overheated imagination, or are we starting to fry in here?"

"I believe I recall someone warning us. . ." Sam began.

Hey!" Becky raced to the glass door and began pounding on it. "Get us out of here before we start popping like corn!"

Slowly, Samuel walked over to her and put his arm around her shoulder. "I've always said it matters not how a man dies, but how he lives. Now I'm not so sure. Dying as fast food seems a peculiarly humiliating way to go."

"Sam," Becky said, turning to face him, her face drawn and pale. "No philosophy. Please. Just help me turn that cup over. Maybe whoever's out there will see the coffee running out."

"Right you are, my sweet," Samuel said, applying his considerable bulk to the cup. "Damn, that china's hot," he exclaimed. "Begging your pardon for my language, Becky."

After a moment of rocking the cup between them, Becky and Samuel managed to tip it over. He quickly snatched her up, before the hot coffee could touch her feet, and winced, as the liquid flowed over his boots, then out the crack under the door.

"You feel too light," he said. "I fear you're beginning to pixillate like the rest of us."

"I'll be fine." Becky clung tightly to his neck. "If I can just get out of this oven."

Sam held her up high, keeping her above the bubbling black coffee that soaked painfully through the soles his high leather boots. "I can hear voices," he said, leaning his ear against the glass door. "Josh and Carmen, I'll warrant. They've noticed the flood. I think they're investigating it."

The door snapped open and the two Lilliputians tumbled out in the flood of hot coffee. Josh and Carmen stared at them as if they had just landed in a spaceship. Not sure what to think, Carmen glanced up at Josh.

"Will you stop looking at him, you bimbo, and look at us?" Becky roared at her, struggling to get to her feet on the slick table.

Carmen jumped back with a small scream. "Santos!" she whispered. "It's your wife."

Her eyebrows a straight, angry line, Becky stared at the nurse and said, "You might start asking me what happened to everybody else while you two were doing your thing." She glared at them. "Whatever that was."

"Who was here?" Josh cried, falling on his knees by the table, so that his head was directly opposite his wife. "Becky, where are Dan and Emily?"

Samuel sat down at the edge of the table, pulled off his boots, and dumped the coffee out of them onto the floor. "It was the colonel who took them, I gather," he said, in his calm, pleasant voice. "That's what the others called him."

"Carmen, you told me he would, and I didn't believe you." Holding his head in his hands, Josh muttered the words desperately. He had always tried to be an optimist like Becky, who believed that negativity would make bad things happen. Now, it seemed like no amount of negativity would be too much to match what confronted him.

"Plus, he took Molly and Henry." Becky's voice was crisp, all business. "We heard the car drive away."

Suddenly her composure evaporated, and Becky was suddenly anxious. "At least I think we did. It's hard to be sure what you're hearing, when you're stuck in a microwave."

Josh pulled Carmen toward the door. "Let's go. We'll have to hope the colonel took them to the lab. Probably he'll try to make Emily produce more of the little people. . ."

"And she won't know how," Becky finished, her voice shaking as she grabbed her bow and arrows. "Hey, Josh, wait up. You're not going without us."

Samuel picked up his sword, which had been tossed alongside Becky's equipment. "Take us upstairs first, Josh. We need to dip our weapons in the poison pot."

"No time for that now," Josh said. "Carmen, pick them up."

Becky stood her ground. "You think we're useless just because we're small?" she challenged her husband, with arms folded across her chest.

"Becky's right, Josh," Carmen broke in. "That's a fight I've had going all my life."

"Right on, Carmencita," Becky said grudgingly, tossing a half-smile in Carmen's direction. "Josh could do a lot worse than you."

"Okay, we'll go upstairs," Josh said, reaching for Samuel. "But make it fast."

Josh stood tapping his foot and sighing loudly to show how much of a waste of time he thought the poison pot was. His head to one side, he watched Becky and Sam touch up the points of their weapons. Sam held his sword next to her arrows and leaned close to her.

The two seemed more compatible than he and Becky had ever been. When his wife wanted him to laugh with her at the funny sayings of Samuel Johnson, back in the old days, Josh had always yawned and said it was time for bed. He was a scientist and had no time for wit or literature. It was unreal, he thought, not like his science, which could change the world. Becky would just snap the book shut and get him some hot chocolate, saying that world events might not be changed by what Samuel Johnson had said, but people who took his words to heart would become kinder to each other. She had never insisted that Josh share her world, but had always been willing to share his.

Josh, looking back sadly, could not begin to count the nights when he had talked Becky to sleep while describing how he was applying holographic principles to virtual reality. Just thinking about his selfishness made him more patient now, and he stopped tapping his foot. He would give Sam and Becky all the time they needed.

"That should do it," Becky said in her cool, business-like voice. "Unless Briglia and Andriette have adapted to the drugs. I'm not sure we have enough left for a potent dose."

"In that case, I have my trusty stunner," Sam said, patting the slight bulge under his waistcoat. "Now, Josh, let's have at them before I lose any more molecular mass. Those children of yours deserve our best effort."

Josh looked anxiously at the little man. "How much time before you self-destruct, Sam?"

"An hour, perhaps less," Sam replied. "But that's not important. We have had our lives. Your children have not had theirs."

"Right," Josh said, suddenly aware that the little man had more objectivity than he himself did. "Carmen, let's move it."

Just as they scooped up Sam and Becky, Josh heard glass breaking.

"They're coming in the back door," Carmen said. "I bet it's Briglia. Be careful, Josh. Briglia is one mean dude."

"You got that right," Briglia snarled, rushing down the hall and grabbing her around the neck.

"Becky, shoot him," Josh cried, holding up his tiny wife on one flat palm so she could use her bow. With the other hand, he gripped the baseball bat.

Balancing delicately on the balls of her feet, Becky aimed, dodged, and aimed again. "Josh, I don't dare," she said, lowering her bow. "Carmen's in the way."

"You betcha, she is," Briglia sneered, tightening his hold on Carmen's neck. "Everybody outside."

Josh dropped the baseball bat on the floor and picked up Sam, whispering in the little man's ear. "It's not the worst thing that could happen. I think he'll take us to wherever Sharpe took Emily and Dan. Let's hold our fire for when we get there."

"Okay, doc," said Briglia, dragging Carmen beside him. "Out the door."

"No sweat, mister. I'm coming." Josh held the two tiny people up, so they could see what was going on. Becky still had a grip on her bow and was looking for a chance to use it.

"And you can toss those poisoned darts," Briglia said, wrestling Carmen into the car.

"Do it, Sam." Becky's voice was urgent, and she dropped her bow and arrows onto the grass by the curb. "He could kill her."

Silently, Sam followed suit with his sword, but left the stunner hidden in his belt.

"You're driving, doc," Briglia said, pushing Carmen into the middle of the front seat and sitting between her and the door. "And watch it. This Porsche is brand new." He kept his gun at Carmen's neck as Josh carefully shifted Becky and Sam into her lap.

Josh drove the Porsche slowly at first, getting used to the feel of the stick shift. He looked up into the rearview mirror and swore softly. Briglia was too intent on holding Carmen still to look back and notice Jamie and Scruff tearing down the street toward the house.

"Shut up, Einstein," Briglia said. "And keep your eyes on the road. Put a dent in this car and you're dead."

Jamie had seen his father and Carmen in the front seat as Briglia's car drove off. He skidded to a stop so fast that he nearly fell over Scruff. The dog was sniffing the grass, running in circles around some tiny, flashing weapons, and making harsh noises in his throat, like he had cornered prey. Jamie took up the weapons in his Kleenex and put them carefully into his pocket. Hearing a noise at the front door, Jamie got ready to take off fast, but it was only Jake, coming out the door of the Ross house with something small that he tucked into his leather jacket. Jamie couldn't help noticing that Jake looked startled to see him.

"I thought you were supposed to be at school," Jake said, hopping on his bike. "So I just walked in and got the flash drive Emily hid under the bookcase. "She told me to take care of it for her."

Jamie frowned at him, glad he had told no one about the Lilliput memory card he had hidden in his teddy bear zipper pillow. It felt uncomfortable to know that the computer, the program, and his mother were in the hands of mean strangers.

"Where are you going to take it?" he asked.

"To wherever Emily and Dan are," Jake answered matter-of-factly. "Only I'm not sure where that is. Any ideas?"

"That colonel must have taken Dan and Emily," Jamie said. "That's all I know."

"So where do we start looking?" Jake pushed up his kick-stand and was ready to ride.

"Scruff can help," Jamie said, unclipping the dog's leash and stuffing it in his back pocket. He leaned over, putting his face next to the dog's ear. "We gotta follow Em and Dan, Scruff. Think you can handle it?"

The dog had been lying on the sidewalk, relaxed and ready for a nap while the humans talked. Since he caught only every tenth word of a conversation anyway, and could never guess how long the chatter would last, he made it his business to snooze at every opportunity.

Suddenly Scruff heard his name and jumped to attention. His tail wagged, his reflexes were alert, and his senses cast about to find the prey. For once, one of his humans was asking him to take charge. He would prove himself, Scruff thought, as his barks poured out dog-music. He would bring his family home safe. Making sure Jamie was right behind him, Scruff uttered snarling, happy noises and took off after the Porsche. He had always wanted to chase cars and had not been allowed to. Now was his chance. Oh joy, he said to himself, giving his mottled gold and brown fur a shake for good luck. Oh pleasure, fun, and satisfaction! I am on the scent and will never let go until my humans are safely home. He took off with a bound, sure this hunt was the most important of his life.

"Hey," Jamie, cried, putting his head down and skating so fast he thought he was going to fall on his face, "wait up, dog. You're supposed to be with me, not the other way around."

Jake was riding at Scruff's heels, his face close to the handlebars. "Don't worry, kid," he called. "I'm on it. You can go home."

"No way," Jamie shouted, flailing his arms to keep his balance. "It's my family we're rescuing." He hung onto Jake's bicycle seat, throwing Jake off balance. The bike went down hard, and so did Jake. Jamie was on his feet while Jake was still untangling his pants from the bike chain. Before the older boy could pick himself up, Jamie had skated far ahead.

"You could drive faster, Hewitt," the colonel said impatiently, as Josh whizzed past them in the yellow Porsche and disappeared in the distance.

"I figured you wouldn't want the law on us for speeding," Hewitt said, going a little faster.

"Man, we are the law," the colonel snapped. "Move it."

Molly perched on Emily's shoulder, steadying herself against the lurches of Sharpe's car. She pulled on some loose yarn at the hem of Emily's sweater.

"Tie your tummy ring to the thread, luv, and toss it out the window," she whispered in Emily's ear. "I can see in the mirror what's coming behind us. It's Jamie and that horrid beast of yours."

Emily glanced at Andriette, who sat beside her, staring happily at the colonel as if she was coming down the aisle to meet him at the altar. The woman was too into her fantasy to notice Emily remove her navel ring and attach it to the loose yarn.

"I'm about to be carsick like you wouldn't believe," Emily said, leaning over Andriette's glitzy satin skirt and reaching for the window.

"Don't think you're going to yell for help, girl. I'm onto you," Andriette said.

"What's going to be onto you in about a second is my breakfast." Emily rolled down the window leaned out.

Andriette jumped back, twitching her skirt close to her body, and climbed over Emily, exchanging seats with her. Seizing the opportunity, Emily threw the ring and the yarn out on the street. To distract the woman, Emily worked up a huge fake sneeze that sprayed spit all over Andriette's skirt. Muttering curses, Andriette wiped herself off.

At least one member of the family would be free and could contact the police, Emily thought, as Jamie receded into the distance. She had no faith in Jamie's ability to do much by himself, for all his membership in the Shaolin Temple.

Emily scrunched down in the back seat of the Porsche, pulling yarn from the hem of her sweater. The sweater began to unravel, slowly disappearing through the open dow. Becky's last gift would go out in a blaze of glory, Emily said to herself, feeling a bit guilty that she didn't mind putting the old-fashioned sweater out of its misery. Her idea of the perfect sweater was one that showed a lot of midriff. What was the good of wearing low cut jeans and a navel ring if your sweater covered up all that once-forbidden skin? It was a question she had often asked Becky in the old days. Emily sighed, wondering if she would ever again have a chance to ask Becky anything. The loss of the navel ring suddenly didn't much matter.

The yellow Porsche picked up speed and was gone from nose-range. Scruff stopped, baffled, and ran in circles. Somewhere, somehow, the scent must be there. In his dim racial memory, Scruff imagined a prey bobbing ahead of him on the horizon, tantalizing him with a smell that came, then went with maddening vagueness. The hackles on his back stood up, and Scruff growled and panted, showing his teeth. Whatever it was would not elude him, any more than a rabbit could have eluded his wolfish ancestors.

Suddenly the dog discovered a new odor. He put his head down to sniff a piece of yarn lying in the street. It smelled familiar. He sniffed again. Emily was what he smelled. He knew that wonderfully stinky sweater. It was the one that hadn't been washed since the days when Becky had been in charge. To his sensitive two hundred million olfactory receptors, the sweater stank as deliciously as roadkill skunk. It was attached to a small item that smelled like Emily, and Scruff took it in his mouth. He would track the string, delirious with nose-joy, until he found the source or dropped dead trying. Then he would roll in it until he smelled just as wonderful as roadkill. Scruff barked a triumphant bark and ran like a wolf in the wild, long legs flying in the air, nose to the ground. He looked back only occasionally to be sure his boy and Jake were struggling along behind him, and then redoubled his furious chase.

Chapter 18

"Slow down, Josh," Becky cried, hanging onto Carmen's thumb as the Porsche veered back and forth across the road. "You'll get another ticket."

"Actually, a cop might come in handy just now," Josh said, letting his foot fall harder on the gas pedal.

"Think I can't handle any cop who stops us?" Briglia bragged. "I'm the military police. The cops around here know me."

"I'm counting on that," Josh murmured.

"Turn here, doc," Briglia said, taking his attention from Carmen for a moment.

"Think you can grab his gun, Carmencita?" Becky whispered, her hands curved around her mouth, megaphone-style.

"Think you can give me a distraction?" Carmen whispered back, ducking her head near Becky's.

"You got it," Becky said, nodding to Sam to put some pre-arranged plan into action.

The two Lilliputians hopped from Carmen's hands into Briglia's lap. Both hanging onto his pants zipper, they pulled it down fast. When Briglia grabbed his zipper, they clambered up his arm and onto his head. Hanging from the hair over his forehead, they kicked at his eyes with their tiny pointed boots.

As Carmen grabbed Briglia's gun, she leaned over and opened the door. The two Lilliputians hopped onto her shoulder as she pushed Briglia out. He rolled into a ditch, yelling and kicking.

"Okay, cop," Carmen cried. "That's for all the bazu the Rochas family has ever taken from guys like you."

Becky held onto Carmen's long hair and gave her a big kiss on the cheek. "You tell him, Carmencita!"

Just then a police siren sounded and flashing lights let Josh know he was being flagged down. He drove faster, but kept an eye on the rearview mirror. "We have company," was all he said. "And they've picked up Briglia. I can guess what he's telling them." He sped up, letting Briglia's Porsche do its thing.

Sam hung onto Carmen's ear while they swayed back and forth as Josh zoomed up to pass a truck. "On the whole," Sam remarked, "I would have preferred death by microwave. At least one would have privacy."

"Josh," cried Becky frantically, "I've already died once in a car crash and I'd rather not do it again. Can't we just get out and run?"

Swerving again, leaning toward the steering wheel, Josh replied in a low, steady voice, "It's another half mile to the lab. We've got to lead the police to my equipment before the colonel starts messing with it."

He revved the Porsche, just as the police caught up with him. Alarmed at the impending collision, Josh cut the wheel and slammed into a fire hydrant. Leaning to one side, the hydrant spat a stream of water onto the road. The Porsche, low-slung as it was, ground to a halt, sputtering in the flooded street.

Briglia sprang out of the police car and surveyed the damage to his precious Porsche with murder in his beady little eyes. As he watched, the hood popped up, and the radiator burst with a noisy, despairing sigh indicating irreversible damage. A few metal parts clunked onto the pavement, and water shot up from the front end, hissing and foaming.

"You owe me, Einstein, for creaming my Porsche." Briglia voice sounded like he was being strangled. "For that, you're gonna pay big-time."

The police got out of their car, nodding at Briglia.

"You can use our car, Lieutenant," one of them said, "since you have a military emergency."

"Okay, Chiquita," Briglia said. "Toss my gun on the ground." He leaned over to pick it up. "Into the cop car, you two. Now, drive, Einstein, but remember I'm in the back seat with a gun pointed at this chick's head."

Hewitt, who was driving Colonel Sharpe's car, glanced around as he pulled into the military complex. "How do we explain the kids, Chief?" he asked Colonel Sharpe.

"All I gotta do is pinch the little people in the stomach till they squeak, and the kids will keep quiet. Right?" He half-turned toward the back seat and held Molly up between his thumb and forefinger.

"Okay, okay," Emily muttered. "We won't say anything."

"I'll smack her in the mouth if she does," said Andriette, obviously looking forward to the prospect. Sitting between Emily and Dan, she held both fists up, ready for action.

The autocom buzzed and the colonel picked it up. "Sharpe here." He paused. "Good, Briglia. Bring 'em straight to the lab." He clicked off and leaned toward Hewitt. "Briglia's got Josh and Carmen. And the other two little cybernauts. We're in business."

Emily eyes burned with rage. "I don't believe you," she said. "My father will be looking for you with the police."

"They are the police," Andriette hissed, pointing at the men in the front seat.

Sharpe checked his watch, pleased with himself. "Clean sweep, except for the little kid and the dog," he said, clicking on the autocom again. "Give me Mel Glatt, fast."

He waited a moment, checking his watch again. "Colonel Sharpe here. Get your butt to my lab ASAP, Glatt. We got critical mass."

Andriette leaned forward, getting her face as close to the colonel's as she could manage. "That little Jamie is smart, Colonel Pete. He could be trouble."

"I'm in charge here," growled the colonel. "Just keep your eyes on the kids we've got. Turn here, Hewitt. We'll go in the back way."

Colonel Sharpe rolled down the window and smiled at the kiosk guards. "Evening, sergeant," he said, like the night was any other night. "We're expecting a second car. Send it right along to my lab. Just wave them through. Got that?"

The sergeant leaned toward the car. "Nice looking kids you've got, Colonel, Sir." He paused a second, knowing he ought to compliment Andriette. "And the wife, too."

Andriette grinned at him with her huge red mouth like she was Julia Roberts or somebody equally worth looking at, and waved as they drove by. Disgusted, Emily pulled off what was left of her sweater, rolled it up and threw it at the woman's back, wishing it was a bowling ball. Andriette was busy chattering in the colonel's ear, and he was busy trying to ignore her.

As soon as the car stopped, Hewitt took Emily by the scruff of her Grateful Dead t-shirt and Dan by the shoulder, pulling them into the low, dark building. After they got inside, Hewitt tied their hands together in front of them. Emily craned her neck, trying to see what the colonel was doing with Molly and Henry. When the colonel shoved both little people into a Have-a-Heart trap, Emily was relieved. Now, at least, he wouldn't pinch them.

Her mind was whirling. Had Becky, Sam, and Josh managed to escape from Briglia? Was Jamie safe at school? She brushed her tied hands across her damp forehead and wished that she had a Kleenex in her pocket, the way Becky had insisted she always should. And what about Jake? She couldn't believe he would help turn Josh and the others in. It made her burn with fury and shame to think she had actually trusted this perfidious fink because he was cool. Yet he seemed so kind, so concerned for Jamie, putting him in the closet to protect him.

Emily shook her head, wishing all her thoughts would just fall out of her brain and leave her alone. It did no good to be thinking about what might happen or what had happened, she told herself. All that mattered was what was up for her right now. Anything else, she couldn't do zip about. She concentrated on the cage carrying Molly and Henry. They were the ones most at risk and the ones she would try to liberate if she could. If only she had the extra Lilliput flash drive with her. Thanks to the colonel's brilliant idea of pulling the plug, the Lilliput game was probably history, and by the time she had reclaimed her spare copy from under the bookcase in Josh's study, Molly and Henry would be history, too. Emily shuddered, not wanting to think about what would happen to her mother, who was God only knew where.

Okay, okay, she said to herself. You're doing it again. Thinking about what's going to happen instead of what's happening this minute. Keep your mind on something that might do some good. She focused again on the trap and tried to think of a way she or Dan could open it without being noticed. Glancing up, she saw a shiny, hi-tech tennis racket hanging over Sharpe's desk. Maybe it could do double-duty as a weapon, she thought, wishing she could grab it. Only if she could jump to the desk, she figured, and that wouldn't happen if Hewitt didn't untie her hands and let go of her t-shirt.

Hewitt and Plummer repaired the torn plug and set up Josh's computer on a white metal lab table big enough for ping-pong. Emily noticed that Plummer was moving slowly and that he kept wiping sweat off his face.

"Plug it in, boys," Sharpe said in a cold, far-off voice, like he had turned into Robo-Cop. "Let's get that program up."

Briglia drove the police car to the back gate with a shriek of brakes. He wanted to let the guards know that he was the sunrise all the world had been waiting for. It was time people understood he was more than just a crummy gym teacher.

"Open up, guys," he shouted out the open window. "I'm with Colonel Sharpe."

"Right you are, sir," the sergeant said, waving him on.

"You want to see my military police badge?" Briglia asked, pausing to make the most of his moment of glory.

"Naw, the colonel told us you'd be coming," said the sergeant, yawning.

"Here it is," Briglia said proudly, holding up his gleaming proof that he was a person of importance. For once, he could be proud of himself. Briglia checked his watch, imitating the colonel, and felt like a man in charge.

Nobody noticed that while the police car lingered at the checkpoint, two boys and a dog slipped behind the kiosk and ran toward the lab.

"We're here, colonel," Briglia said over the autocom. "Got everybody with us except the little kid."

"Come to the lab," the colonel replied. "We're ready to go."

When Briglia arrived with his prisoners, the computer was running, but the screen looked oddly blue and blank. Colonel Sharpe was bending over the keyboard, tapping hard, not looking up.

"So, Dr. Ross," he said as Briglia brought his captives into the cavernous room. "Join the family."

"Emily, Dan," Josh cried as he stepped into the lab. "Are you okay?"

Carmen was right behind him, carrying Becky in one hand and Sam in the other. "Your mom's with us."

Emily laughed, forgetting that the colonel and his men were in the room. "Mom! I was so scared you'd fry in the microwave."

"Nice try, Em," laughed Becky. "Next time, use the freezer." She looked up at Carmen. "Watch this kid, Carmen. She'll be ahead of you all the way."

Carmen was obviously relaxing a bit with her rival. "I hope she gets the chance. Looks bad, Becky. We've got nothing to work with."

"Against the wall, all of you," Sharpe said. "I'll take that little lady in green." He roughly pulled Becky from Carmen's hands into his own. Becky bit his thumb hard, and Sharpe grunted, nearly dropping her.

"A fighter, huh?" the colonel said. "We'll see how good you are."

Samuel popped his head out of Carmen's fist. "Unhand her, coward. You disgrace the dignity of soldiering."

Sharpe grinned. "Fond of the little lady, are you? Then you'll want to watch her at work. Glatt, are you finished over there?"

Mel Glatt had been gasping over Josh Ross's computer as he patched it into Sharpe's. He was shaking with excitement as the screen lit up. "Got it, colonel," he cried, his voice shaking with greedy expectation. Then he frowned and kicked the leg of the lab table in frustration. "No, it isn't happening. The program is toast."

"I told you so," cried Emily triumphantly, pointing at Colonel Sharpe. "You were the one that told them to pull the plug." She hoped nobody would break the news to Sharp a copy of the Lilliput game was hidden back at the house.

"Shut that brat up," said the Colonel to Andriette, who covered Emily's mouth with both hands, jerking the girl's head backward. "So the program's down. We've still got the goods."

"I don't see why you need the little people," Glatt said, giving the lab table a final, furious kick. "With my software upgrades, Plummer says his new robot can do almost anything a human can."

"If we can get the damned robot out of the program," Sharpe replied, studying Becky closely, like he was trying to figure out if she was edible. "Once Fat Boy is free from the software, we'll test them in battle together, the robot and the woman. If she bombs, we have three others." He checked his watch again.

"This timepiece must be the man's god," Samuel said loudly, "since he consults it on every occasion."

"Watch your mouth," said Hewitt, warning Samuel with an upraised hand, ready to slap the little man down.

Busy thinking out loud, Sharpe paid no attention. "She'd fit just as easily into anti-missile circuitry as the robot would. And she can think."

"Apparently, I didn't get my PhD for nothing," Becky said ironically.

Josh tried to fight loose from Hewitt's grasp. "Keep Becky out of your war games, Sharpe."

The colonel didn't even bother to look at him. "We have a country to protect. I'll do what I have to do."

"I have always believed that patriotism is the last refuge of a scoundrel, and now I know it," Samuel roared at him. "Colonel, I beg you to use me instead of her."

"You'll get your chance, little man," Sharpe retorted, with a nasty half-smile on his face. "If she doesn't make it, you're on next. First, I want to check her reflexes against the robot's."

"Becky doesn't know anything about missile circuitry, Sharpe," Josh cried out, his voice shaking.

"You heard the little lady," Sharpe put Becky on the table and gave Plummer the high sign to get the robot. "She's got an education. We can train her if she's got the right stuff in a fight."

Becky folded her arms across her chest and jutted her chin out in the determined way Emily knew too well. "I don't know what you want me to do, but whatever it is, I'm not doing it."

Sharpe stepped over to Emily, pulled her away from Hewitt and held a letter opener to her throat. "Oh, I think you will," he said softly, his icy gray eyes gleaming.

190

Chapter 19

Out of the corner of her eye, Emily saw faces at the slightly open window and suppressed a gasp. Jamie and Jake were looking in, and between them was Scruff standing on his hind legs, his black, twitching nose fogging the pane. Both boys were pale and open-mouthed, staring at the letter opener touching Emily's neck. The colonel had his side to them, and his men were busy with their work. Not daring to look at the window and tip off Colonel Sharpe, Emily kicked Dan, knowing he would pick up her signal to pay attention. As she had hoped, Dan glanced at the window, then waved his tied hands frantically at his brother, gesturing to him to go away.

"Who you wavin' at, kid," Briglia said, smacking his arms down and squinting at the window with his beady, near-sighted eyes.

But by then, the three had disappeared from view. Emily hoped Jake had decided to give up and take Jamie home. Jake would be of no other help since he was apparently in the colonel's pay. For all she knew, Jake had captured Jamie and was bringing him to Sharpe, so the whole family could be held hostage. But Scruff wouldn't have allowed that, she told herself, her head spinning with plans for rescue and fears that rescue wouldn't happen. She felt the steel of the letter opener tight against her throat and hardly dared to breathe.

"Okay," Becky called out, "Let her go. I'll do whatever you say."

Suddenly Jake burst in the door, waving a small packet in one hand. "I've got what you wanted, colonel," he cried. "I've got that copy of Lilliput. If you let the Ross family leave, I'll give it to you."

"No, Jake," Josh called to him, pulling loose from Hewitt's grasp. "Take the flash drive and run."

Emily fell to the floor with relief when the colonel released her. Having a knife at her throat had made her feel for the first time that she could die. Somehow, death had never been a possibility before. She had foolishly thought she was immortal, Emily said to herself, like nobody her age could die. Now she knew differently, and huddled on the floor, wishing she could warn Jake that he could die too. All that came out of her cotton-dry throat and parched lips was a faint croaking sound that communicated nothing at all. She tried again, wanting to tell Jake that she was sorry she had doubted him, but her voice choked up.

Taking advantage of her position on the floor, Emily reached over and, with her tied-up hands, released the catch on the Have-a-Heart trap, letting Molly and Henry out.

Jake backed up toward the door as Hewitt rushed him. "If you don't let them go, I'll drop the flash drive and stomp it to death," the boy threatened, his voice going high and squeaky with fear. Jake glanced at Emily, embarrassed.

She beamed back at him, thinking that he could squeak forever and it would sound to her like music. Somehow, his being cool was no longer a big issue with her. Cool was the last thing on her mind. Saving Becky was the first, but she saw no hope of it. At least Henry and Molly were free, and rushing toward the lab door. Her smile faded as the colonel pulled her up next to him and stroked her throat with his letter opener again. He stared Jake down.

"I got a feeling, kid, that you care about whether this scrawny brat lives or dies. Your call."

Emily gasped as the steel cut into her skin. Jake turned white and held out the flash drive.

"Just don't hurt her, is all," he whispered. "I don't care about this thing, just about Emily."

"Good man," Josh breathed, not taking his eyes from Emily and the colonel. "I like your priorities."

"Now, all we need is that combination," Sharpe said. "One of you has it, and I don't care who it is." He snatched

Becky up by one leg and dangled her upside down. "Just give it to me or this little lady will have one busted head."

Josh pulled the stained, tiny piece of paper out of his pocket. "Here. Let her down."

The colonel put Becky on the floor. Smiling, he examined the paper, then tapped the formula into his computer. Hewitt grabbed the flash drive from Jake and got to work. A few moments later, he and Glatt had the program up, and soon the holographic square was glowing like a solar nova on the cold, white floor of Sharpe's lab.

Plummer returned with his robot program and entered it into the colonel's computer. Then the man stood aside, looking ill at ease, his dark skin shining with sweat. He looked afraid that Fat Boy would poop out again, bringing down the colonel's rage upon both robot and creator. It wouldn't be the first time.

More than once, Emily had heard Plummer tell Josh of his regret that he hadn't taken the job offered to him at NASA, which would have returned him to civilian life. Emily knew the head of NASA had told Plummer to call anytime if he changed his mind about taking the job. Plummer was clearly mulling over his options, she thought, wanting to be anywhere but where he was.

"Bring Fat Boy into the square," Sharpe ordered Plummer, putting Becky down in the middle of the lighted area. "Take this pellet gun, little lady," he said, shoving a tiny weapon into her hand. "Your objective is to score against that robot." He pointed as Fat Boy materialized in the square of light. "Just hit him with a paint pellet, is all you have to do."

Becky glanced down at her weapon. "And if I knock out the robot, you'll let my family go?"

"Cross my heart," Sharpe said, grinning like a rabid wolf. "If you win. Plummer, let Fat Boy roll."

Following Sharpe's orders, Plummer, with shaking hands, had set the small, gleaming robot into motion. One tiny fist clutching a gun and the other spinning with lethal blades, the robot moved toward Becky. Its face looked a bit like Sharpe's, but was cold and shiny, like the metal points of what should have been its right hand.

Becky backed up a little, and Emily could see fear in her eyes, something new for Becky. Mom, she said silently, be strong. You can take this guy. In the past, she had always resented Becky's strength, but now she prayed it would hold, that Becky would smack down the hateful little robot.

Stepping forward, Becky splashed Fat Boy at close range with a blood-colored paint pellet, so forcefully that the robot fell. "Got him, colonel. Your guy is down for the count. So let my family go."

"Man, has she got some attitude," said the robot in a flat, computerized monotone. "Gimme more juice, boss. I'm dyin' here."

"You got it," answered the colonel, tapping commands into the computer keyboard. "Now, get up and go."

Emily's heart felt cold. The colonel had cheated. He had no intention of letting Becky win with paint pellets. She would have to face the whirling knives. Remembering the cold steel against her own throat, Emily shuddered.

"Spin the red dial on the right," Sharpe said to Plummer, his voice high and strained. "It turns the robot's pellets into laser blasts."

"That wasn't the deal, Colonel, sir." Plummer's voice was suddenly deep and firm. "You said these two would have a fair fight. The little lady has nothing but a pellet against the robot's laser weapon. I don't like it."

"Don't mess with me, Plummer," the colonel snarled. "I've bought and paid for you. Follow your orders."

Plummer winced and started to obey, but stopped when Carmen yelled at him.

"Bro, you got no shame. Nada. You oughta know better, coming from where you did."

Plummer looked first at Carmen, then down at the floor.

"Deal me out, dudes," he muttered and backed out the door. "I'm gone. Murder's not what I signed up for."

They could hear his footsteps clicking as he ran down the tiled hallway.

Carmen had dropped to the floor, her hand reaching into the golden square. "Come on, Becky. I'll keep you safe."

Becky waved her pellet gun at the robot. "I can take care of myself, Carmencita. Just get the kids out of here, if you can."

"Not without you, Carmen insisted. "We're going to send you home."

It crossed Emily's mind that Carmen's motives might be mixed, but by and large, they were in sync with her own. She and Carmen each had a reason for wanting Becky back in Lilliput.

As Sharpe and Briglia leaped for Becky, she shot them in the face with her paint gun. The two men cursed and wiped their eyes with their sleeves, while Becky turned to level another blast at what seemed to be the eyes of the robot. Tiny windshield wipers worked, instantly clearing the robot's visual receptors. Fat Boy responded with a projectile from his hand launcher, and the fiery missile chased Becky wherever she dashed for cover.

Sam waited until Becky had run near Carmen's feet, then tossed down the stunner, calling out, "This device might help more than the paint gun."

Dropping her useless weapon, Becky picked up the stunner and aimed it with both hands at the robot rushing toward her. The charge from the stunner hit the robot squarely in the chest. Fat Boy spun around in a full circle, but kept coming. Another laser missile popped out of his weapon and Becky had to throw herself on the floor to prevent the fireball from hitting her.

"Alas, Becky," Samuel cried out in despair. "The stunner must work only on humans."

"Carmen, Josh, get the kids out of here," Becky panted as she ran to avoid the laser shot. "The missiles might hit them. You cheat," she fumed at Colonel Sharpe. "You gave me blanks and him the real thing. Whatever happened to military honor? Or don't they teach that at West Point these days? Hell, is honor even a word anymore?"

At that moment, Jamie and Scruff rushed in through the door. Henry was riding on the dog's back and was stretching his bowstring to its limits. The small blacksmith let a dark-tipped arrow fly at Sharpe, then slung the bow over his shoulder. His weapon of choice was the cannon, now that he had come to know modern artillery.

Jamie had balanced the plasma cannon on the dog's head and Henry crouched over it. Scruff stopped and held still at Jamie's command, so that Henry could take aim.

"You'll have to do better than that, little man," Sharpe said contemptuously, plucking the arrow out of his arm.

Pointing the muzzle of the plasma cannon at the colonel's bleeding arm, Henry shouted, "Take heed, dude. Have you gotta trip comin'," mixing his newly learned punk talk with eighteenth-century diction.

Blood poured from Sharpe's sleeve, and the Lilliputians cheered. Their cannon might be small, but it was at least capable of opening a vein, Emily said to herself. Henry had managed to hit the same place his arrow had landed before, speeding the poison through the colonel's blood stream. Meanwhile, she hoped, the colonel's wound would weaken him, making it easier for the drug to take him out.

Sharpe glanced down and frowned at the spreading stain on his uniform. He held his bleeding arm high in the air and applied pressure to the wound to stop the blood flow, while calling out to his men.

"Glatt, Hewitt, send Fat Boy and the woman back into the square. Be sure his knives are operating."

Fat Boy moved stolidly ahead toward Becky. The robot raised its weapon, but no laser missiles emerged, Emily saw with relief. The tiny gun seemed to have exhausted its power pack. But the robot's other arm went up and pointed at Becky, knives whirling like blender blades.

Emily screamed. "Henry, Jamie, stop him or he'll cut mom to pieces!" She and Dan both struggled against Hewitt's restraining grasp.

"Don't ever underestimate a living weapon," Jamie cried, rushed toward the glowing square, positioning his palms at an unyielding angle.

"Back off, Jamie," Becky said, beginning to run first in one direction than another, zig-zagging like a rabbit. "I can take this guy. Watch and learn."

Chapter 20

Pausing at his mother's command, Jamie looked back at the others. Carmen had put Sam down on the floor between her feet and was struggling to pull Briglia's hands away from her neck. Maybe he should aim a low kick at the gym teacher where it would do the most damage, Jamie thought. Briglia deserved it for choking Carmen. As he swung his leg back to build up the kind of energy the kick would require, Jamie figured Carmen could grab Sam and run for the door. But what about saving Becky? Even Carmen didn't come before his mom, in Jamie's priorities. As he hesitated, Carmen brought her bound hands up fast and hard between Briglia's arms, knocking his fingers away from her throat. She kicked one heel back, hitting Briglia right where Jamie had planned to and just as hard. The man howled and doubled over, forgetting all about hanging onto her.

"Jamie, me boy," Henry cried, aiming his plasma cannon at Hewitt. "Grab Molly and run. I have this matter well in hand."

A blast from the plasma cannon and Hewitt spun around, scrabbling at his bloody shoulder with desperate fingers. Then he seemed to remember that his colonel had made him swear a mighty oath to keep the little people from escaping and would not take kindly to losing even one of them. Despite his bleeding wound, Hewitt made a dive for Henry, leaving Dan and Emily unguarded. They nodded to each other, communicating without words, then immediately separated, moving closer to where Becky was fighting for her life and theirs.

"I won't go without you, 'Enry," Molly cried out, hanging onto the dog's furry neck. "The odds are against us, small as we are. Jamie, come with us. We need you."

"But my mom. . ." Jamie wailed.

"Go with Henry and Molly, Jamie," Becky ordered over her shoulder as she ran, evading the robot's twirling knives. "Take care of them. I have a plan. Don't worry about me."

Henry sent one more arrow flying, this time into Briglia's backside, which was easy to hit, since the gym teacher was still doubled-up. Briglia screamed and groped for the arrow. Grabbing Sam had apparently ceased to be his top priority.

Noticing that the poisoned sword Jamie had given him was still tucked in his belt, Henry pulled it free and tossed it at Sam's feet.

"Cut down the last of these villains, scholar," he said. "You can do this. Go for it." Henry chuckled at his own mastery of twenty-first century diction and hoped the children were noticing how much he had learned from them.

Emily snatched him up and put him on Scruff's back, along with the tiny cannon. "Use it to protect Jamie," she said. "He's just a little kid. We should never have gotten him into this mess. Make him go home, Henry. Tell Scruff to run for it."

"In a bit, Emily. For now, I think my plasma cannon would be better employed here." Sinking back into Scruff's warm coat, Henry murmured to the dog his hope that he had struck at least one vital spot in Briglia's anatomy.

Sam had picked up the sword, with its lethal blackened point, and held it in both hands. He saluted Henry with it and called out an answer to the tiny blacksmith's order, "I will happily oblige you, Sir. Have no fear. Your sword is in capable hands."

Leaping away from Hewitt's lunge in his direction, Sam ran between the man's feet and jabbed the sword point into Hewitt's ankle, right to the bone. When the man hopped, swore, and swatted at him, Sam hid behind a leg of the computer table. He looked longingly at the stunner that Becky had thrown across the room when it failed to take down the robot.

"It might do better against a human," Sam said to himself. Once the drug-dazed Hewitt had fallen to his knees, Sam headed for the stunner, determined to retrieve it.

Emily couldn't help noticing that the mushroom drug was having less effect than when they had used it at home on Andriette and Briglia. Molly had told her that there had been very little poison left in the pot when the Lilliputians had coated the tips of their weapons with it for the second time. The dose was apparently not strong enough to knock out their captors. Emily breathed fast, feeling like she couldn't get enough air no matter how hard she tried. The stunner seemed to be their only hope, but Sam would have to work his way around a roomful of people to get his hands on it. He slid along the wall slowly, so as not to attract attention, keeping his eyes on the weapon. Just as he reached it, Andriette saw what he was doing, picked up the tiny weapon and tossed it on the computer table.

"Think again, wig-head," she jeered, reaching down again to snatch the scholar.

At that moment, Jake wrenched his arm from Briglia's grasp and knocked Andriette away from the Lilliputian. She staggered back, and Sam escaped, running under the computer table. Cursing, Briglia smacked Jake on the side of the head with the butt of his revolver.

Emily gasped, knowing that such a blow could kill. If Jake was dead, she would never have the chance to apologize for doubting him. It was the same feeling she had about Becky, that the worst thing about death was how it kept you from telling people you loved how much you cared. If only she had told them when she had the chance, Emily said to herself miserably. If only she hadn't been so afraid to let down her guard and say what she really felt. She put her tied hands over her face as Jake collapsed on the floor and his eyes closed.

Meanwhile, in the hall, Scruff had delivered Henry and Molly into Jamie's waiting hands. The dog growled, blocking Jamie from returning to the room. He had a strong desire to run back into the lighted square and grab the robot, then shake him like a squeak toy. One thing was sure, the dog thought. His boy must be kept away from the whirling knives at all costs.

Dan nudged Emily. "Sam was trying to get to the stun gun. See if you can reach into my pocket for the other one and drop it on the floor. It's no good to us where it is."

Freed from the drugged Hewitt's grasp, Emily could turn just enough to get her tied hands into Dan's pocket. She coughed as the tiny stun gun dropped to the floor, hoping no one would hear the clink. At least one person heard. Becky stopped running long enough to swoop in, grab the weapon, and tuck it in her belt, despite the whirling knives that were only a foot away from her face. Then she sped off again, heading for the electric socket. Looking over her shoulder, checking how close the robot was, her eyes widened in terror at the gleaming points of Fat Boy's knives.

Scruff waited at the door, rump in the air, front paws stretching out on the floor, ready for action. He knew humans thought this was a play posture, but they were wrong. Sometimes, it was attack mode, and this was one of those times. Scruff growled deep in his throat, getting his nerve up. He was glad his family was all in one place, making protection easier. Scruff thought about sinking his teeth into Sharpe's fancy spats and snorted happily. The task would be easier, now that Sharpe and his men were having trouble staying upright. Scruff cocked his head to one side and examined the men. They smelled funny and acted funnier. Something was totally wrong with these humans. He wouldn't bite into them anymore than he would eat wormy meat.

The dog turned to watch the robot spin around, chasing Becky this way and that. Scruff's eyes went back and forth between Becky and the robot, which didn't smell like anything at all. The dog made a sound in his throat that he hoped was vicious enough to scare the small metal creature, and crouched, ready to spring.

Becky ducked in time, barely dodging the thrust of the knives. Out of the corner of her eye, she saw Sam being pursued by Andriette across the room. She pulled out her stun gun and fired at the woman's knee, which was the highest target the little weapon was likely to reach. Since Andriette was beginning to feel the effects of the drug, she went down easily. Sam shoved his tiny sword into the fallen woman's plump thigh and kept on running.

Pulling herself up a little, Andriette crawled toward the colonel. She was clearly too whacked out to feel much pain. "Hey, Colonel Pete, I'm in trouble, here. Help me up, sugar." With her free hand, she hung on his pant leg, burping and giggling.

Slapping her hand away, Sharpe turned a dial futilely and swore when the robot's laser missiles failed. Andriette flung herself against Sharpe and hung on like a tick. She was grinning clownishly and her smeared red lipstick glowed on her teeth. At least for now, Emily figured, the poison was working well enough to keep the woman out of the fight, though it wasn't as potent as before. With luck, that stab from Sam's mushroom-coated sword would hold her down a little longer. Emily could only hope that the shock of the stun gun had made up for any weakness in the drug.

"Out of ammo," Sharpe muttered to Fat Boy. "So think, you stupid little tin can. What do you do now?"

The robot droned drearily and then spoke in a high, mechanical voice. "Search me," it cried, falling on its back, waving its arms and legs helplessly.

"Get with the program," Sharpe cried. "Move!" His hand twirled the dials, looking as desperate as a laboratory rat trying to hit the lever that produced cheese.

Andriette hung onto the colonel, bobbing up and down, her large teeth chattering from the shock of the stun gun. With a spasmodic jerk, she wrenched Sharpe away from the controls and pulled him toward her, as she sagged to the floor. The colonel tried to fight her off, but gave up, reeling from the poison of Henry's arrow. He had not been exposed to the mushroom brew before, and it was hitting him hard. Still, he had managed to push the robot's controls before collapsing.

Fat Boy leaped up, juiced for another attack. As the robot came closer, Becky dropped to the floor and rolled away from her attacker. With a snake-like hissing sound, Fat Boy rushed at her, rotary blades whirling as they approached her legs. The machine seemed to know where she was most vulnerable. If her legs were slashed by its whirling knives, Becky would be helpless.

At this moment, Scruff charged back into the room, Henry standing tall on his back. Scruff's eyes were narrowed into slits and his lips pulled back from his teeth in a snarl. He had finally understood that this tiny Becky had once been his very own two-legged can-opener and surrogate mom. Scruff rushed toward her enemy with intent to kill, while Henry struggled to keep his balance on the dog's back.

Blades flashing, the robot turned from Becky to face the charging dog.

"Watch out for your nose, Scruff," Jamie screamed from the doorway.

"Stay out of the room, Jamie," Henry cried out over his shoulder. "Guard me Molly with your life."

Jamie peered anxiously at the dog and then at the little barmaid in his hand, unsure what to do. After looking around the room for a hiding place, he skated into the corner and set Molly down gently next to the tangle of electronic circuitry behind the computer.

"Just don't touch anything," he whispered to her, and turned back to watch what was happening, waiting for a chance to get into the fight.

Henry was shrieking into Scruff's ear, hanging onto it with both hands. "Yo, beast! Grab Sam first. Then we'll save Becky."

Scruff whirled around and ran from Becky, whimpering his objections to the order. Becky, in his opinion, should be saved first, since in his experience, she was both Alpha female and primary food source.

"Let's go, Sam," Henry cried, reaching for the little scholar. "Climb up the beast's fur."

Holding the sword between his teeth like a pirate, Sam went hand over hand up Scruff's side, then leaned into the dog's ear. "Go for the lamp cord," Samuel whispered to Scruff. "Now!"

The dog obeyed, in a single leap, allowing Sam to grab the cord and swing down, landing in front of Becky. Andriette and Briglia, rolling on the floor from the effects of the drug, cheered when the robot charged the two Lilliputians, his tiny gleaming knives rotating so fast that the blades seemed no more than a blur.

"Go, robot," Briglia shouted. "You got the knives. Get the little bitch first, then the guy."

"Stand back, Sam," Becky cried. "This robot's mine." She took the electric cord from Sam and rammed the end of it into the wall outlet.

Taking the slack wire in both hands, Becky swung it at the robot like a lariat. "Death by fire, tin man," she cried as the robot's whirling knives hit the wire. "May you get no posthumous medals."

Then she jumped into Sam's arms, burying her face in his shoulder as sparks flew. Fat Boy lit up and began to sizzle.

"Dad! Carmen!" Emily screamed. "Grab Mom and Sam! That robot's totally out of control!"

Carmen darted forward and put Becky and Sam on the computer table out of harm's way. "Give it a rest, señora," she said to Becky. "We're impressed, already."

The shiny metal man circled crazily around the room, slashing with his knives at every ankle in sight. With what small intelligence it possessed, it tried to complete its assignment, until sparks began to sputter from every opening in its head. At last Fat Boy dropped helplessly to the floor, kicking and tunelessly humming. Briglia crawled over to it and breathed into its tiny metal mouth, as if trying to do CPR.

As soon as his lips touched the electrified robot, Briglia let out a cry and flapped one hand next to his face, trying to cool his burning mouth. He collapsed on top of the robot, gasping as the flailing knives slashed the buttons off his uniform.

"Never mind him," Carmen said to Josh. "He's done." She picked up Briglia's gun. "This time, let's keep his toy."

Josh stepped in front of her, pointing at Hewitt, who was limping toward them. "Get the kids out of here, Carmen. Go!"

"Not while you got no back-up," Carmen said.

She pointed the gun at Hewitt, her hands shaking. Carmen might talk tough, Emily thought, but she wouldn't hurt anyone, even if they deserved it. Hewitt's face looked faintly green, and he stumbled sideways, falling forward into Josh, knocking him against Carmen. All three went down in a tangle of arms and legs. The revolver skittered across the floor toward the computer desk.

Emily cried out as she saw Jamie aim a flying kick at Hewitt. "Jamie, you're too little for this fight! Back off!"

Hewitt staggered up and flung himself at Josh, his hands grappling for the other man's throat.

"Leave my dad alone," Jamie shrieked, smacking the colonel's aide with a hard-edged blow to the temple, so that the man's head ricocheted painfully between the floor and Jamie's stiffly extended hand. Dizzily, Hewitt turned away from Carmen and Josh, watching the revolver as it spun through the square of light on the floor. Squinting at the gun, he crawled to the glowing square, like a moth into a flame, and fell in the middle of it.

"One more down," Josh cried, pulling Carmen to her feet. "Emily, our Lilliputians are going to be nothing but pixels in a few minutes. Try to get to that computer."

"I can't," Emily cried in despair. "They tied my hands."

As if on command, Scruff bounded across the room and began chewing and pulling at the rope around her wrists. Emily felt her bonds loosening, and whispered encouragement to the dog, until her hands were free. Both Henry and Molly were sparkling like they'd been sprayed with glitter glue. If she could just get all four of the Lilliputians into the holographic grid before they fell apart, Emily said to herself, she might be able to undo the terrible moment when she had killed Becky with her smart talk and that fatal watermelon.

The only trouble was that a crazed Colonel Sharpe was hobbling toward the computer with his revolver in his hands and murder in his cold gray eyes.

Maybe if she could get Sharpe away from the computer, Emily figured, she might have a chance at the keyboard. It was a plan, at least. Emily nodded at Henry, jerking her head first at the plasma cannon and then at the colonel. Henry swung the weapon around and aimed, just as Scruff took off for the golden square. The dog's sudden move made Henry slip to the side, and instead of hitting the colonel, he hit Andriette in the back.

Andriette grabbed Colonel Sharpe, reaching for support as she went down. Together the two of them fell backward on the floor in the middle of the lighted square. Scruff guarded the prisoners, careful to stay out of the light himself. Somehow, he knew the light was a bad place to be, which was why he kept his prisoners in the middle of it. When Hewitt tried to crawl out, Scruff growled and snapped his teeth at the man.

"Joshua," Sam cried, "You could hurry a bit. We're in meltdown." Samuel's shirt was sparkling like a midnight sky.

Josh leaned over the keyboard. "Now," he muttered. "Where'd that robot come from? Ah, here." He punched a few keys and a scene came up on the monitor. It was a battlefield, strewn with dead and wounded, weapons and rusty armored vehicles. Josh slapped out another command and the golden square expanded to enclose Sharpe and all his people. Emily thought the scene looked just right as a permanent home for killers.

Just then a shout rang out from the coat closet, "Wait, Josh. We gotta save the colonel!" Glatt's high-pitched voice shook as he jumped out from his refuge. He shook his finger at Josh like a teacher threatening detention. "Give it up, Josh. Sharpe's our boss. You got no idea how much money he's promised the company."

Glatt failed to notice Jake, who had gotten dizzily to his hands and knees. As Glatt charged forward toward Josh, Jake threw himself at the man's legs in a tackle as inspired as any he had made on the high school football field. Glatt stumbled over him and fell flat into the spreading lighted square, alongside the other prisoners. As he fell, he knocked Sharpe to the side of the square so that the colonel was half out of the light.

"Maybe he's *your* boss," Josh said, not turning around. "But he isn't mine. I'm exercising a hallowed American prerogative, Mel. I quit."

Glatt saw immediately his predicament. "Wait! at least let me go, Josh!" Glatt bawled, trying to drag himself out of the square. "Don't send me into that program!" Scruff parked himself at the edge of the light and nipped Glatt hard on the wrist when the man tried to move past him. Confused, Glatt stayed put, more terrified of the immediate danger than the distant prospect of life in a computer game.

"You won't die, Mel." Josh said, working at the keyboard. "Anything happens to you in that game, it starts all over again. You're all immortal. Like defense contracts and the American Idol."

Emily's eyes were focused on Sam and her tiny mother, who were both fading in and out of sight. Emily placed her hand on her father's, digging her nails into her his skin.

"Josh," she whispered, "We haven't much time left. Don't stop to talk. Just send the colonel and his guys into the war zone."

"Right, Em." Josh said, sitting down before the keyboard. "Sam, clue me in."

"It's all set up," Sam said, in a high, thin voice. "Just hit the sticky keys, row by row. They're marked with sherry and pizza. An infamous combination, I must say. Appropriate to your mad twenty-first century."

Josh nodded, flexed his fingers, and tapped the keyboard rapidly, but not fast enough for the square to keep the colonel contained. Sharpe rolled outside the boundary just as the square began to shimmer and glow around the other four prisoners. As Josh hit the keys of the computer, the square took on a life of its own, fading and pulsing, absorbing its contents with an electronic gurgle.

Glatt, Hewitt, Briglia, and Andriette vanished in a shower of golden light. On the holographic monitor, Emily and the others could see the four conspirators sitting on the ground in what looked like a desert. Everybody but Glatt was singing and giggling and throwing sand at each other. Glatt was lecturing them, waving his finger and yelling. He was probably telling them that if the government would pay eight hundred dollars for a toilet seat, imagine what it would pay for a holographic battlefield.

Having crawled outside the lighted square, Colonel Sharpe leaped to his feet with gun in hand. He lunged at Josh, knocking him against the computer table so hard that Molly and Becky had to hold onto each other to keep from being thrown to the floor.

"I have you now, Ross," shouted the colonel unsteadily, as the drug had given him a sick stomach and a reeling brain. "Bring my people back or you'll see your whole family shot, one by one."

Josh trembled, thinking about how everyone in the world he loved was in this room, at Colonel Sharpe's mercy, which obviously couldn't be counted on. "They're civilians," he said. "Soldiers don't kill civilians."

"And where'd you hear that sentimental slop? Berkeley?" Sharpe sneered at him. "This is war. Anything goes." He raised the gun, using both hands and whirled around to aim it at Emily.

"Hit the floor, Emily!" Jake cried as he grabbed Fat Boy. Whirling like a discus thrower, he threw the heavy, inert little robot at the colonel.

Fat Boy bounced off Sharpe's head and the colonel sat down hard on the floor in the middle of the lighted square, his eyes crossed. Jake snatched the gun it from the man's limp fingers.

"You have a choice, Sharpe," Josh said. "You can either let me turn you in to the military police for drug abuse, or join the war game program. Pick your poison."

Sharpe didn't hesitate. "I'll take the war game," he said woozily, his lips trembling like they were made of rubber. "Bring it on." He looked up at the monitor, where his guys were waiting for him. "We have a mission, people. Not sure what it is, but we'll think of something."

Josh slapped at the computer keys, and the light turned many-colored, making the square look like a disco dance floor. In a shower of brilliant sparks, the colonel vanished from the brilliantly lit area, reappearing on the holographic screen with the others. The colonel staggered to his feet and pointed to the horizon, where tanks were kicking up sand.

"Move it out, men!" he cried, checking his watch. "We've got no time to lose."

Josh hit a few keys and brought Colonel Sharpe's war game into focus on the big screen. Shiny robots danced across the horizon, flashing their rotating knives, and tanks crawled heavily behind them, kicking up dirt with their rubber treads.

Josh stood back, his eyes on the screen where Sharpe and the others appeared. They stood still, looking around them in a daze, then took off running after the tanks. Still hollering that he should never have made Josh his partner, Glatt ran along behind them, begging them to wait up. Bullets whizzed past him, kicking up yellow sand. The colonel and his men staggered, disoriented. Lights flashed around them, and the ground shook. A large armored vehicle skidded to a stop beside the colonel, who jumped into the front seat beside the driver.

"Follow me, everybody," he shouted, beckoning to his crew. "Andriette, you're in charge of the mess hall. Men, we finally have the perfect war, the kind that will never end."

"You got your wish, Colonel Putz," said Josh, taking one last look at the holographic screen. "Live till the end of time, and may you eat okra casserole till you choke on it."

The screen went blank as Josh hit 'close,' and the four Lilliputians cheered with faint, tinny voices.

Leaping into the air and brandishing her bow, Becky cried out joyfully, "They're happy as pigs in . . . " She glanced at Emily and closed her mouth firmly. "Merde," she finished.

Chapter 21

For a brief moment a wave of relief went through all of them, large and small, two-legged and four, as they realized the battle was over. Josh's shoulders relaxed and his hands rested on the keyboard as everyone took a deep breath.

Appreciating the quiet, Sam looked at Becky, then at himself. They were almost gone! He waved his arms to get Josh's attention and finally threw his dingy wig at Josh's nose, where it hung, dangled for a moment, and then fell.

"Dr. Ross, I hate to be a nag, but we're about to pixillate entirely," Sam said, his voice calm as if he was sitting down to dinner. "The molecular breakdown is right on schedule. We may have no more than five minutes of life left. Can you re-program the holographic field fast enough? We would prefer not to join the soldiers in that distinctly unappealing desert."

Alarmed, Josh looked at them, taking in their disintegration at a glance. At once, he set to work, pushing keys on the keyboard.

A moment later he looked up, worried.

"I don't know, Sam. The Lilliput program's not responding." He studied the computer keys and shook his head helplessly.

"I have it all set it up," Samuel cried, holding a sparkling Becky in his arms. "Just hit all the sticky keys, the ones marked with sherry. Do it, man!"

Josh bent his head over the keyboard, his fingers flying. He bit his lip, concentrating, trying to follow Sam's instructions. The little man's voice was fading and hard to hear. Emily leaned over one shoulder and Jake over the other.

"Here's a sticky one," Jake called out, reaching over the keyboard to hit a key Josh hadn't noticed.

"And here's another." Emily finished the job and stood back, holding her breath.

Suddenly the screen above them sprang to life showing Molly's pub, drinkers at the bar raising their mugs, cheering and beckoning. As the virtual reality drive whirred, the whole pub filled the screen, shining like heaven.

"Time to go, guys," Josh said, sitting back gazing at the revelers with relief. "Who wants to be first?"

"Make it Molly and Henry," Sam said. "I have a few words to say to your wife." He held out his hand to Becky, his voice faint but clear. "I know you want to be with your children, but don't chance it, my sweet. Come with me."

"No," Jamie cried, snatching his mother into his arms. "Stay!"

"Jamie, boy," Henry's fading voice said, "be reasonable. I lost me whole family to the cholera. You're not the first to lose someone you love."

Molly reached out her almost transparent arms to Jamie, like she wanted to hug him. "I was hardly bigger than Emily, child, when me mum died. I had to run the pub all by meself. Do what's right, luv. Let yer mum go with us"

Jamie looked at his tiny mother, realizing he could almost see through her, and loosened his hold. "I get it," he said. "I don't like it, but I get it. She can't stay, and I'd be really selfish if I tried to make her."

Emily put her arm around him and hugged him close, being careful not to squeeze her mother in the process. "You're not selfish, Jamie. I think you're a hero."

He looked up at his sister. "Honest? You think so? All I ever wanted was for you and mom to be proud of me."

"We are," Becky said. "You're growing up fast, Jamie. I don't think you really need me anymore. Maybe Emily doesn't either."

"Come on, Becky," Molly cried in a voice almost too faint to hear. "You're sparklin' like bloody fireworks. Jamie, put 'er down righ' now!"

Jamie carefully set his mother down next to Molly. "Go on Mom. You'll have a good life there in Lilliput. Here you'd have no life at all. I couldn't stand to have you die again."

Gently releasing her hold on Jamie, Becky looked over at Sam, and their eyes stayed linked. The kids could barely hear her voice as she said, "I think you are my new life, Sam. What do you think?"

"I think you had better go with me before you turn into pixie dust, Becky, my sweet. Why is it taking you so long to grasp the inevitable? Did your mother drop you on your head?" He smiled and reached out to her. "Let's go home."

Emily blew a kiss to them both, then looked down at Molly. "And you need a husband too, Molly. You could marry Henry. He'd help you run the pub."

"Becky, we'd need yer help." Molly turned to her friend and tossed her yellow curls. "Otherwise I'd kill the dear man for interferin'."

Henry took Molly by both hands. "'Ow about it, luv?"

"You've got a baby girl to take care of, Molly," said Emily. "She needs a dad. I'm counting on you both to raise her right. Mom, you need to help her. Nobody but you could raise a kid like me."

Becky smiled at her daughter. "I did a good job, didn't I? And the job seems to be done. Josh?" She looked up at her giant husband, tipping her head back so she could see into his eyes. "Should I go or stay. Which?"

Josh rubbed his eyes, which were suddenly red and damp. "If I could keep you from disintegrating, Becky, I'd tell you to stay. But I can't save you. I'd rather see you live on with Sam than stay here and die with us."

Nodding slowly, Becky smiled. "I see how it is, Josh. You've given me another life, and I'm grateful. I'll start all over again with Molly's Emily. Practice makes perfect. You and Carmen take care of Jamie for me."

All the little people were on the floor now, ready to enter the holographic space.

Stepping into the middle of the lighted square, Becky looked up at her husband and then at Sam, who was right beside her. "Josh, can you make me a tennis court? Sam needs exercise if he's going to lose that lard around his waist."

Josh nodded. "Lilliput's about to take the quantum leap into the twenty-first century. You'll have a cell phone and an internet hookup, even MTV, sweetheart, if that's what you want."

"I want all I can get," Becky said, beckoning to Sam. "Always did. Come, love, before there's nothing left of you to hug."

Sam took an enormous leap and landed next to Becky in the golden square. "I'm with you," he said, taking her hand. "I'll always be."

All four Lilliputians shimmered, disappeared, then came to life again on the VR monitor.

Carmen tossed Sharpe's tennis racket into the bright square, where it began to sparkle before vanishing. "Maybe you could make some more of these, Josh," she said, smiling at Emily. "Along with that tennis court."

Emily shouldered her father out of the way. "Let me do it. I know what she likes."

On the screen, a glowing, Eden-like Lilliput shone, and as Emily worked, a green tennis court soon filled the foreground. Tears ran down Emily's cheeks as she worked, and for once she didn't care who saw her cry. Becky looked out of the screen at Emily, her face crumpling in a way Emily had never seen happen before.

"I'm crying, too, Em. Always remember that it's okay to cry," she called to her daughter. "Help Josh keep my girl out of trouble, Carmencita. No street language, y' hear?"

Carmen winked at Emily. "Street language?" she said, acting like she'd never heard of it. "What's that?"

Jamie suddenly changed his mind. "Mom! Take me with you!" he cried, jumping into the light square.

Jake dragged him backward. "She's got a new life, kid," he said, one arm tightly around the boy's shoulder. "So do you."

"But the temple priests say I gotta be with her," Jamie cried, holding out one hand toward his vanishing mother.

"There now," Molly called to him from the screen. "Ye're a fine, capable lad, Jamie. Rescued us all, ye did. No more priests and temples now. Just be yerself, dear boy."

Jamie hung his head, letting his arms fall by his sides. He had a feeling he would never again be a living weapon or any kind of weapon at all.

"Okay, I guess. Molly?" he said in a low voice. "How did you stand it when you lost your mom?"

In the foreground of the screen, Henry came up to Molly and held her around the waist. "Same way as I did, boy. Feels like 'ell for a while, it does. Then ye look around, smell the flowers blooming, get a whiff of a roast on the spit, and life goes on."

"Promise me you'll be civil to your little brother," Sam said, holding his hands around his mouth like a megaphone pointed at Dan. "You live in a greedy, rude century, dear boy. Remember that a life spent grubbing for power is no life for a decent man. Cultivate kindness. You understand?" He reached out as if he could touch Dan through the screen.

"I do," Dan whispered, touching a finger to Sam's, through the glass. "I won't call Jamie a dork and hurt his feelings. Never again."

"Good-by, Becky," Josh called, his voice breaking. "May you never lose a game or an argument. Sam, a word of advice. Let her win. She'll love you for it."

Molly blew a good-bye kiss to Emily. "You make a family by kindness, luv," she called out before going into her pub. "Not by what you think is cool."

"Can't I just go in and visit them for a minute?" Jamie cried, as he watched his mother and Sam hold hands in front of the pub.

"Sorry, Jamie," Josh said, turning back the computer. "I need you here, son. We need the whole crew to mind the store. Pacific Electronics has a job to do, making VR games. And I need you to keep me healthy. I don't want to turn workaholic again."

Carmen laid her arm around Jamie's shoulder. "Not to worry, Josh. You've made friends with a nurse, remember?"

"More than friends, I hope," Josh said, looking at her with a bit of a smile. "And now we'll make the Lilliput world history." Josh hit a few keys.

On the screen above, the Lilliputians ran into the pub, greeted by a cheering crowd. Only Becky looked back, with a wistful expression, and extended her hand toward them. Her lips moved, framing the names of her children, and she had tears in her eyes. Then, as Sam pulled her toward the bar, she laughed and accepted a mug of ale, toasting their return.

With a final tap on the keys, the screen briefly blazed, then went dark. Josh turned off the computer. "Live forever, Becky!" He smiled, but the corners of his mouth didn't turn up like they usually did.

Chapter 22

Scruff was waiting politely under the computer table. He was hoping someone would mention his heroism. He wasn't at all sure that the Ross family had the faintest notion what would have happened to them if their dog hadn't been on the job. Not that he wanted a medal or anything. Just a belly rub and a hearty 'good dog' would do fine. He stood staring up at Josh with his head cocked to one side so that an ear flapped over one black, shiny eye. Well?' he thought, directing the word at Josh, hoping his human had at least a tenth of the telepathy dogs had. 'Am I a fantastic dog or what?'

Josh finally turned away from the computer screen, and saw the dog looking at him. Grinning, he took Scruff's paws in both hands, raising him up so his head was on a level with everyone else's, "You're a great dog, Scruff!" Josh said, nuzzling his face against the animal's neck. "The best. When we get home, you get a milk bone."

Scruff sank down in disappointment. He had been hoping for at least a Beggin' Strip, which everyone assumed he thought was bacon. As if a dog's nose couldn't tell the difference between a plasticky mouthful out of a box and the real thing. But he would take whatever he could get. Whatever he had at any given moment was, in Scruff's opinion, the best.

Gathering them all into a circle, Josh put his head close to Carmen's. "Let's go for a pizza, guys," he said. "Lilliput's not the only game in town."

"No way," Carmen smiled, "I got enchiladas at home, hombre," She put her arm around his waste, "With lots of green chilies. Your palate needs educating."

"It seems, kids, that the era of junk food is finally coming to an end," Josh said, looking half-glad and half-sorry that Carmen had closed his favorite escape hatch.

"Mom would be glad to hear it," Emily said. "I bet temple priests have no problem with enchiladas, right, Jamie?"

"I'm not a temple priest anymore." Jamie closed his eyes, thought for a moment, then opened them and smiled. "I think I'll be a Lilliputian and learn how to swordfight like the Shaolin warriors."

"And you can teach Jake and me," Dan said, looking at his little brother through his geeky glasses with such earnestness that even Emily hadn't the heart to make a snide comment.

At the thought of homemade enchiladas, everybody followed Carmen like she was the pied piper. Only Jamie hung back, glancing at the darkened computer monitor and smiling as he remembered the Lilliput program that he had zipped into his teddy bear pillow. When he had mastered T'ai Chi swordfighting, Jamie promised himself, he would visit his mother. Josh's virtual reality computer was a piece of cake, now that Sam had shown him how to use it.

"I'll see you again, mom," he whispered "And you can teach me to play tennis, like you always promised. Sam says kung-fu can take a man only so far." He turned, bumping into his big brother.

"Jamie," Dan said, putting an arm around his little brother's shoulders. "Mom's program is gone. We won't be seeing her again."

"But I got a. . ." Jamie broke off quickly and smiled his phony, endearing smile to put Dan off the scent of the hidden Lilliput copy. "Lilliput can't die, Dan. I got it safe in here."

Jamie patted his chest over his heart, hoping Dan would fall for his sentimental gesture, which Dan did. Bending over Scruff, Jamie whispered in the dog's ear, "Where they'll never find it. You and me, dog, we'll go to Lilliput anytime we want."

Emily took Jake's hand and smiled up at him. "I'm glad you didn't snitch on us," she said.

"And I'm glad you're going with me to the Homecoming Dance," Jake murmured into her ear. "No guy ever worked harder for a date."

"Now I get it," Dan said. "You were stringing the colonel along, trying to get information we could use."

"Yeah, and a great job I did." Jake looked at the floor and sighed.

"You saved my life," Emily smiled up at him. "I'm not complaining. Hey, I'd like a gardenia for the dance."

Jake bent down so their faces were close. "You got it, sweetheart," he said, touching his lips gently to hers. "You got it all."

Emily graded her first real kiss an A+ and said to herself that she really did have almost everything. The Lilliputians were safe and would even have a TV at their pub. Henry and Molly would get married and raise a miniature Emily. She and her mother had parted friends. That they had to part at all was tough, but she could handle it. To have almost everything, Emily decided, was suddenly enough.

THE END

About the Author

Barbara Gardiner Rogers Wilson writes about the things she loves for the people she loves.

A retired professor of literature and creative writing, she has written and published many books on spiritual subjects in which we meet people who are seeking understanding of their faith as the world changes around them.

Barbara's current life is centered on a farm in Uruguay, where she and her dog are happily living with friends practicing sustainable agriculture.

Find out about her other books at

www.portalcenterpress.com/authors

Other books by B R Wilson

Deva and the Soul Snatcher tells of a young Irish girl who is sent by the King of Faery to help save the world from disaster and ends up creating a musical with a high school class to get the word out.

Little Man in a Dog Suit and *The Dog Who Loved Jesus* lets us see the world from the dogs' point of view.

The Ring and the Cross, set in medieval times, shows us what life was like when being a Christian was very new.

www.ingramcontent.com/pod-product-compliance
Lightning Source LLC
Chambersburg PA
CBHW070937190726
48292CB00004B/1223